RED ROCK ISLAND

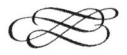

ALEC PECHE

BSW Publishing

Thank you for downloading this eBook. This book remains the copyrighted property of the author, and may not be redistributed to others for commercial or non-commercial purposes. If you enjoyed this book, please encourage your friends to download their own copy from their favorite authorized retailer. Thank you for your support.

This book is a work of fiction. Names, characters, places, and incidents are products of the author's imagination or are used fictitiously and are not to be construed as real. Any resemblance to actual events, locales, organizations, or persons, living or dead, is entirely coincidental.

All rights reserved.

Text Copyright © August 2016 Alec Peche

Published by GBSW Publishing

Cover Design: Vila Design

Photography: Rachael Paulsen

No part of this book may be reproduced or transmitted in any form or by any means, electronic or mechanical, including photocopying, recording, or by any information storage and retrieval system, without the express written permission of the author and the publisher, except for the use of brief quotations in review.

PROLOGUE

1988

The summer of 1988 in Morgan Hill, California was shaping up to be dry and hot. Tempers were flying as people had the radio on too loud listening to Faith by George Michael, or Need You Tonight by INXS. Yellowstone National Park had been on fire since June and it was already August. Debbie Altman was tired of the heat, the music and the endless ads for the United States presidential candidates. Really, the election was several months away and yet the news had been incessant about the political race.

She grabbed her keys off her kitchen counter and decided to head north to her friend's house in San Jose. At least she had air-conditioning included in her apartment rent. Holly had invited her to stay at her house earlier in the day, after Debbie complained about how hard it was to sleep in the heat. She'd take Monterey Highway past the cherry orchards up to San Jose. The road could be scary at times as it earned the name Blood Alley for the bad accidents that occurred as a result of head-on collisions at high speeds. On this Friday afternoon though, hopefully the traffic would be light with the majority of cars heading south for the weekend. Debbie left the traffic lights of Morgan Hill and crossed the signpost indicating it was San Jose. Then she heard her car's engine make a few weird noises. She drove a nearly ten year old Datsun 240Z. It got decent gas mileage and was fun to drive. The car coughed and started slowing down. Darn she'd have to pull over and walk to find a telephone to call for help. The day just kept getting worse and worse.

She locked up the car, grabbed her purse, and set out on foot to the nearest business; fortunately she knew there was a concrete pipe company about one mile ahead and since it was only three in the afternoon, it might still be open. After walking just a few steps, she felt like she was going to explode from the heat bearing down on her. She heard the noise of a truck behind her and looked over her shoulder to see a pick-up truck slowing down. A woman in the passenger side seat rolled the window down and asked if she wanted a ride somewhere. Debbie smiled, said yes, and hopped in the truck's cab and that was the last time anyone saw her alive other than her killer.

CHAPTER 1

*D*amian Green stood on the red rock looking west. On his right was the Golden Gate Bridge, and in the distance Alcatraz Island and the San Francisco skyline. Directly in front of him, floating on the water, were three floral wreaths. It was the seventh anniversary of the murder of his wife and two daughters. He'd had them cremated and spread their remains on their favorite ski run at Lake Tahoe during a heavy snowstorm and so he honored their existence with the wreaths and an imaginary conversation with the three of them on the anniversary of their deaths.

Behind him on the hill of this little island in San Francisco Bay, stood retired detective Natalie Severino. She'd solved the case, shot the bastard dead that killed his family, and had remained in his life the seven years since. She brought the wreaths on the first anniversary and it had become a ritual each year. His oldest would have graduated from high school this year, but that and all of his children's other milestones would never come to pass.

He had survivor's guilt and his life since that time had drastically changed. He'd bought the island, built a house and designed a computer alert system to prevent any further errors like the one that had taken his family from him. Using his computer skills he went to work erasing his existence after his family tragedy; reporters had been relentless at the time of the manhunt and subsequent killing of the convict. Part of his core after that was making sure he was impossible to locate or for people to figure out whether he was dead or alive at any given moment.

As he lost sight of the wreaths on the waves, Natalie said, "I have a job for you," and then she winced. She'd left Damian to his own silent thoughts for the past twenty minutes and she was itching to tell him about her latest case. Talk about throwing cold water on the grieving man, *damn it Natalie you're so uncouth.*

She'd met him in his office at a research lab of a major technology company in San Jose to notify him that his wife and children were dead and later, after a short manhunt, she notified him their murderer was dead. She'd come to know him better over the years since and when she opened her own detective and security agency, he'd help her in a variety of ways, usually related to technology, computers, or some amazing engineering feat. She was a decade his senior in her late fifties and she found him to be a renaissance man – traditional, polite, and very, very smart. He'd invented so many things and either sold the patent for a large sum, or the invention would be added as a new line item of his ongoing large royalty checks. She became familiar with his background when she'd researched him at the beginning of the investigation into his family's murder.

Damian stood a moment longer searching for sight of the wreaths, and then he sighed and turned. Another year without his family; it seemed like an eternity and yet it seemed like yesterday. Each year as the anniversary of their deaths moved upon him, he was depressed and morose, and yet the wreaths sailing away on the waves somehow eased his grief and he could go on again for another year, each slightly less painful than the previous one.

The man was six foot, and rugged looking from both the permanent lines of grief and from the climate of living on this rock of an island. His blond hair was in transition between blond and white depending on how the sun hit it. He was muscled from swimming in the bay in a wetsuit, clambering over his rocky cliff to his house and the twice weekly treadmill runs. His island wasn't big enough for him to run around it. Besides, parts of it were a bird sanctuary and he wouldn't want to disturb the natives. His eyes were blue and if he passed you on the street, you would wonder if he was a tourist from the Nordic area of the world - perhaps Sweden or Finland, but you would be wrong. His ancestors came from the North Sea region of the United Kingdom and his heritage was Norse. All in all, Damian was a very pleasant man to look at.

"What's the job?"

"I need a computer analysis," replied Natalie.

To Damian, a brilliant computer analysis creator, it was like saying you needed a white shirt. There were so many options that he couldn't even respond to Natalie's request.

With a sigh he asked, "What specifically do you need analyzed?"

"So you know that my former department, the SJPD is short on officers. It's hard to live in Silicon Valley on a cop's salary. They're down nearly twenty percent of the force. So they contracted with me to work their cold cases since they have no personnel to devote to them at the moment. It's sort of a dream job for me, and I was really excited to go to work on them until I discovered how bad the backlog is. There are over two hundred cases and no one has worked these files in the last three years. That's just wrong, those families deserve justice!"

"Have they all been electronically catalogued?"

"Yes."

"So what do want me to do with them? You're the retired detective," Damian said.

"I want to use that brilliant brain of yours to find a process to approach these cases. They aren't calling out to me, saying 'solve me first!' I'm afraid to waste time on cases that I'll never be able to solve in my lifetime even if you, genius Damian, gave your every waking breath to solving a case. I don't want to waste time on lost causes."

"Aren't they all lost causes? That's why they weren't solved the first time around."

"Aren't you the pessimist? I said this would be hard, not impossible. With you helping me, I would think your brilliant mind would come up with some angles that weren't thought of the first time around. If your brain fails me then I have to think your computer will come through."

"There is that. Can you send me a few cases so I can see what the data possibilities are?"

Natalie did a happy dance in her head at his interest. She was sure that with his help she would go so much further and faster. She watched him for a while longer knowing this was always the saddest day of the year for him. She felt bad for his suffering but since she'd never met his family, she felt no personal loss; rather it was his suffering that weighed on her. She wondered if he would ever ask her not to bring the wreaths on the anniversary, but she wouldn't ask, wouldn't intrude on his intensely private thoughts.

CHAPTER 2

Damian watched the boat depart heading for the Richmond Yacht Club marina. He had an arrangement with a boat owner at the marina to bring any guest to his island as well as supplies. He rarely left the rock except to leave San Francisco Bay. He did his shopping online and the supply boat would deliver any packages to a shallow beach he had on one side of the island. He then used a drone that he'd designed to move packages from the beach to his house. The drone could handle up to two hundred pounds and he enjoyed the exercise of operating the drone to pick up packages. He'd designed a lot of gadgets for his island getaway. He used wind, water, and solar energy to provide electricity for his home. He had a pulley system, much like a zip line to get from the top of the rock to the beach and back again. He debated various technologies to get on and off the island - helicopters, hot air balloons, motorized hang gliders, and jet packs, but they all had somewhat high failure rates, so he settled for the boat.

He bought the island after his family was murdered, cleared the poison oak, and then created a sanctuary so that he never had to fear another convict mistakenly released from prison. A convict from Soledad's death row had murdered his wife and children. A series of mistakes by the correctional system had led to the release of the wrong prisoner. Once released, he headed for San Jose, killing two other people along the way. He was looking for cash and targeted their neighborhood looking for money, jewelry, and a car. He struck gold with Damian's family, and since he'd been on death row for murder of another family, killing Damian's family was the most expedient way to meet his need and get out of town. Fortunately Detective Severino and her squad had quickly identified the man and run him to ground, killing him in the process. Damian had cheered the convict's death, but it hadn't brought his family back.

Now he would occasionally look across the water at San Quentin prison and fantasize about sending his drone there to annihilate all of the prisoners on death row. He'd study the blueprints and then look at payloads his drone could carry but then he thought of the guards that would be in the area of his drone strike and he couldn't do it; kill innocent men. Then his rage receded and his normal mind returned. Instead he played with the prison software, doing hourly surveillance to assure himself that no more mistakes would be made that would allow a murderer to be released. He contemplated adding things to a convict's record to close the door on any Parole Board hearings for releases, but he hadn't taken that step so far. The Parole Board was doing a pretty good job of keeping Charlie Manson locked up so he hoped that common sense existed among their members.

He looked down, feeling a presence at his side and found his cats looking up at him. These two were highly intelligent and trained cats; trained as he taught them to leave the birds alone that visited, nested, and otherwise called his island home. They enjoyed climbing the steep walls and he kept them in fresh fish from the bay.

"You guys hungry or just out for a stroll?"

They eyed him as though assessing his mood, then looked at

each other and set off together toward one of the cliff edges. He worried when he'd first brought them here, but they were agile climbers, their nails assisting their climbs. They used the small sandy beach for a litter box and were great companions. Two solitary males and one female had made this rock of an island, home. He turned and headed uphill to enter his home. The island, at one time, had been mined for manganese, he'd drilled into the rock to make a second level below ground. The top level contained his kitchen, living room and bedroom with each room having breathtaking views of the bay. From a distance, it was hard to discern the structure as he had designed it to fit in with the terrain. He didn't want people curious about his island and most people couldn't see it unless the sun reflected off the windows. He had signs posted below on the beach about it being private property and if someone cared to ignore the signs, they got an audible warning, and then they were sprayed with bay water if they crossed a line in the sand that they couldn't see. He averaged one idiot a week that apparently couldn't read.

His subterranean level contained his gym, computer room and laboratory and workshop. He had no overnight visitors so there was no need for a second bedroom. His wife and he had no immediate family and that was part of their early attraction in their relationship.

Acquaintances that knew Damian called him a modern day MacGyver, an American TV character from the late 1980's. The character solved complex problems by making things out of every day stuff. Yes that was Damian, beside the numerous patents he held; his island and his home were testament to his engineering prowess. In addition to what the television star could do on his show, Damian could also work magic with a computer.

He was working on a couple of ideas for transporting himself and his supplies off and on the island. Conceptually, it was an ever present challenge to see if he could do better than his current process. Anything less than the transporter from the Enterprise on the Star Trek series was a failure in his own mind, but he hadn't figured it out yet. He put aside that idea as Natalie sent him an email with instructions on how to reach the database that would be her source for the cold cases. She must have emailed him as soon as she reached the marina.

Following her instructions, he was quickly inside her police database looking at the types of data fields. He read five of the cases to get a handle on the scope of the information. Then he sat back, closed his eyes, and swallowed around the huge lump in his throat. Suddenly, he was grateful to Natalie for tracking down his family's murderer and killing him. If the case had remained unsolved all of this time, he wasn't sure he would have his sanity. Then a sudden sliver of humor hit him as he considered whether his closest acquaintances considered him sane for living his life on this rock of an island. They'd asked him why not own a private island in the Caribbean where he would have more land, a bigger house, and water that didn't require a wetsuit to swim in, and he'd answered that the rock suited him. In his own way he was living off the grid closest to the most technological culture of the world.

Looking back at the cases again, he checked how old some of them were. The first use of DNA to solve a police investigation was in 1986 according to the Internet. So a crime committed before then would be harder to solve as a cold case. Instead he decided to think about what new information, evidence, or criminal case approach would impact the status of a cold case. He called Natalie to ask her a few questions.

"That was quick; did you look at the database already?" Natalie asked upon receiving Damian's call.

"Yes, and I have some questions for you. Has the approach by police to process a case changed substantially recently?"

"Hmmm that's a good question, let me think." And there was silence over the phone line. Damian could hear road noise as she was clearly driving south to home. Then finally Natalie came back on the line and said, "Yes I think so. The 1990's were a time of police innovation. With computers and DNA, we did more objective investigation. Prior to that, a suspect caught your eye or you had a hunch, or you saw the crime committed in front of you, then you had your suspect, case closed. It wasn't exactly a time of innocent until proven guilty. When I was a new cop on the force, it was always interesting talking to the guys that were about to retire. They had practiced policing before the Supreme Court decision on Miranda rights so you could almost go about framing someone for a crime or at least intimidate them into a confession. Now if we find you guilty, then you're really guilty."

"So in regards to the older cold cases, there is no DNA but there might be new evidence or a new way of looking at the same crime scene to develop a suspect. Do I have that right?"

"Yes, that's correct," Natalie replied.

"So the easiest cases to solve are those that DNA evidence was collected on and the hardest will be a case going back forty years with no new evidence since the initial crime."

"Correct."

"Okay, I have some ideas and I'll get back to you later today."

Natalie was the closest thing to an older sister he'd ever have. She kept tabs on him and did her best to keep him connected to the real world. He knew she was married with adult children. She'd been a hard-working detective and now she was a hard-working private investigator. Glancing at his watch, he decided it was time for lunch. The time he put into assembling his lunch would be used to think about different angles to analyze data and so he returned upstairs.

CHAPTER 3

Given the stressfulness of the day he was surprised he had any appetite. He thought that with each passing year he was slightly less sad on the anniversary of his family's murder. Maybe that was why he had an appetite. He made a lot of items from scratch as it was far easier to import a single fifty pound bag of flour than a loaf of bread every week. He was planning to eat a multigrain wheat bread sandwich consisting of turkey, cheese, and avocado. In the scheme of things, avocados were easier to transport and stayed ripe longer than lettuce so he had taken to dressing up his sandwiches with the fruit. As he worked at his kitchen counter, he was distracted with thoughts of the greenhouse. He'd like to have more fruits and vegetables on the island but the soil was incompatible with growing his own food. He could work with the architect that had designed his house to build a hundred square-foot greenhouse which according to his calculations would be sufficient for his needs. His problem was he'd really had no one out to the island to do any work in over five years and frankly he didn't want anyone on his island other than Natalie. He tuned back in and looked down at the sandwich he was making, adding pickles, mustard, and mayonnaise and topping with alfalfa sprouts. He sat down at his table with his sandwich and some water and thought about the over two hundred families that never had their crime solved. Given the age of some of the cases, he would've thought that the immediate family was long dead. As much as he wanted justice for some of the older cases, he knew Natalie would get the best case solve rate if he concentrated on the more recent cold cases.

The State of California and nearly every other state was behind in processing DNA tests, and so he'd take a side trip to DNA testing to see if there was any way he could speed it up or otherwise automate it. Perhaps if he could develop a process that would make the DNA testing say, seventy percent correct, then he could move forward and submit fewer samples for the more refined DNA test. He visited a few websites and read about the process. While he thought he could shave perhaps 10-20% of the time off of processing, he really could see how a specimen needed to be as carefully analyzed as it was. One website he visited, suggested fifty-four hours from receipt of some item of clothing or sample containing DNA to its resolution. The trouble with handling and analyzing DNA was it was so easy to contaminate because there was DNA everywhere.

'Okay' he thought; he wasn't going to come up with some genius solution to DNA testing today.

He then did a search on some recently solved cold cases to see what they had in common, and it was back to DNA. From an engineering point of view, DNA testing was the crimp in the pipeline of an otherwise smooth flow of evidence. He was back to the theory of how to speed up the DNA analysis and it wasn't just the two hundred plus cases of the SJPD, it was the nationwide processing of DNA specimens. Perhaps some of the crimes under the jurisdiction of SJPD were committed by someone whose DNA was collected in Arkansas. The whole matching of DNA to potential cold cases would only move as fast as the state crime labs were at processing samples currently within their possession. He needed an analyzer that wasn't invented yet; that would be much quicker at processing DNA. Okay he'd leave that for another day as he put the concept on the to-do list.

Maybe he would do a computer run and collect any name of a person interviewed during one of those cold cases who had since interacted with the criminal justice system. It might be coincidence and it might have an impact on a cold case. It was a starting point and so he wrote the program to do the analysis.

Then he couldn't resist so he took high powered binoculars and rushed outside to see if he could catch a glimpse of the floating wreaths. Each anniversary he promised himself he wouldn't go looking for the wreaths and each year he did. It was as though by seeing them floating, it meant his family wasn't gone for the briefest of moments. Of course they were gone, but as long as he could see the wreaths in the distance, it was like they were waving to his soul. He searched for maybe fifteen minutes and then gave up; there was no sign of them. He knew the flowers would eventually sink as there was no Styrofoam in the wreath or anything else that would harm the bay or it inhabitants. There was an incoming rainstorm creating higher waves, which usually caused the wreaths to sink quicker. He knew because he had conducted experiments about the sinking of wreaths in his lab. He sighed and said another prayer for his departed family and turned to go back inside, wondering what his family would have thought of his little ceremony and his life since their deaths.

His phone dinged with an email and he saw it had arrived from Trevor, Natalie's son. He'd met the boy at the funeral of his family. Natalie had seen something in Damian that matched something in Trevor. They were both probably geniuses, but Trevor was just starting out as an assistant district attorney. He had sailed through law school at Berkeley and passed the California Bar having missed just one question, a record among test takers. The death of Damian's family influenced Trevor to put the bad guys behind bars.

Trevor was more outgoing than Damian, but then he hadn't lost his family. The two men occasionally took in a Giants baseball game or a Warriors basketball game. There they would argue statistics of the various players. Despite his affection for the other man, Damian had never invited him to his home, nor had he been to Trevor's condo in San Jose. Trevor loved to hear about Damian's latest engineering inventions; though his genius was for the law rather than engineering, he understood enough to bounce ideas off. He'd also reviewed any patent issues or sales contracts for Damian's inventions.

'I've got two tickets for the Warriors game tonight. Do you want to grab a hamburger and beer at our favorite pub and then move on to the game?'

Damian had two emotions warring within him. On one hand he wanted to take his mind off the anniversary and on the other it was sacrilege to attend something fun. In the end he thought that his family would want him to move on; certainly if he'd been the one murdered, he would have wanted his wife to remarry and for his kids to have a supportive stepfather. Perhaps it was time to start living again and see where it took him. He wondered why he was feeling this way? Had the cold cases caused this yearning for more meaning in his life somehow? He decided to act on this new feeling and start by attending the game tonight.

He typed back, 'Sounds like a brilliant plan. Meet you at six at our pub.'

The game tip-off was at 7:30pm so that gave them enough time to eat and drink a few beers before walking over to the arena. He'd take a boat to the marina closest to the arena, while Trevor would likely take a BART train. They'd found on a prior game night, a pub that was a mile away from the arena, small and quiet, with a great selection of Belgian beers and the best cheeseburgers that they'd ever tasted. There was no glitz or glamour about the place, and they'd both gotten to know the owner over the years and helped him in different ways.

One night Damian had come in by himself sick of his own company, depressed, and craving one of Pete's cheeseburgers. Pete was depressed himself as he'd just fired another bartender for stealing alcohol from the bar. He'd really liked this person and bemoaned that if only he could design a foolproof system that would measure and dispense alcohol, he could stop firing bartenders that were wonderful with his customers. Sure there were fancy systems he could purchase for thirty thousand dollars, but he would be a long time getting a return of investment. Damian took up the challenge and within the month had designed a system made from sprinkler system parts, and a few valves and sensors he purchased. He then developed the software that required a bartender to enter a code to get anything dispensed. The system worked so well that Pete had called back the last likable bartender he fired, and rehired her since he knew she couldn't cheat him anymore. It also earned Damian free cheeseburgers for life and another patent which he sold to someone that would commercialize his concept, but not bankrupt small bar owners like Pete. With the plans in motion to perhaps change his life, he returned to Natalie's cold cases.

CHAPTER 4

He thought he'd focus on two groups of victims – those cases where a family member disappeared or those cases in which a body was discovered; be it in hours, days or years, but they started out as missing persons. At least there was a little evidence. There were, of course, people listed as Jane or John Doe who were never identified, but ended up as homicides based on evidence found in the remains. It would be hard to work on cold cases that were simply about establishing an identity for the remains.

He sorted the thirty-five cases that his first analysis had kicked out and added these new parameters which knocked the case total down to twenty-nine. Still a lot of cases to focus on, so next he tried doing a run to see if any of the cases were connected; common location, common method of a crime, any commonalities at all. That knocked it down to five cases. Perfect, he thought that was a manageable number. He explained his reasoning to Natalie and sent her the list. Later he'd take a look at the cases to see if there was anything else he could do computer wise, but he needed to do his own work. He checked in with his correctional system software and all was calm and correct, no heinous murderer was about to be released. So he entered his lab to work on his new invention which was a wave powered energy cell. He'd been experimenting with different devices in his lab to collect the energy of a wave crashing against it. He thought it might solve the energy needs of some poorer island countries like Tonga or Haiti.

He blinked when his alarm system went off. It might be a sea lion or a salmon or a human. In his seven years of living on the island, the perimeter alarm had rarely been triggered. It was about fifteen yards out from the shore in a circle around the island buried in the bay's dirt and rock layer. Boats didn't trigger the alarm; rather it was something large and about seven feet below the surface, which was lower than a boat hull. He checked the object's location on his system and went upstairs and outside to check. He thought about putting cameras with the sensors, but they would be big, subject to frequent replacement, and it was murky. He walked toward the cliff edge nearest the alarm, his island's closest point to San Quentin prison ironically. He couldn't imagine a convict escaping by putting on a wetsuit and snorkel apparatus.

He stood looking down, weapons in hand; he had a slingshot and a high powered water gun. The water gun, another invention of his, contained a liquid form of pepper spray. Enough to turn back a human, but not ecologically hurt the bay. In the slingshot, he had pellets of a fishy substance that wildly attracted birds. He tested both out in terms of aim and function. When he fired the slingshot pellet, birds had seemingly come out of nowhere to bomb the pellet. He also knew his pepper spray was harmful to eyes and he practiced aiming the gun to ensure he was adept with the weapon. Glancing over the edge in the general direction of the tripped sensors, he saw bubbles floating to the surface.

'Interesting,' he thought, his first human intruder. He moved back from the edge and lay down on his belly so he could see what the person was up to. Soon enough, he saw a scuba diver rise from the rocks, walk over to a boulder and sit upon it. The diver pushed a mask off, taking a few strong breaths. That was when Damian noticed that it was a mermaid that had landed upon his rock, confirmed when she pushed the wetsuit hood off and shook her hair out in a most feminine way. He was curious to see what she did next.

She took out a cell phone and tried to call, but he knew it wouldn't work as he'd installed a jamming feature to prevent any cell phone from working on and within about twenty feet of his island, but his own. The Federal Communications Commission had no knowledge of his technology and he aimed to keep it that way. He heard her mutter a few curse words as she re-examined her gas tank gauge. Then she looked toward San Quentin and then Richmond, sighed and prepared to go back into the water. Damian guessed she was having problems with her scuba equipment and was judging which shore was easiest to swim to. There was no happy answer to that question as a swimmer could get side-swiped by a boat that would be unable to see a lone swimmer in a dark wetsuit against the dark waves. Damn he'd have to offer his help; he wouldn't want her death on his conscious.

"Do you need some help?" He called out from his now standing position, his weapons well out of sight.

She startled and slipped off the rock into the water and came up sputtering. Once she had herself under control in the rocking of the waves, she called out, "Maybe. Who are you?"

"I live here; you've beached yourself on my island."

"Your island? I thought the government owned all of the islands in the bay. Is there a house up there or a working cell phone?"

"Yes to both questions. What's the problem with your gear?" Damian asked pointing to her scuba tank and regulator.

"I was exploring the floor of the bay when I discovered my tank was leaking air. It's completely drained and I was debating which direction to swim ashore. Do you have a boat that will get me across the water?"

"No, but I could probably repair your scuba gear. I'll go fetch my drone to pick up your equipment. Why don't you find a comfortable seat down there and give me a few minutes. Do you want something to drink?"

Damian had scuba dived and had memories of how dry his mouth felt after using the apparatus.

"Yes to the drink, I'd love something hot, like tea or coffee."

He nodded and walked out of her sight. He was back in less than five minutes with a thermos filled with ginger tea for her, attached to his drone. The drone gently brought the thermos to her and it sat patiently in the air while she loaded the tank and regulator on its legs which served as hooks. Damian had her equipment in no time and he checked it over. Then he yelled down to her, "Was there a leak or did you lose track of time and just run the tank dry?"

"Could have been either, what time is it now?"

Damian just shook his head at her cavalierly ignoring the time. That was scuba 101.

"Who gave you your certification to scuba dive?"

"Why?" She asked him suspiciously.

"Scuba 101, you never ever lose track of time. Speaking of which, enjoy your tea while I go recharge your tank."

Damian left her there knowing that other perimeter alarms would alert him if she tried to climb the wall of his island. He hoped she wouldn't try.

He was back in ten minutes directing the drone down to her with her gear. She looked at the regulator and tested the manifold and judged everything to be fine. She could return to the shore by staying well below any boat hull levels and make it back safely.

"Thanks, whoever you are. Can you send your drone back here for the mug?"

He did just that and after she loaded the thermos, she slipped her hood on and was shortly underway, swimming toward Tiburon. Even with fins she had perhaps a thirty minute swim in front of her. Oh well, the little mermaid had entertained him for half an hour. He walked back into his house and moved to put the thermos in his dishwasher when he discovered she left behind a business card inside.

It read, 'Ariana Knowles', with an email address and phone number in Belvedere, a very posh city next to Tiburon. No occupation listed. 'Weird', he thought.

Oh well, back to his lab, though he felt pretty good for assisting the woman, while managing to protect his own privacy. He was going to check her out, but then he noticed another email from Natalie.

CHAPTER 5

Ariana had a long swim back to her own cove across the bay in Belvedere. She'd been reckless not watching her tank pressure until it was too late. If the man from the island hadn't rescued her, she could have had a dangerous swim home. There were ferries that crossed her path overhead and if she had been swimming at the surface, it was very conceivable that she would have had a hard time avoiding the boats. She rather liked pretending she was a fish and swimming at a depth that avoided boats. It was easy to get lost in the darkness of the water and her own fascination with the floor of the bay. She planned to look up who the man on the rock was and thank him for filling her tank.

It had been a bizarre encounter. She'd thought the island was deserted and she was still puzzled as to why her cell phone hadn't worked, since it worked in every other part of the bay. She nearly jumped out of her skin when the man had called down to her, but she'd liked his drone technology and the hot tea had been good also. He looked about her age, smart, and she liked his brand of ginger tea. Maybe she'd send him some as thanks. Except how did you deliver anything to that island? It wasn't like UPS or the postal service made it a stop. Maybe she'd have to match a gadget with him. She owned a small boat that she could drive back to the island and then operate her own drone to drop some tea on his doorstep. Not that she'd spotted his house to even know where his doorstep was. She dropped her scuba equipment off in her boathouse, hosed down her wetsuit and the equipment, and then headed up to her house to shower and research the man on the rock as she would call him until she had a name.

Twenty minutes later, her brunette bob of a haircut clean and dry, with yoga pants and flip flops and a soft hoodie, she sat at her computer excited to have something new to research. She'd bought this house four years ago when she relocated from New York City to the West Coast. Her husband of ten years had lost his battle with pancreatic cancer and everything about New York had reminded her of her loss. He'd been a hedge fund investor while she was a whiz at sniffing out business interactions that would impact companies that her husband would or wouldn't invest in. They'd been the perfect pair. At first they put off having children, but then once they started trying, Jared had soon after been diagnosed with cancer. He'd lived longer than average for that cancer, but it hadn't been the time to try getting pregnant as he'd been on powerful chemo agents and she wanted to be focused on helping him at first fight the cancer, then in time to have a comfortable death. He hadn't had a bucket list to fulfill rather he played the investor game up to about the week before his death. It had left her a very wealthy widow, but she'd rather have been poor just to have had Jared around a few more years. She'd up and left New York, her friends and family included, and bought this beautiful house just north of San Francisco. She'd found that by using the same acumen that assisted Jared, she'd increased her net worth by operating a private venture capital fund successfully investing into some highly successful Silicon Valley start-ups.

Her future assured, she'd been trying to find a purpose for herself. Making companies successful was intellectually fulfilling, but she'd yet to find meaning to her life. How could she make an impact on the world? She'd hiked all over the region and thought about ways to protect this incredible natural beauty that she was surrounded by, but she hadn't found her passion yet. Recently, she'd taken to exploring the bay with scuba gear, but still nothing was striking a cord. Oh well, cracking her knuckles she went to work creating a dossier on her man from the rock. She would approach him like she would one of her start-up companies.

A while later, she sat back and frowned. He was a hard nut to crack. The island was indeed owned by a private trust, but she'd been unable to locate who was behind the trust. It was like someone had gone into several public systems and erased data that was usually available. She felt a cold nose nudge her, and looked down to Miguel, her Portuguese water dog. The dog was so smart that she was sure that if he could talk human, he'd be an even better investor than herself, and he loved to swim. He demanded rain or shine to go swimming in the bay every day.

"What's up Miguel? You don't like being ignored? You need to go for your swim?"

He smiled happily up at her and so she took a break, grabbing a floating toy for him to chase in the waves. While she stood at the shore's edge, she thought again about her mysterious man, checking off in her head different sites to visit to research him. She couldn't come up with anything new so once the dog was satisfied with his exercise, she went back inside and ordered a drone that could carry up to five pounds of tea. She would practice with it dropping toys into the bay for Miguel and once she got the hang of it, she would journey out to his island and drop some tea as thanks.

CHAPTER 6

Damian opened Natalie's email and thought about her request. Could he access the FBI's fingerprint system? Of course she didn't ask the question in those exact words; that would be setting up the two of them for some jail time. He thought he could get her an answer. The five cases he'd picked for her all had fingerprint evidence and that had changed in the last twenty years. In the past, if you had a suspect's name you could have a fingerprint expert compare fingerprints at the scene versus the particular suspect. Fingerprints collected on paper cards left detectives to sort through thousands of cards, assuming the criminal was fingerprinted in their own jurisdiction. There were simply too many cards to search for a suspect and that was assuming the fingerprinting occurred in your own city or county. Fingerprints collected in Florida were impossible to search for a match.

The FBI setup a computer system that collected and computerized fingerprint cards from about 1990 onward and had over 100 million fingerprints on file to match. As four of the five cases that Damian highlighted were from 1980-1990, there was a chance that the fingerprints from the old cases were never matched against the FBI's computer system. Could Damian reach inside the firewalls of the FBI to check on the fingerprint matches? Of course what she was asking him to do was illegal, but it was for a very good cause and he understood her request as cold cases like this might take fifteen weeks to get results officially from the FBI. If he could instead peek inside their system and run the analysis himself, Natalie would be that many weeks ahead in solving the case.

It was an intriguing request. He was sure he could break into their system because he, as yet, had never failed to access a computer server. However, the key here was rather ironic. He needed to not leave any 'fingerprints' behind when he broke into their system. He replied to Natalie that he could fulfill her request, but he wanted to think overnight about the implications of doing so. That settled, he turned to researching his mermaid from earlier.

Damian spent about fifteen minutes assembling a dossier of sorts on Ariana. His conclusion was that she meant him no harm and was actually a person he'd probably enjoy knowing, not that their paths would ever cross again since he didn't dabble in venture capital and he hoped she learned her lesson about watching her air tank while scuba diving. She had to be a risk taker as it was never recommended to scuba alone. He glanced at the time and decided it was time to get his work out in before heading across the bay to the Oakland harbor.

Two hours later he sat in Pete's pub talking with Pete on how his alcohol dispensing system was working and whether he should make any changes to it to better meet Pete's needs. Each upgrade he created for Pete was then worked into the system sold to other small pub owners. Pete asked if he could include an inventory system, that would calculate his weekly alcohol consumption and then he could use that for ordering from the various distributors. He presently felt he was carrying more inventory than he needed, but it would help if he had the data to better decide what his weekly alcohol needs were. He also thought he might be able to spot some trends sooner from his patrons such as the recent rage with Fireball, a cinnamon whisky. He'd run out of it for about six weeks in a row before he wised up and kept spare bottles in his office that he purchased from a local big box store. Damian took notes and thought he could work something out for Pete in a few weeks. They'd just finished their conversation when Trevor walked in. Trevor must have looked like his father as Damian could see little of Natalie in him. He was slightly shorter than Damian's six feet, with a nearly bald head. He had a severe receding hairline and had given up having any hair on his head in his twenties. He liked to run 10K races and so had the long lean look of a runner. Despite the seriousness of his job, he always had a huge smile that nearly blinded anyone nearby.

Pete provided Trevor a cold Blue Moon as soon as his butt hit the barstool. There was no need to look at the menu because the two men always ate Pete's cheeseburgers and fries when they appeared at the bar. In time they moved over to a table and dug into their meal.

"How did you find tickets to tonight's game?" Damian asked.

"Pure luck. One of my office mates sold his set, but then the sale failed at the last moment. I offered him twice the face value and he took it. It helped that I'd helped him on a case of his last week, of course, and he owed me."

"It's so exciting to be there and potentially witness history, perhaps we'll see seventy three wins in a single regular season in just under three hours. It's going to be an electric crowd."

"I hope to see Curry hit the four hundred 3 pointers mark. It feels like each of those records will stand for my lifetime. I love the fact that their skill records are amazing, rather than sheer physical strength on the floor. It's like watching a basketball genius at work."

"Yeah, it's going to be a historic night," Damian said. "What else is going on in your life?"

"Haley and I are talking about getting engaged, so expect to hear the announcement soon," smiled Trevor. Then he frowned and said, "Sorry man, I shouldn't have said that on this day," and he looked crestfallen.

Damian had felt just a dim memory of when he asked Jen to marry him, and thinking about his earlier resolution said, "It's okay, this has been a taking stock of my life kind of day and I'd concluded earlier that I needed to start living more, beginning with accepting your invitation for tonight's game. Attending a game on the day of the anniversary of my family's murder, rather than wallowing in depression for the entire day and night, is a new event. I guess time is beginning to soften the wound."

Trevor couldn't think of anything to add to Damian's statement, so he just nodded and decided to head to less emotional waters and said, "Mom mentioned that she'd pulled you in on a new assignment of hers. What does she want you to do this time?"

"Since you're a respected member of the California Bar, I can't tell you," Damian replied grinning.

"Oh God, she must have asked you to hack into the Governor's account or something; you should really consider whether you want to go to jail. You won't have unlimited computers there."

"Yeah, but with the way I engineer things, I'll spend the first month improving the place for the convicts and the second month planning my escape. I might even make it back in time for the NBA finals."

Trevor just groaned and added, "The NBA finals in what year? 2030?"

Poor Trevor, the line of questioning had just gone from bad to worse, so Damian decide to steer the conversation into calmer waters.

"So I had a mermaid visit my island today," Damian remarked.

Trevor choked on his beer with this last comment. Damian waited for him to catch his breath and he finally croaked out, "What?"

Damian had watched the emotions chase across Trevor's face; concern, briefly wonder if it was hallucinations, and then decide that whatever happened he would sit back and enjoy the story.

"I was working on a wave power invention when my underwater perimeter alarm sounded. I grabbed my slingshot and water gun and went outside to investigate. A woman surfaced with her scuba gear; she'd run out of air."

"Wow," was all Trevor could say since he never visited the island and his mom said it was more protected than Fort Knox.

"I used my drone to lift her tank up the cliff to me and sent her down some tea. A few minutes later I was back with a filled tank that I sent down to her. She returned the tea thermos to me with her business card inside and she set off to swim underwater back to Belvedere."

Trevor blinked trying to think of something relevant to add to the conversation, but he was stuck back in the vision of a mermaid on the rocks of Damian's island, using a drone to move objects, the fact that there was an air compressor on the island, and finally that someone would want to swim underwater across that area of the bay. Where to start? Finally Trevor admitted, "Damian, since you're turning over a new leaf, you need to invite me out to your island so I can see these quirks – mermaids and drones in the middle of San Francisco Bay."

Damian paused and then nodded, "Okay, there's a guy in the Richmond Marina that I make arrangements with to bring your mother out to the island. So when you want to come, let me know and I'll arrange it."

Trevor, never one to let grass grow under his feet said, "How about this weekend? Say Saturday at 11. Do you have a TV? We could watch the first playoff game."

Whoa thought Damian, uneasy about the thought of having anyone inside his home for the length of a basketball game, but then he thought, turn over a new leaf and start living your life.

"I do have TV, but no beer, so you'll have to bring a six pack with you. If game time is 12:30, you just need to be at the marina by 12. That will give you plenty of time to get out to the island and climb the hill or ride my zip line."

"Okay," was all Trevor said; unwilling to put any hesitation or roadblocks in the way of visiting Damian. Having made arrangements for the weekend, the two men left the bar to walk to Oracle Arena to watch basketball history being made.

CHAPTER 7

The next morning, the two cats and Damian were sitting at his breakfast counter. They were eyeing his bowl of milk and cereal, and he was giving them the evil eye to keep them away until he finished. It was like this every morning and he tried giving them just a plain bowl of milk, but they let him know they liked the additional flavor provided by his cereal remnants and so this routine started. He said to them, "We're going to have a guest this weekend; are you guys going to show yourselves?"

They blinked at him, then Bailey leaned over to clean his leg as though Damian wasn't worthy of an answer, Bella just looked at him and blinked her eyes, giving him a look that said 'cut the conversation and hurry up and give me my milk.' When Natalie was on the island, they stayed out of sight, but she was never there for more than an hour. Trevor would be there for three hours so they might come out of hiding. All three of them liked to hide from the rest of humanity, but it would be interesting to watch them adjust as he interacted more.

On today's agenda was to see if he could hack into the fingerprint system at the FBI without detection. His money was on his own technical skill. He checked out the news to see if any hacker announced getting into the security system, but all he found was fingerprints stolen from the federal government's Office of Personnel Management which contained the prints of those employees with security clearances. That wasn't the system he was after or likely the fingerprint sources. He would hope that none of the employees with security clearances had fingerprints that belonged in a criminal justice system.

Natalie sent the fingerprint request for matching to the FBI in case he couldn't get into their system, but he loved the challenge. Stretching his arms and cracking his knuckles, he went to work. He could approach the hack a variety of ways, but his first choice was to borrow a username and password from someone with access to the system. His presence would be much harder to detect, and frankly it didn't feel as criminal as exploiting the fingerprint software. He set to work figuring out who had access to the system. Once he had their names and the username for FBI employees he went to work trying passwords. Two hours later, he found what he was looking for and was in the system. He then sent the fingerprints in for a match that were lifted from the crime scenes of the five cases he selected and Natalie confirmed as being the first cases to work on. In total, there were fifty sets of prints to match. He checked the database, looking for ways to mirror it onto his own computer. Sure it wouldn't be the most updated as he assumed that new entries are added to the database every day, but given that these were cold cases that they were researching, it should work for most if not all of their cases.

The first set came back with a match, and he set that information aside for the moment while he looked for a way to copy the database. It was so large that he couldn't do a single copy and go. He recognized the company that created the database for the FBI and knew how to write queries to copy entire columns of data from their database. The difficulty with copying a column at a time was that it was a relational database, data in one column having a relationship to data in another column. It wouldn't do him any good to have just a column of fifty million fingerprints, without the corresponding names to match. Even the names were probably not enough given the frequency with which people's last names were Smith or Garcia.

This was such a huge database he thought his best bet was to implant a backdoor command string into the database that would allow him endless access. The fingerprint data he located in the database would give Natalie a head start on her investigation, while she waited for the same information to come through the proper route from the FBI. Since he understood commands for this database, he had the backdoor access implanted in no time and then he looked at the coding that produced matches of fingerprints. He decided that at some point he would leave an anonymous message with the Bureau of how they could speed up their fingerprint matches.

Their program matched the thirty points of one fingerprint to another. Damian thought it would go faster if you matched the first six points and then moved on to more decisive matching with sixteen points of match which seem to be the criminal justice standard. Mathematically, it would be faster to run a large data search in that manner, than trying to match the first sixteen from the start. Having set up his backdoor and his data run, he walked away from the terminal to look again at the cold cases. He had some ideas that he listed on paper and sent to Natalie along with a summary of what he'd done with the database. Of course the second part of the message was written in code as he wanted no trail to his doorstep of his hacking successes.

He'd let the fingerprint matching program run, and over the next three days, he was able to identify about eighty percent of the prints found at the scenes of the five cases. As it came in, he would send it to Natalie, then forget about the cases as he went back to inventions. In the back of his head was a worry about having Trevor visit the next day. It would be his first social call in seven years, before the death of his family. He decided, when Trevor arrived, he would use his drone to move the beer and then give Trevor the choice of riding his zip line or walking up the hill. His boat captain would let him know when he left the Richmond Marina and then Damian would know that Trevor would arrive in about twelve minutes. He had chips and dip and meat to barbecue. The house was clean and he could offer his guest tea, coffee, or water. His couch had plenty of space for two guys to sit and watch a basketball game.

The Bay was his source of water. Damian had built a small desalination filter that pumped water out of the bay and up to a tank close to his house and he used that for everything but drinking. He had a few more filter gadgets that he put his drinking water through inside the house and the water tasted so good he thought about setting up his own home brewery. Maybe he'd ask Trevor's opinion on the taste of the water. He had the equipment for a microbrewery as well as yeast, but he'd have to import the hops. He could have his own beer on the island in two months and perhaps if he made enough, he could supply Pete with the brew for his bar. That thought brought a smile to his face.

He checked his satellite receiver, something else he'd built to make sure he could get the station that the game was on. He could lock onto any satellite, but since he wasn't a subscriber he had no idea what he was watching until the commercials ended and the show began. To move from one major network to another took his computer finding the satellite then locking on it, but he couldn't complain as it was free. Okay, he was ready for a guest.

It was time to step outside and fish for tonight's dinner. He opened his door and was shocked to see a package sitting there. Never in his seven years here had there been a package on his doorstep.

CHAPTER 8

Could it be a bomb? He paused and did calculations in his head of what kind of damage something explosive inside the small package could do; and then he shook his head at his negative thought and bent down to reach for the box.

Then he smiled. It was a rare use of his facial muscles. He hadn't had much to smile at in the past seven years.

The box was addressed to 'The man on the rock, whose name I don't know.'

He was sure he knew who the box was from, the question was how had it arrived without his alarm systems going off? How had she gotten on the island without him knowing it?

He opened the box and found two flavors of tea from a tea shop in Sausalito and a thank you card from Ariana.

He read, "I tried to find out your name but you've done a great job of hiding that from the world. No, I didn't step on your island, instead I matched you for technology. After practicing dropping toys in the bay for my dog to retrieve, I dropped this package close to your doorstep. I appreciate your help with my air tank; it would have been a dangerous and long swim home without your help."

Cheers,
Ariana

HE ADMIRED her approach and decided to acknowledge her gesture. He picked up the phone and called the number on the card she originally gave him as she had not included one in the package of tea. The phone rang six times before he heard someone pick up the other end.

"Ariana"

Damian tried to remember if this was the voice from a few days earlier, but he couldn't confirm it, but since she said her name, he figured he had the right person. Then he froze, what was he going to say? It'd been an impulsive gesture on his part, just wanting to say thanks.

"Ah, hi, it's the man on the rock." Wow, Damian thought, *aren't you 'a brilliant conversationalist.*

"Hello man from the rock," Ariana replied. "Did you get my package?"

"Yes and thanks. I assume you used a boat and a drone rather than just launching the drone from your house."

She laughed and replied, "I ordered the drone the minute I got back to my house and practiced the next two days before attempting the delivery to you. No way could I have made it from my home to your island without dropping the package or the drone into the bay. As it was I took two packages with me in case one of them ended up as fish dinner."

"I don't think fish like tea leaves. They like to eat each other or kelp or algae. I can't imagine tea made from kelp or algae being at all tasty."

Again, Damian thought, always hide behind science rather than asking her about herself. He'd never work up the nerve to invite her to his island. Whoa. He felt like his brain had hit the brakes so hard that it slammed into the bone of his cranium. Where had that thought come from? First he invited Trevor and now he was thinking about inviting Ariana? What about his treasured solitude and privacy? His thoughts were going a million miles an hour, so he tried to disengage his brain and tune back into Ariana.

"These are Silicon Valley fish, so they probably eat sushi or kale."

He liked her sense of humor and replied, "Did you see any sushi underwater on your swim home?"

"No, Man on the Rock. Do you have a name? I admit I looked you up but I couldn't find your name anywhere and I'm good at that kind of thing. So in my mind I've been calling you Manny as in Man of the rock."

"Manny?" Damian exclaimed, wincing. "I'll have to tell you my name just to get away from that awful nickname. I'm Damian."

"Damian, hmmm. That's a Greek name. Are you descended from Father Damian who saved the Hawaiian Lepers of Molokai, or are you Dr. Damian, the patron of physicians?"

"I never looked at my name that way. I have a PhD, so I'm a doctor of sorts, but not one of medicine."

"Okay Damian, call me when you need another order of tea dropped on you. I'll keep you supplied with tea as long as I have the hang of operating this drone. I really do thank you for the scuba air, I was thinking about my body being hit by one of the ferries crossing the bay and was just going to try and drown myself off of your island to save myself from being chopped up in a boat propeller, so I'm serious about keeping you in tea for a long time."

"I had the same vision; you take a lot of risks when you don't pay attention to scuba air. I hope that event made you more aware of that."

"I'll admit it did and in fact I haven't been out for a long distance swim since then."

"Why do you scuba dive in San Francisco Bay? I wouldn't think there would be much to see as the water isn't very clear?"

"You're right about that, sometimes it's creepy coming upon stuff suddenly, but I have the sense not to go outside the Golden Gate Bridge for fear those currents would sweep me to Japan."

"Why don't you fly to some place warmer like Hawaii or the Caribbean? From what I know about you it's not a matter of affordability."

"You looked me up?"

"Yes, you left me your card, otherwise I would have looked for you under the title of mermaid, and you were the first person to breach my security in seven years, so I needed to know what you were up to."

There was dead silence on the other end of the phone, while she thought about his words then she said, "Then I'm glad your first visitor was a mermaid. If you're ever over in Belvedere, give me a call and I'll cook dinner for you at my house, where you can just see your island off in the distance."

"Thanks for the invite, and I'll do that sometime. Are you a good cook?"

"No. I'd probably fake it and order something from a restaurant around here and throw it into a saucepan or my oven to make you think I'd made it."

He laughed at her candid response and said, "I've got to go and it was a pleasure talking to you, Ariana. Be safe."

After Damian ended the call, he decided he would do just that, cross over next week and look her up. He liked her adventurous spirit and intelligence. They were kindred spirits in that they were both widows and of about the same age. He'd certainly enjoyed their call.

Now it was back to fishing for tonight's dinner. He learned years ago, that it was best to fish in the afternoon as sometimes it took a long time to catch fish suitable for eating and he and the cats could go hungry if he failed. There were a variety of fish in the bay but he mostly caught halibut or flounder and the occasional striped bass. If the fish was small, he released it back to catch another time. His cats needed two fish for food throughout the day, while he liked one to two for dinner. Sometimes he fished just for the cats when he had beef or chicken or pasta for dinner. On the rare times he left the island, it was dry kibble for the cats, but they hadn't starved, nor had he found dead birds on his return.

Fishing was also thinking time. He'd worked out many puzzles while catching dinner. He also depended on the wind direction or current, fished from different spots on his little island and the different views never ceased to power his creativity and problem solving. He had so many things going through his head; the anniversary of his family's murder, inviting Trevor out to the island, Ariana, the cold cases, his wave powered energy unit. He hadn't had this much on his mind in years. He decided to focus on the cold cases as all the other emotions roiling through his head would hopefully work themselves out in time.

CHAPTER 9

He'd sent about forty five fingerprint identifications to Natalie, but could he do more for her? Maybe write a program that would search a bunch of databases to say where these people were now, so she'd have an immediate summary of each person without having to research each one. Likely the FBI database was out of date and didn't include every death, or prison stay. As he pulled up the second and final fish for the day, he was anxious to get inside and filet the fish, then get downstairs to his computer lab.

A short time later he was sitting in front of his terminal looking at the results from the first algorithm that he wrote. Sometimes it took several modifications before he hit it right and other times he nailed it the first time and this was one of them. He picked up the phone to call Natalie.

"Hey Damian, thanks for the run," Natalie said upon answering her cell phone.

"Well, I've got something even better, I've got two people you need to immediately focus on."

"What? What did that brilliant brain of yours do?" and Damian could hear the excitement in her voice.

"I thought you needed some help narrowing down the huge list of prints and while I was fishing, I thought of an algorithm to create pulling in a bunch of different databases to create a bio on each person, otherwise you could waste a lot of time researching people with just a random connection to the case."

"Yes," and "what did you find?" asked Natalie, impatience in her voice.

"One of the cold cases is for a woman named 'Debbie Altman'. She disappeared one night in south San Jose in the summer of 1988. Her car was found on the side of the road, but she has never reappeared, so she's classified as a missing person, not a homicide."

"Yes, I remember that case," replied Natalie with growing impatience. Damian could feel her voice urging him to move faster.

"So a fingerprint from that case is connected to other cases that are not on your cold case list. I believe the police lifted prints from her car and her apartment since they never did find Debbie, dead or alive."

"Who is the person with prints in these two cases?"

"It's a man named John Avery. He was placed on trial for the murder of another person in 1990 but was acquitted on a technicality."

"Yes I vaguely remember that case. I was working patrol at the time, but I kept an eye on the detective division as that was where I wanted to end up. He wasn't tried because of something with paperwork," Natalie said trying to reach back in her memory to the case.

"He was released because the district attorney filed the case on the 91st day and the law requires it be done in 90 days. His prints were taken at the time of his arrest, so they were in the system. Besides the run I just did, there was another incident of his prints in an apartment of a woman that went missing from Santa Cruz County. Granted all of the cases are at least twenty years old.

What's the likelihood of his prints being connected to two different missing women and one murder victim?"

"It's small Damian, very small. Did the bio you created say where he is now?"

"Yeah, it did. He works at a small convenience store and he is reputed to be connected to the Aryan Brotherhood gang. So I guess that means he's probably trafficking drugs through that store."

"Wow! That is quite a break and since there is no statute of limitation on murder, we can haul his ass in for questioning, or rather I should say the detective I'm working with can haul in this suspect. I forget I no longer have police powers. Even though you already know it, Damian, you're a genius! Tell me about the second name."

"The second name was also a missing person who was eventually found, but the case wasn't solved. Her name is Barbara Watson and she was reported missing by her husband in 1982. The husband was suspected, but other than being the first person police usually look at, there wasn't a shred of evidence and no weapon was located. Her remains were found on a hillside with brush covering the ground that utility workers came across when they constructed an area called Communication Hill."

"I was a detective at the time for that case, but I remember hearing about it. I think the body had been there five to seven years when they found her, so they used dental records and DNA to identify the bones. The husband had gone on to make a life with another woman, and while he seemed happy that her remains had been found, his affect hadn't seemed right at the time. He seemed more uneasy than relieved. So what connection did you find?"

"It's an odd finding, there was a knife used in a stabbing case around 1983 and prints were lifted to match the suspect in that case. The knife had two sets, one was the person in custody and he was convicted and sent to prison. He served his time and was released. The second set of prints matched Mr. Greg Watson whose prints were taken five years ago when he provided consultant services to the Federal Government. His prints weren't matched to the knife as that case was considered solved. I accidentally landed on the prints by the way I did the algorithm."

"Do you know where he is now?"

"He relocated to Phoenix, so he's not in your jurisdiction."

"I wonder if the knife is still available for a forensic pathologist to compare to the wound evidence in Barbara's remains."

"Are her remains still available?" Damian asked, thoughts roiling through his mind. "Even though the case isn't solved, the remains would still get a burial right? The police don't hold on to the remains indefinitely waiting for new clues right?"

"No we count on our medical examiner and crime scene techs to collect all the available evidence. Think about it, we have some two hundred plus cold cases. Where would we possibly store the bodies related to those unsolved cases? Granted not all of them have a body, but you get my point."

"Okay." Damian said, relief in his voice. "Keep me posted with what happens, Natalie. I'm going to see if I can find any other leads like these. Good luck with these suspects."

Natalie said curiously, "So, you already think the first guy murdered three women?"

"Yes, I ran a statistical analysis of my finding and it came back at 99.994 for the first case and 85.7 for the second case. Statistics rarely lie."

"Good to know. Great work, Damian, and I'm going to try to nail these guys."

"Talk to you later."

CHAPTER 10

Damian was kicking himself for being nervous about Trevor visiting his home. What was he so worked up about?

'Okay' he'd admitted to himself that Trevor's opinion was important to him; he felt like an uncle to him as he'd known him for a long time and they had a special bond. His house and island were spartan and he had no visitors to the island after the workmen left other than Natalie. She barged onto his island with her wreaths on the first anniversary of his family's death. She'd had a friend bring her by boat and she forced her way into his life and yes he would admit it, easily, that beginning opened a relationship both personal and professional that enriched his life. He also appreciated her idea for the wreaths ceremony as it both helped him mourn and to say goodbye. He might be able to tell her next year, if his life opened up a bit, to stop the ceremony. He hoped he might be able to say that as he somehow thought his life would be richer with more to focus on.

He did one final check of his house and land to make sure that nothing was out of place and he had food available for the game. He kept no alcohol in his house, in the beginning because he was worried about resorting to it to deal with the pain of losing his family, now sometimes he had beer and wine, sometimes he didn't. He'd have wine or beer when he left the island but he didn't miss it if he had no inventory.

He checked his watch and looked toward the Richmond Marina; he should see Trevor's boat approaching soon. He would stand on top of the hill and direct him to the path that was the easiest way up. When it was time to leave he could take the zip line down. Damian would use his drone to bring the beer up, he didn't want Trevor slipping and breaking glass on the side of his hill. It might hurt Trevor and it would be a mess to clean up.

He saw Mike's pontoon boat approaching with Trevor. He was expecting a box of supplies in addition to Trevor and the drone was resting at his side. For once, Mike could motor back to the marina rather than staying to help Damian with putting packages inside the net that the drone picked up. The pontoon boat was great as it could come up on the sand and no one had to get their feet wet. Trevor hopped off then reached back to lift a cooler down as well as about five boxes. Mike was also Damian's garbage man, taking recyclables and cardboard back with him, Damian composted his regular garbage, but he would have drowned in cardboard by now if Mike hadn't helped him remove the stuff. Soon Mike was pushing off the sand and giving a wave goodbye as he headed back to the marina.

Trevor yelled up to Damian, "This entire morning's been an adventure! How do I get this stuff up to you?"

"Welcome to Red Rock Island, just stay where you are and you can help me with my drone." Trevor did as instructed and soon the boxes and cooler were close to his front door. He asked Trevor if he wanted to ride the zip line or hike the cliff. Trevor had somewhat non-gripping soles on his feet and so indicated the zip line. Damian disappeared from Trevor's view, but then he saw an empty harness go over a rock and head for him.

Trevor moved over to the harness and stepped into it and gave the ready sign. He was soon moving over a rocky cliff in a circle around and up to the top of the island where Damian was waiting for him.

"I built the zip line for your mom. On her first visit, she skinned her hands and knees trying to scramble up the cliff. The ride makes her nervous but she prefers that to bleeding hands and knees."

"It's a rather daunting view when you're moving over the rocky cliff knowing that if the thing drops you, it's going to hurt a lot."

"I built it; it won't drop you. I over engineered it and I occasionally ride it myself."

"I imagine the trip down is even scarier than up, but I guess the same is true about scrambling down that cliff. Do you need help with those boxes?"

"I'll unpack them later, there's nothing in them I need at the moment. The weather's good, so we can just leave them outside for now. You didn't need to bring an entire cooler, I have a kitchen here you know."

"Yes, but when I got here the beer wouldn't have been cold," Trevor replied. "This way we can open it immediately rather than waiting for it to cool in your refrigerator."

Damian looked at his watch and said, "We better get inside, the game starts in seven minutes."

Trevor picked up the cooler and followed Damian inside the house and over to a kitchen counter. It was a normal looking interior including a comfortable looking couch and big screen television.

Trevor looked around and said, "Where does your electricity come from?"

"A combination of solar and wind power. I'm working on a wave technology as well, but I haven't figured it out completely yet."

"Damian, this is a beautiful house you've created and I like that you figured out how to live off the grid but yet have all the modern conveniences. What's next on your list to invent?"

Damian thought a moment and replied, "A greenhouse and a home brewery, after the wave power technology."

Trevor just nodded then grabbed a beer and a sandwich from the cooler which he handed to Damian.

"I didn't know what to expect here, so I brought sandwiches from your favorite fast food place. It's pastrami and probably with a few seconds in the microwave it'll be perfectly heated."

"I had snacks and hot dogs to throw on my barbecue, but I'd much rather have that pastrami."

They watched the first half of the game eating the huge pastrami sandwiches and washing it down with a couple beers. They discussed the performance of the Warriors team and then groaned as they saw their MVP go down with a knee sprain. At halftime Damian took Trevor down to the lower level to see his workshop and computer set up. Then they went outside so Trevor could try picking something up with the drone.

Soon they were back on the couch, worried about the outcome of the game without their star player, but they needn't have worried, as their team blew out the opponent in the end. Mike was scheduled to come back and pick Trevor up in about thirty minutes, and so they sat there chatting about other things.

"Damian, you've served as a mentor for me for the past seven years and I'd love to bring my fiancée to meet you soon. I've talked to her about you and she'll likely expect you to be twenty feet tall and able to foretell the future."

Damian thought about the request and replied, "My brain might be twenty feet tall, but the rest of me is just a regular guy. You could come back next weekend as I'm sure the Warriors will have another playoff game if she's interested in basketball."

"Of course she's interested in basketball, I couldn't date a girl who didn't have interest in sports. She played B-ball in high school and went to college on a softball scholarship so she's a force to be reckoned with."

"Good to know, I won't challenge her in either of those two sports. Once we know the schedule, I'll make arrangements with Mike and email you. I see his boat coming now; he's always perfectly on time. Do you want to hike down or ride the zip line?"

"I'd hate to ruin a perfectly good day by falling down one of your cliffs, so I'll ride the zip line down. Maybe when I come back next week, I'll try the hike up and wear the appropriate shoes."

"Sounds like a plan, safe travels home."

Damian watched the boat depart before going back into his house. He sat down on his couch to think about how he felt about the day. When he thought about it, he guessed there was something right about Trevor being his first guest to the island. The visit had gone well and he'd be back next weekend with his fiancée. She'd be the first true stranger to visit his home. Even Mike had never come up the cliff, to see the house he made so many deliveries to. He'd had a good time this afternoon and looked forward to repeating it next weekend.

He wondered how Natalie was doing, running down the two suspects.

CHAPTER 11

Natalie was excited to follow up on Damian's leads. She had a feeling that if she gave him the data that he would figure out how to put it together effectively with a computer so that it was a more efficient use of time. She had tried doing what he did manually and hadn't been getting anywhere as there were simply too many facts to comb through.

She made an appointment to meet with her SJPD detective contact, Kevin Shimoda, and discuss the two cases. She knew that Kevin, on the one hand, hated that the work had been contracted to her, but rationalized the need to solve the old cases and at least they had worked together before she retired. Once Damian had the fingerprint matches, she went back and pulled the same stuff manually in the SJPD system. She didn't want Kevin to know that Damian had hacked into the FBI system. Kevin would be doubtful about how she'd gotten the print matches, but that didn't matter, he would be more excited about pulling the two suspects in for questioning and trying to solve the cold cases.

Sitting in a drab conference room in her old division, she discussed the two cases with Kevin.

"They both appear worthy of questioning. I think we can bring

Mr. Avery in for questioning, and we'll ask the Phoenix PD to go out to Mr. Watson's home and question him for us," Kevin said.

"Are you going to get a search warrant for either suspect?" Natalie asked.

Kevin paused, thinking of the pros and cons and then nodded. "It will take longer, but I suspect our thug at the local convenience store won't willingly come in for questioning and if he does indeed belong to the Aryan Brotherhood, he'll have a sophisticated gang behind him."

"I agree and with the information about Greg Watson. Phoenix PD will have a sophisticated client for a different reason. Before we interview that gentleman, I want our coroner to look at the case and tell us if the knife's edges match the victim's remains. It will take longer but it will be an amazing piece of physical evidence if the coroner can make the connection. Thankfully, the man who committed the other crime with that knife is still incarcerated; otherwise we might not have the knife still in evidence. Is Dr. Patterson still on the job at the coroner's office? He was always excellent with knife wounds on the body," Natalie mused.

"He's still working and that was exactly who I was going to tag for this investigation. He'll have to compare the photos taken by the CSI techs when we recovered the bones. I know they photographed what they thought were knife striations according to the case report."

"Let's hope for a match."

"Yeah. I wonder about John Avery. He appears to have had three kills attributed to him about twenty years ago and would appear to meet the FBI's definition of a serial killer. I wonder why he stopped killing women? Or did he? Maybe I can do more fingerprint searches and see if his prints were found at any other older crime scenes before we computerized prints to the degree that we have today."

"Natalie, the problem with that is so many prints for the time period you're talking about exist in individual jurisdictions and haven't been computerized yet."

"True, but it's worth a look. How do you feel about taking on the AB gang?" Natalie asked curiously as she hadn't had any real dealings with the group during her career.

"I'd almost rather take on any other group of people including ISIS. They are a large white extremely violent prison gang that operates drug manufacturing and distribution outside of prison. I bet that convenience store is a source of meth distribution. I think I'll call my contacts in gang investigations and the covert response unit. I think the three of us could work together to set up surveillance on Mr. Avery. It would help to have something criminal to hold him on while we wait for other pieces to fall into place."

"Maybe this will be a two-for and we'll stop a slice of the drug trade. Kevin, is there any information you need for this interview of John Avery?"

"No this is good work Natalie. I hated when the brass contracted this work to you, but I'm not sure we would have found new clues on these two cases, so if it had to be someone outside the department, I'm glad it was you."

"Thanks Kevin. You know my contract is not a reflection of poor work on your part, the SJPD is just understaffed."

"Yeah, I know," he said as they stood up and shook hands before Natalie left the building. She greeted acquaintances on her way out. It'd been several years since she worked here, but she knew a lot of people in this building. She considered herself a good interviewer and hated not being in on the action when they brought Avery in for questioning. Hopefully the case would be cracked wide open next week she thought as she approached her car while checking her emails. Kevin promised to keep her informed with the findings in the case and she'd have to be satisfied with that.

Out of the corner of her eye, she watched a man walking

through the parking lot on a collision course with her. There was something about his behavior that made her suspicious, starting with the fact that he looked like a thug. She decided to change course and return to the building as if she'd forgotten something. At the same time, she wanted to keep a few cars between her and the thug.

She surreptitiously looked around the area thankful that the sunglasses could hide the movement of her eyes. When she'd changed course, she noticed that he had also. They were on the side of the building for public parking, unfortunately all of the patrol cars as well as officer private cars were in a separate parking lot. If she was still a member of the force, she would have had a body armor vest on and a gun in her holster. As a private citizen, she had neither, although Damian had rigged a water pistol for her with pepper spray. It was lime green and plastic, so as to be immediately recognizable by the police as not a real gun. She could, however, shoot a thirty foot stream of pepper spray at anyone bothering her. She'd once told Damian she felt insecure no longer walking around with a gun on her. He told her that she'd get into a lot of worthless trouble carrying a gun and had mailed her the water gun with instructions to practice shooting it. She did and walked around with it loaded with a home based recipe for pepper spray. Her husband had at first laughed at the solution and then called Damian to express his thanks for the gift. His eyes had pained him for hours after he accidentally touched the solution then rubbed his eyes. He liked that his wife was happier and protected.

The thug continued his beeline for Natalie, clearly intending to cut her off before she turned the corner of the building where there would be a lot more people and officers using the building entrance. She pulled out her water gun and yelled, "Freeze right now!"

The thug ignored her warning and reached for something in the back of his pants.

CHAPTER 12

Natalie took aim and fired at the thug as he did likewise. He saw that she was holding a plastic water gun and gave her an evil grin, assured of who would come out the winner in this gun battle. Fortunately, while his bullet was faster, she'd gotten off her stream and he was hit in the face by it causing his shot to go wide. The noise of the gun brought people around the building to where the thug was moaning in agony with his hands over his eyes, his grin gone from his face.

Police immediately swarmed the two of them and took the guns off both of them. One of the officers recognized Natalie and asked her to make a statement as to what had happened. The thug continued to moan and would do so until his eyes were washed. Natalie's water gun was put in a police evidence bag, by a detective who was trying not to be caught laughing at a crime scene.

Natalie made a note to herself to ask Damian to send her another water gun as it would be months to years before she got her lime green gun back. She trooped back inside the station knowing there were going to be a lot of statements she would have to give and it would be hours before she was released. Since the thug had fired a gun and the police had the shell casings, and gunpowder residue on his hands and the security footage of their little gun battle, Natalie was in the clear a few hours later minus her handy little toy gun.

She had the thug's name and put in a call to Damian hoping to get him in person.

"Hey Natalie, how did your meeting with your detective go?"

"It went well. He's getting a search warrant, and bringing in both the gang and covert operations folks to see if we can kill three birds with one stone."

"Covert operations?"

"That's the new age name for cops that go undercover concerning illicit drugs."

"Oh, I guess I haven't watched enough cop dramas recently."

"Damian, I was shot at in the parking lot at the headquarters and,"

"What! Are you hurt? Which hospital are you at?"

"Damian I'm fine thanks to you. In fact, I haven't told my husband about the incident, I'm so fine. I need a new water gun; yours worked perfectly, but they confiscated it as evidence. That is after they all got done laughing at a retired girl detective running around with a plastic water gun. I'd also like to see what you can find on a guy named 'Michael O'Brien'. He was the thug arrested for shooting at me."

"No problem, I have a spare or two here. I can't get off the island today, but I can use my drone to drop it at the marina and then have Uber pick it up and deliver it to you. Do you want it delivered to your home or office?"

"Home, and thanks."

"As for your thug, give me half an hour and I'll see what I can find. Is that O'Brian with an 'A' or O'Brien with an 'E'."

"It's an 'E', he was Caucasian, about 5'9" tall, tattoos all over his face and body and somewhere between twenty and thirty years of age, and quite creepy looking."

"Got it! Are you sure you're okay?"

"Yes, we fired at each other, and his shot went wide. He laughed when he saw the lime green plastic gun, but he isn't laughing now. Last I saw him, he was moaning and crying over that pepper juice recipe that you advised me to use. You know I've carried that gun around since you gave it to me over two years ago and never had occasion to use it. My former co-workers were having a hard time not laughing at the water gun, but I wonder how many of them will go home and arm their spouses with your ingenious weapon."

"So they can't accuse you of aggravated assault, right?"

"Nope, the thug's actions were caught on the security video and it's clear he stalked me, ignored my order 'to freeze', and then fired first. Until they saw the security footage my fellow officers had laughed about my silly bright green water gun, now I'm free and clear of any part of this drama. I just don't recognize this guy or the name, but he must be connected to me somehow."

The moment they hung up, Damian called Mike and fortunately he was at the marina and could collect the package. Then he went down to his workshop to collect a water pistol. This one would be princess pink, which should make Natalie laugh. He purchased a variety of kid's water guns and then ran them through a series of tests to determine which was the strongest gun. Once he settled on a brand, he modified the gun in a variety of ways. He'd covered it with a light, but strong polymer that made the gun stronger; allowing it not to be damaged by the pepper spray juice, and allowed him to form a better nozzle for more precise aim and power in the spray. The water gun was like putting a Ferrari engine in a Ford Pinto; it looked ugly and frail on the outside but it could do just fine in the heat of battle as Natalie just proved. He went outside with his package and the drone. Perhaps once a year he tried to fly something over to Mike. It was always something small and the camera on the bottom of the drone did a fairly good job of directing the drone so it didn't run into a boat if it was too low or a small plane/helicopter if it was too high. Twenty minutes later he managed to drop it on the deck of Mike's boat. The driver would pick it up within the hour.

Natalie next made the call to her husband to tell him about the day. He was grateful to Damian for creating Natalie's weapon and even more glad to know that she was getting a new weapon the same day. He would have laughed at the thought of her pointing a bright green water gun at someone except it was his wife who'd been shot at. He laughed at it the first time he saw it and laughed again when he watched her put it into a holster. He'd laugh no more and would instead check that she always had it with her. Natalie got a text from Damian telling her the new weapon was on its way. She'd have to make a new recipe of pepper juice for it and find some time to practice aiming and shooting, but otherwise she was good to go.

Damian went to work on finding out who Michael O'Brien was. The last name was Irish and it was spelled with an 'e' usually. He'd already served time in prison and had been released about a month ago after time served. He was twenty-four and served time for burglary and narcotics. His arrest was made after Natalie left the force. What was the kid's connection to Natalie? It was time to look at his family; maybe there was a brother or sister that Natalie arrested.

Then Damian leaned back and put his hands over his eyes.

CHAPTER 13

Michael O'Brien had kept his mother's name, his father was Ryan Murphy, the man that Natalie had killed and who had killed his family. It was a second generation of poor quality men in that family. After he got his emotions under control, he picked up the phone and called Natalie.

"What'd you find on my suspect?"

"His father is Ryan Murphy."

Natalie responded with a hiss and then said "Fuck". Ryan Murphy was the only man that she'd killed in her twenty-five years with the SJPD; she would remember that name forever.

Damian had to agree with that reaction. Ryan Murphy had so wronged his family, he never thought of any of them coming after Natalie for his death.

"There's more…." Damian said waiting for Natalie to be ready to listen.

After a moment, Natalie said, "Go ahead."

"He belonged to the Aryan Brotherhood while in prison. He might have belonged to it before he went to prison as they do recruit outside the prison walls. His father also belonged to that gang, so Natalie you may have been targeted for quite some time if you read the history of their creed and behavior."

"You think I was a marked woman seven years ago?"

"You can talk to your gang specialists there, but I wouldn't be surprised if this was a job they were saving for the son. Patience is one of their qualities; you have to have patience to survive prison."

Natalie hadn't thought of that but knew he was probably right, then another thought crossed her mind. "Do you think they'll come after you, Damian?"

Now he paused and thought, and then he replied, "Yes. They probably see it as my fault that I was unhappy with the murder of my family and brought the police in on the case. Certainly I was quoted at the time as being grateful to the SJPD for hunting him down and killing him. Not in those exact words but you get my meaning. If I hadn't recently read about the Brotherhood for the John Avery case, I wouldn't have made that connection. They'll have a very hard time finding me though."

"I wouldn't be too sure about that. This guy was really bold going after me so close to police headquarters. I wonder how he knew I'd be there today? It's not a logical location for someone that retired three years ago."

"Good question Natalie! The gang is generally not known for computer skills, but I suppose that since they support credit card and internet fraud that some members of the gang must be very computer literate. With no other explanation, I would offer two theories for why the guy knew you'd be there today. First, it could have been sheer luck and impulse that had you two cross paths; or someone is high tech in the gang and knew you'd received this assignment and who your contact person was. Then it was only a matter of hacking into his computer to see your name on his appointment calendar or in his emails."

"You're scaring me by painting a picture of a prison gang being tech savvy," Natalie sighed. "I think I'll ask for increased patrols in my neighborhood to hopefully avoid getting killed on my front doorstep. I am very curious to see what comes out of the interview with him. Attempted murder will get him five to nine years at a State prison, but I doubt if the DA will do a bargain for information. Let me talk to the detectives that are interviewing him and see if I can get in on the process. I'm heading back there now and I'll have Eddie bring my new water gun when it arrives at our home."

"Keep me posted," Damian urged as they ended the call.

He leaned back after the call and thought about what an unsettling day it had been. He hadn't enjoyed reading about the Aryan Brotherhood; hated that someone had shot at Natalie, but was thrilled that in a true test, his technology did what it was supposed to do; allowed Natalie to defend herself but didn't get her in trouble over firearms. Now to find out that her assailant was related to his family's murder and that they had somehow known that she would be in a particular place at a certain time was sickening. Time to go to work to figure out how all of these loose ends connected, because instinct was telling him they were.

On Red Rock Island he felt safe given his security set-up and it had recently been tested by Ariana. If this gang arrived by helicopter, he would have some problems defending himself, but he'd planned for that and had slingshots armed with nets that should disrupt any helicopter rotors. He'd not heard of a gang owning a helicopter, but he supposed that anyone could hire one for such an assault on his home. His top level of the house was bulletproof, but wouldn't survive bombs or rockets, but the lower level would. Of course that was all speculation on his part. He'd never actually tested it, but rather his contractor had used certain materials that contained those qualities.

First, they had to find him.

He would proactively log into the systems at the various California prisons and see how far any of them had gotten in researching him, but first he had to figure out how they found Natalie. To do that, he'd need to decipher the code the gang communicated in. He obtained three different samples of their language then spent some time studying the repetition of the letters. Within a few hours he had the code figured out. He should have been a decipherer for the military, he thought grimly amused. With their language decoded, he set about hacking into their communications. He was an expert hacker and it took him just under a minute to access any account.

While he could hack into each email account quickly, with over ten thousand members in and out of prison, he'd spend a lot of time reading worthless emails. Instead he wrote a program that would hack into all emails that used the gang language and a second program that searched for Natalie's name after he translated it back to the gang's language. He let his console run and decided it was time for a change of scenery. He'd built a small storage room at the base of one of the rocky cliffs. It was well hidden and you had to be able to slide your fingers over the rock to see the door. Inside he kept his water toys - a kayak, a dinghy with a tiny motor, and a jet ski.

He could reach the room from the lower level of his house or from the exterior. He had a ramp that he could use to launch any of the water crafts and then using an app on his phone, the ramp would fold up and return to the storage room and the door would close. It was a hidden escape route if his island was ever attacked by criminals. It was a nice day, sunny and not too windy. He debated which water craft to use and settled on the jet ski as he was going to try and visit Ariana's house. If he ever visited a second time, he'd try one of the slower methods. He wore long pants and a jacket that dried quickly as he was likely to get wet on his ride. Once he reached her dock, he'd call to see if she was home, that way if he changed his mind on the way, he wasn't committed to meeting or talking to her. Yes, he was still set in his ways, generally avoiding other humans.

CHAPTER 14

Ariana was on her private beach playing fetch with Miguel. Since she mastered the drone, she'd been using it to drop toys into the water for the dog. He seemed to enjoy that more than when she threw them; probably because the drone went out farther.

She looked into the distance when she heard the noise of a jet ski and frowned when it seemed to be coming her way.

Miguel returned to her side ready to defend her as no one had the nerve to drive up to her private beach. She squinted into the sun but couldn't identify the rider. There was something familiar about the white blond hair and then it clicked as he approached her dock.

Then she smiled and said to the dog, "It's okay, Miguel, it's Damian and he's a friend."

She left the sand and walked on to her dock as he was scaling a ladder up to the dock deck.

"Hi," Damian said. "I needed a break from work and thought I'd journey over here. Lucky for me you're home."

"Hi back and this is Miguel, my protector."

Damian held out his hand for the dog to sniff and then

scratched the dog's head. He observed the drone and remote in Ariana's hands and said, "Ah, I see it serves a dual purpose, tea delivery and dog toy launching."

"Are you out of tea?" Ariana asked.

"No, you gave me a supply that will last for at least another month. I have few visitors to my island and I can only drink so much tea each day."

"Would you like to come in for a drink? You must be thirsty after your ride across the bay."

Damian looked down at his pants, wet from the spray and said, "I wouldn't want to drag bay water into your house. How about if I play with Miguel while you grab drinks and anything will do - water, tea, whatever. He's a Portuguese water dog, right? So I don't have to worry about him going out too far."

"Miguel drags bay water into the house all the time so don't let that deter you, but it's a nice day and we can sit outside and amuse ourselves. Be back in a few minutes."

She handed the drone and remote to Damian and made her way up to the house. She was prettier up close than her picture or her scuba gear framed face had let on. He looked at the dog holding his toy clearly expecting Damian to drop it in the bay for him to fetch and got to work. He soon had Miguel acting like a dock dog. He'd suspend the toy below the drone and Miguel would have to jump off the dock to grab it which he clearly found a great experience. Ariana returned with a drinks tray containing two pitchers of liquid and two glasses. She set the tray down on a table located on another part of the dock deck and invited Damian to sit down.

"I brought lemonade and ice tea so pour whichever one you want," and then looking over at the dog said, "Miguel, I'm going to have to learn this new trick with the drone that Damian has been entertaining you with."

Ariana put a bowl down on the dock and poured water into it

for the dog, who was clearly winded from his play. He then sat at her side ready to protect her from any other strangers.

"What made you come over to my beach?" Ariana asked.

"I needed some fresh air and felt the siren's call of a mermaid."

"That sounds nicely poetic, and considering I nearly marooned myself in the bay, I'm sure the mermaid race would be horrified of my underwater skills."

"I wasn't sure how far a ride this was or what the qualities of the water would be so I brought the jet ski. I also have a rowboat with a tiny motor and a kayak, but was afraid it would take me more than an hour to reach your beach and of course there's the danger of the ferries. It was less than fifteen minutes on the jet ski and I was fortunate to not only find you home but outside on your beach."

"Yes, you were lucky, but then at this time of day you can usually find me here. If I'm working from home, Miguel pesters me to play outside with him about the same time every day. What were you working on that you needed a break from?"

Damian hesitated, sorting through what to tell her, "I designed a program to search for certain pieces of information in a large database and I assume the search would take several hours and the day looked promising outside, so here I am."

"I bet you did a background search on me and so you know I invest in Silicon Valley startups, many of them related to the use of data in one way or another. What kind of data search were you doing?"

For some reason, Damian felt relaxed in this woman's company. It was a weird feeling this companionship. It was an emotion he hadn't felt in a long time, and it felt strange to feel it now. He decided he would try shocking her with the news of what he was actually doing and see if the companionship disappeared. He doubted she had any connection to the Aryan Brotherhood and so there was no risk to him if she knew the truth of what he was doing. About the only person that would be concerned with someone related to the brotherhood would be a civil rights attorney and she appeared to have neither attribute.

"I'm searching through the email communications of men both in and out of prison that belonged to the Aryan Brotherhood." He just let that sentence rest between the two of them. He was curious to see where her mind would go next. His research had told him that she was an intelligent woman and so he knew she wouldn't ignore his statement. The question was would her reaction be one of curiosity or perhaps disgust?

He soon got his answer.

"That sounds like a long and complicated story and it says a few things about you. You apparently know how to write programs for data and you know how to hack into other people's email accounts, both skills point to perhaps a near genius level of computer language. What I don't know is what your connection is to the Aryan Brotherhood or to prisoners. Are you in some secret government homeland security thing?"

He laughed at her usage of the word 'thing', and said "No I work for no one but myself, however, in this particular instance, I'm helping a retired detective from the south bay on some cold cases."

"Ah," was all Ariana said.

What did 'ah' mean coming from Ariana? Damian knew he was overthinking her every word, so perhaps it was time to go.

"My computer program should be done running, so I'd better get going," Damian said as he stood up. "Thanks for the lemonade, Ariana." He then leaned down to give the dog one more pat on the head. Straightening up he asked, "Miguel won't follow me out into the bay will he?"

"He might, but I'll hold onto his collar until you disappear from sight. Stop by again sometime. I'm often home at this time of the day, but not always."

With a wave he was on the jet ski and soon heading back to his island. What a mysterious man, she thought. She was sure he was testing her with his explanation of his work; but she rather thought it fit with the story she had created about him. A story was all she had as she still didn't know his full name or even much about his life. Miguel liked him, but then the dog liked anyone who dropped toys for him in the water and since Damian had devised a new play strategy, Miguel was in love. Oh well, it was a nice break to her day and he'd probably show up again some time. He was such a unique person.

Damian was thinking of Ariana as he bounced on the waves across the bay. She was a nice person, respectful of his privacy, had a great dog, was smart and knew something about technology. Looking around her exterior, he had engineering ideas for her and the dog. Since the dog loved water so much, he planned to design her a dog wash. He could envision it working just like a car wash, but he'd have to figure out a quiet blower system so as not to scare the dog. His mind designed one that would use filtered bay water, with soap that wouldn't harm it and the blowers would run on energy stored from the wind in her area. Yes, he'd build a cool dog wash.

He pulled up to his island and hit the remote and waited while his dock slid out. Soon he was inside his home, writing notes on his dog wash idea. He checked his security systems and noted a few boats in his area as well as a helicopter with one of the local news stations on it. No one had tried to breach his home while he was gone. Changing out of his wet clothes he was soon seated in front of his computer scanning the results.

"Crap."

CHAPTER 15

Damian had set three programs running before he left with the third program translating the gang's code back into English so he could immediately read through a string of emails. It was clear that there was a move afoot to kill Natalie. He saw reference to the fact her name was 'in the hat' meaning there was a contract kill announced within the gang for her. He was tempted to call her immediately and discuss his findings, but he wanted the whole picture about what this group was up to. He shook his head at the irony that he'd go to jail for hacking into their email system even though the gang was using it to plan murders; what a strange world!

He spent about twenty minutes reading through all the email. They had plans to end Natalie's life, but they also knew about Trevor and Eddie which sent a chill through Damian. It was worse still when he read an exchange about Trevor putting one of the Brotherhood in prison. There was also mention of himself, but they hadn't been able to locate him yet. Natalie and her family needed protection but it wasn't like she could share the email trail with the police. If need be, he could relocate her entire family to his island but somehow he guessed that wouldn't be a solution.

Dammit, he was an engineer; he should be able to think of a more creative solution. He leaned back and thought for a while. He made a list then called Mike to see if he was available to ferry him off the island in an hour or so. He packed his supplies and made sure his cats had food as he thought he'd be gone overnight. As soon as he got into his truck that he left at the marina, he called Natalie on his car phone.

"Hey Natalie, I'm on my way to your house. Where are you now?"

"What? Why are you coming to my house? Not that you aren't welcome, but you've been there twice in seven years. What's going on?"

"I wrote a program to search for the language of the AB and then it would hack the email and translate the message into English. I read an entire trail this afternoon and you and your family were mentioned."

"Mentioned how?" Natalie said with urgency.

"You are targeted for a kill and it's okay if they take Eddie and Trevor as well."

"Fuck! Are you sure, Damian? Of course, you're sure. So why are you heading to my house?"

"You can't turn these emails over to the cops as I obtained them illegally. So I'm on my way to build some protection into your house and supply Eddie and Trevor with water guns among other weapons."

There was silence on Natalie's side as she thought about what Damian said and realized he was right. He was most worried about Trevor; he needed to work and he couldn't do that from his mother's house.

"I'll call Eddie and Trevor and ask them to drop whatever they're doing and head home," Natalie replied.

"Natalie, until I add some fortifications to your house; it may not be the safest place. Let's give you and I a little time to set things up and then bring them home, but you should definitely warn them and see if you can get them close to a police officer in the interim. If Trevor is at the courthouse, tell him to stay there since there are armed bailiffs in the court room."

"This is going to be an ugly conversation with both of them. They'll want to come home and take care of me."

"Why don't you conference the two of them into our line and I'll talk with them. I'll be bloody cold about the dangers they're facing."

"Okay, give me a moment."

A short time later he spoke with the entire Severino family about the emails in detail. They were all horrified, and so Damian described his plan. After some discussion, they couldn't think of any other way to approach their own protection than the plan that Damian had outlined.

"I'm in heavy traffic, so I'll still be thirty minutes reaching your house, Natalie, and I'll call you when I'm close. Let's meet at the little café down on Second Avenue, and I'll take you in my truck to your house so we can do surveillance of the neighborhood first."

"You're really worried about this despite the fact that their hand-picked murderer is in custody."

"Natalie, these guys are like ants at a picnic, you kill one and there's an army of one-hundred behind them. The prison system and the FBI haven't found the bug spray to eradicate them. Once your name goes in the hat, it stays there until you're dead and both of our names are in the hat, they're just not sure if I'm alive or where I am. Did the police learn anything from Michael O'Brien during the interview?"

"They learned that he hates my guts for the death of his father and he has no conscience, but not much else. He gave no indication of how he knew I was at the police headquarters, or if he had any other gang bangers in the vicinity. I did enjoy the small victory of his eyes; they'd taken him to the hospital and they washed his eyes out but they were badly red rimmed and he was keeping ice on his face. I think he hates even more that he was brought low by a child's water gun. So I have those small satisfactions."

"Do you have a few fellow retired cops that could serve as watchdogs on your street while I get the technology set up? You could bring Eddie and Trevor home much quicker if you do."

"Good idea, Damian, I'll give some friends a call. Do you have any special weapons for them?"

"I do. I have water guns, ink smoke bombs, and a precision slingshot."

"They'll want to come for the weapons alone. How long do you think my house will need to be fortified? I don't see an end to this."

"I have a few incentives for the gang to take your name out of the hat, I just need to reach their leadership."

"Damian, I don't know if you're brilliant or crazy!"

"I'm a little of both."

As planned, they met at the little café and proceeded toward Natalie's house. Damian's dark blue Ford F-150 truck was not exactly inconspicuous, and if he hadn't needed the cargo space and been pressed for time, he probably would've tried to find an older gray Honda Accord that looked like every other car on the road. Her street was quiet, tree-lined and part of the grid housing development. There were streets in front and back that perfectly paralleled the street she lived on. Each block was about fifteen houses long. They sat in the truck looking down her street with Natalie looking at each car that was parked in the driveway or on the street. She could see a delivery truck farther down, but it was the requisite brown color of UPS. There was a car she didn't recognize parked in front of the house across the street. She knew that the family had a teenager with lots of driving friends. This car appeared to look as though it belonged to one of them, and she gave her assessment to Damian.

Of course they couldn't view into her backyard, but they had already driven down the two parallel streets to Natalie's and seen nothing obvious. She didn't know the cars of those two streets, so indeed some gang banger could've parked and hopped over the fence in the backyard, but hopefully they had a few hours before, as Damian put it, more ants arrived at her picnic.

Damian pulled into Natalie's garage and they closed the door behind them and began unloading stuff from the truck. Some things Natalie recognized and other stuff, she wondered at. Once they unloaded it, Damian pulled out his laptop and had Natalie read all the translated emails. Her retired cop friends were expected any minute and so Damian was taking care of them first. Natalie wasn't sure they would want the weapons that Damian designed, since they hadn't tested them and they likely had their own firearms, but as she proved this very day, his weapons worked.

"What are ink smoke bombs?"

"I took old lightbulbs and removed the filament, then I filled them with a green ink that will take months to get off the skin and never off the clothing. I also added iodine and turpentine to create a nice purple smoke. All they have to do is toss the lightbulb at these guys and they'll be covered in green ink and blinded by purple smoke."

Natalie had to smile. It'd been a very stressful day; nearly getting killed and then finding that she and her family were targets of the most violent prison gang. Damian's inventions had a way of lifting her spirits; they protected without killing probably anything more than weeds in her grass. The thought of a violent offender walking around with green dye on his skin made her day.

He looked out the glass of the top segment of her garage door to see a car pulling into her driveway. It didn't look like a gangbanger car, but he knew she wasn't tall enough to see outside the garage windows. He said to Natalie, "There a short African-American man exiting a Subaru SUV; does that sound like one of your friends?"

"That's Sherman and yeah he's a friend," Natalie replied as she went to the side door of her garage to let him in.

After introductions were made, Damian demonstrated the water gun and smoke bomb for Sherman. He brought a You Tube video with him so he wouldn't have Natalie's neighbors calling the fire department. Sherman nodded his understanding and pulled aside his jacket to reveal a Smith and Wesson M&P Shield, a favorite of off-duty and retired police. Sherman liked the water gun especially since he had seen a replay of how Natalie had disarmed the thug that afternoon. The exterior video footage of her water gun had made the rounds far and wide that afternoon in the law enforcement community. He asked Damian if he could keep the gun for his wife once his guard duty was finished and Damian nodded.

"It's a small payment for your help protecting Natalie and her family. I wouldn't mind outfitting the entire world with hot pink colored water guns as it would really help control the bad guys."

Damian went through the same motions with the other friend who showed up, Andy had also wanted to keep the water gun for his oldest daughter who was at a distant university. Soon the men were in place and Eddie and Trevor were given notice they could come home while Damian went to work setting traps around the house.

Gangs liked to carry out their hits via drive-by shootings; often this was the easier way to fire a gun and escape the scene. Bullets had no problem going through wood or glass. Damian had brought with him cloth sheets of a lightweight structured polymer composite made of alternating rubbery and glassy layers. It served to absorb the kinetic energy of things like bullets. He draped the front of the house and garage in the fabric and then used another quantity so that each of the Severino family could walk around with an invincibility cloak rather like the invisibility cloak that Harry Potter owned. He also went about adding both alarms and booby traps around the house. If the suspects entered the property underneath any of the trees, they'd find their bodies flung upward in a net. He had other wires that would trip and they would be shot with water again colored with a dye that would take a long time to get out. If the shooter managed to avoid all of Damian's traps, then he had nail guns ready to go and the Severino family could nail any intruder's feet to the flooring.

That was unless Natalie shot the intruder dead.

CHAPTER 16

It was close to one in the morning by the time Damian had finished setting up protection for Natalie's house. He felt pretty good about it and her family was impressed with what he implemented.

Now their only vulnerable time would be going to and from work. Trevor weighed in on reading the prisoner emails. He was in a very awkward position as he had knowledge of Damian's illegal activity and he couldn't claim attorney-client privilege. However, he decided to deal with the ethics later as his life was under threat as were that of his parents and he was frankly glad that Damian had the talent to read the email. They were some profoundly bad people; the kind he liked to send to jail for a very long time. As there was no mention of Haley, he had no worry for his fiancée, but they needed to avoid seeing each other. He was grateful he made plans to take her to meet Damian. He would have her go to the island thirty minutes ahead of himself and they would be safe together there, especially since the gang wasn't sure if Damian was dead or alive.

Damian discussed his plan for getting their names out of the hat and Trevor and his mother weren't sure it would work.

Damian wanted Natalie to seek a meeting with one of the three bosses of the Brotherhood. She would show him that their communications were capable of being fully intercepted. If they refused to remove her name from the hat, then her source would start forwarding all emails to both the warden and to the leaders of the other prison gangs. Especially the Brotherhood's number one enemy, a prison gang called the Black Guerrillas. It felt like she was making a pact with the devil, but it was really the only way to stop a hit from taking place.

Damian was itching to get back to his island, but at least he could go now with a clear conscience that he'd done everything possible to protect Natalie and her family. Natalie contacted a friend that still worked in the gang area to understand the leadership of the Aryan Brotherhood. She felt she had only one chance for a rational conversation with their leader. If she got nowhere, then they would exert pressure by sharing a few damaging emails with the Black Guerrillas. If they still couldn't get anywhere, then Natalie might seek out the FBI and allege that she was fighting domestic terrorism. It was going to be an interesting couple of days as she was going to work from home as was Trevor; but he couldn't stay home 100% of his work day as he needed to meet with colleagues and appear in court. He was debating calling in sick for a few days just to gain a little breathing space and be there for his parents if they were attacked inside their house. Maybe his parents would join him at Damian's house this weekend, so for just a little time they wouldn't have to worry about their own personal safety.

Damian knew he would sleep restlessly in one of Natalie's guest bedrooms and as soon as he could, he'd leave in the morning for home where he could get a good night's rest. The next day, he did one final test of the system, and then packed his unused supplies in his truck and he was on his way by ten. He could have left earlier, but traffic was so bad that he would have been stuck and frustrated in that parking lot called the morning commute.

Natalie had the names of the leaders by the time Damian left and was working on an appointment with one of the three. One name was recommended to her but she wasn't going to wait long on his agreement to talk; she'd simply move on to the next gang leader. While the gang had formed at San Quentin in the 1960s, Ryan Murphy, the escaped convict that murdered Damian's family had been at Soledad. The two prisons were about a hundred miles apart, but it appeared that putting Natalie's name in the hat had come from Soledad. She hoped to be visiting one of the two prisons the next day.

When Damian got back to his island, he was going to write a separate program to garner the source of the original kill order. They say that nothing's ever deleted in cyberspace, but he might be looking for a communication from seven years ago. It might not have ever been mentioned in the email system at the time of its origin, still both Damian and Natalie thought they had leverage. As he stashed his supplies aboard Mike's boat and helped him cast off the lines tying the boat to the dock, he took several cleansing breaths of fresh air. He hated having anything to do with these prison gangs; it was hard dealing with people whose only moral code was one of loyalty to a white supremacist band of thugs. Once he unloaded his supplies, gave his cats some attention, and wrote the program for the email, he'd change into a wetsuit and go for a swim. Maybe then he'd feel cleaner.

Usually he chatted with Mike on the way to his island but this time he was silent; questioning what he would do if he met Ryan Murphy or now Michael O'Brien alone with a gun in his hand and nothing in theirs. He'd like to think he would do nothing, just walk away from those sad pieces of humanity, but other times he'd think about shooting them in the different areas of their bodies designed to give them a life-long disability or pain. It was an exercise in futility since Ryan had been dead seven years and his anger toward the son was different from that of the father. He really needed to shake these dark thoughts out of his mind as he was beginning to feel like that first year after his family's death. Then he'd been in such a deep well of anger and depression that he hardly interacted with another human being on any level. For some reason, Natalie's first wreath ceremony marking the passing of his family had lightened his load and allowed him the barest beginnings on moving past the senseless deaths of his family. It was one of many reasons that he would do what he could to protect her and her family.

An hour later, everything on his to-do list accomplished or underway, he pulled his mask and snorkel down over his face and dove into the bay. He wore a sensor on his wrist, so that none of his security measures were directed at him while he swam in gentle circles around his entire island. He thought about swimming straight to the marina or to the Richmond San Rafael bridge, but he feared being too small to see by any ferries or pleasure crafts roaming the bay. Sometime later he felt like he'd excised his demons and he headed inside for a shower and lunch followed by a little fishing to apologize for leaving his cats alone the previous night. Then he'd check on his program to see if he had any answers.

His program was still running so Damian thought he would go back to his cold cases. Natalie said the SJPD was getting a search warrant for one suspect and contacting the Phoenix PD to get the same for the suspect, Greg Watson. The Medical Examiner was going to take a look at the knife wounds to see if the records that they had on the original case matched the knife with John Avery's fingerprints. What could he do with his technology to help Natalie?

What if he went back and traced car ownership of John Avery to see if a vehicle he had in the late 1980's was still around - maybe in a junk yard or maybe it was still on the street. Someone had carted Debbie Altman away in a vehicle since her body was not found on the street where her car had quit. First he did a little research to see if Avery had lived in any other state. No, from a variety of public records he seemed to have stayed in the Golden State and in fact, except for a few prison stints, he stayed in the San Jose area. Damian then searched for any vehicles that he might have owned in the 1980s or 1990s. Looking at the guy's age, he decided to also throw in any vehicles owned by Avery's parents since he would have been just about twenty at the time of Debbie's disappearance.

Bingo, he got lucky and was excited to have some positive news for Natalie after the stress of the last twenty-four hours. The truck was sitting in a junk yard in San Leandro and was being used for parts, it hadn't been crushed yet. Granted it had some thirty years of prints on it, and while they didn't have Debbie's prints as her body hadn't been recovered, she did have some living siblings that might be used for DNA matches. He wasn't sure how a crime scene team would investigate such a vehicle, but it seemed reasonable to say they could search the bench seat, dashboard, or the truck bed for DNA. Considering the truck had been at the salvage yard for ten years, he figured the police were lucky to locate it, but what a pain it would be to collect the evidence off the vehicle.

He called Natalie with this latest information and to check in with her as to activity in her neighborhood.

"Hi Damian, what's up?"

He liked how he never had to go through polite conversation with Natalie, they could just get to the point with each other as soon as the phone call was answered.

"I've got a new lead for you on the Debbie Altman case and it's one that needs acting on today before evidence is destroyed."

"Explain," demanded Natalie.

"I located a truck that John Avery owned at the time of Debbie's disappearance. It's in a salvage yard in San Leandro, so I would use any police powers you have to order them not to destroy the vehicle before any CSI techs get a crack at the truck."

"Wow, Damian! You should have been a cop. That was brilliant! I didn't even think to look for a car the suspect might have owned during the time period in question."

"Your mind's been focused on avoiding being killed by the most violent prison gang in America, so if you weren't so distracted by death threats, I'm sure you would have thought of this."

"No, Damian I wouldn't have thought of that - I was thinking about the case's next steps, the search warrant and interview. I should have backtracked and applied my brain to exploring what new evidence we could collect now that we had a suspect."

Natalie was always appreciative of his efforts to help her, but now he was embarrassed by her over the top compliments.

"Natalie, if you want me to continue working with you on these cold cases, you're going to have to stop with the effusive praise; you're muddling my brain with the compliments. I simply approach any problem as one of data collection. I'm not worried about any of the legal requirements that you're bound by."

"I swear that if you would just give up inventing all those great things you have patents for, that you'd make a supreme detective."

"Enough, Natalie. Let's move on," he replied and then he gave her the VIN of the truck and the junkyard it was presently occupying.

CHAPTER 17

Damian was tired from the long night and the swim around his island and he was sick of there being bad guys in the world. He needed to find a place to relax. He debated calling Ariana to see if she wanted to join him for a cheeseburger at Pete's but that would require effort on his part to arrange for her transportation there. No, he'd just head over alone and soak in Pete's company. Since he had Mike out to the island once already that day he went down to his watercraft garage to launch the rowboat. He put a thirty one pound motor on the back end which would operate for an hour on little more than a quarter tank of gas. That was plenty to get him to the marina and back and he'd just drive his truck to Pete's.

He stopped by the harbormaster's office to let him know that his little dinghy was parked in an area of the docks with little traffic.

"Hi Tom, I left my dinghy in its usual spot and I'll be back in about three hours."

"Hi Damian, I was about to call you. I had some kid sniffing around your truck earlier."

Damian stiffened wondering how anyone from the Aryan

Brotherhood had found him. Had they followed him from Natalie's house? He'd watched his mirrors and hadn't seen anyone following him and he exited two different off-ramps to see if anyone followed him off and then on again and no one did. What the hell?

"Can you describe the kid?" Damian asked.

"She was young, Caucasian, and checking the doors of various cars in the lot. I think she was just looking for a place to stay tonight, maybe homeless or a runaway. Sometimes those kids fantasize about sneaking aboard a boat and leaving this town."

Damian relaxed, the only women in the Brotherhood were wives or girlfriends who carried drugs or messages. This girl seemed too young for that role.

"Have you seen her here before today?"

"No, but she isn't the first kid that strayed into the marina."

"Thanks, Tom, for keeping an eye on things. See you later."

Damian walked over to his truck and walked around it looking for anything out of place. He didn't find any problems so he hopped in and set off for Pete's. It had been a very unsettling day and Pete's beer, cheeseburger, and companionship was exactly what he needed to right his world. He hoped that Natalie had been able to get Avery's truck checked for DNA or at least make sure that it wasn't wrecked or touched overnight. He'd thought about going over to the yard and buying the truck so Natalie would have the evidence while she processed the paperwork, but that would surely screw up any chain of evidence order that the police and the district attorney liked to see, so he'd let it go.

When he got to Pete's place, it was a slow night; and so he sat at the bar and chatted with Pete about operating his own home brewery. By the end of the evening, he'd made a decision that while he could pretty much engineer anything, perhaps brewing beer would not be satisfying considering the variety of beer he liked and the small quantity he imbibed when home. He had this feeling that he'd brew beer but he wouldn't be able to keep up with the quantity he made and he'd either end up dumping it into the bay, or perhaps on his compost pile. He'd stick to buying it from his local grocery store. Much like the swim earlier, the time at Pete's had served to relax his mind. He thought he could go home now and get a good night's sleep. He was soon back at the marina and waved at Tom as he went by.

It was dark now, but he knew his way to his dinghy as he had docked it in the same place for years. He wasn't worried about anyone stealing it as it was a cheap boat locked behind the entrance gate to the slip. No one would bother it. He stepped down into the boat and cast off. He'd be in trouble if the Coast Guard stopped him as he had no lights on the boat. He didn't worry about it though as he knew the path to his island in the dark and he could always see other boats in the lights of the cities surrounding the bay. If for some reason he needed illumination, he could turn on the app of his cell phone for light.

Just as he hit the remote door for his watercraft garage, he caught the blanket moving in the front of the boat. He put his hand on his own water gun ready to aim and fire at whomever was under the dark blanket in the front of the boat. With his water gun in his hand, he reached forward and flung the blanket to the side to uncover a frightened young girl.

Oh God, it was probably the same one who had been sniffing around his truck. She was clutching what looked to be a stainless steel dinner knife.

Damian debated what to do for a few quick seconds - whether to turn around and head for the marina or shoot the kid with pepper spray. Instead he aimed his remote at the garage and the dock began to fold out. His passenger watched wide eyed, dividing her attention between Damian and the water craft garage.

Once the dock clicked into place, he asked, "What's your name?"

She was mute for so long, he wondered if she spoke a different language, but then she finally said "Hannah."

"Well, Hannah, I'm Damian and this is my home. I'd like you to put your knife down as my water gun is loaded with pepper juice which will make your eyes hurt for several hours if I have to fire at you. It's dark outside here; why don't we go inside and talk about why you were in my boat?"

Why after seven years of no visitors had he had so many in the last week? Were the gods trying to tell him something?

He directed the boat toward the dock and gave Hannah ready access to the ladder on the side of the dock. She took another look at him and then out at the dark water and apparently decided to take her chances with him. She scampered up onto the dock and advanced into the garage. Damian could see she was thin with brown hair tucked up under her hat. She kept his tarp around her as she was cold. He decided he needed some female help with the situation and quickly texted Ariana, seeing if she was awake.

She replied back immediately, "Yes, why?"

So standing on his dock he called her.

"Hi, what's up?" Ariana hadn't known Damian very long but she knew that if he contacted her at this hour of the night that something was off.

"I just returned to my island and discovered a female stowaway in my boat. Can you come out to my island and help me with her?"

"Is she injured?"

"Not that I can see, but I don't know what to do with a teenage girl."

"How do I get onto your island?"

"There is a watercraft garage with a dock on the bridge side of the island. I'll leave the lights on for you to find it and call me when you're approaching."

"I'll bring Miguel since it's a kid."

"Thanks, Ariana. I really owe you for your help with this one."

"No I still owe you for refilling my tanks. I'll be there in about twenty minutes. Does she need any clothing? How tall is she?"

"She needs a jacket and I'd guess that anything you have would fit her."

"Okay, I'll call you when I'm close."

Damian ended the call and looked over at the girl.

"Hannah, I know a lady who lives on the opposite shore, who is going to come here in a boat with her dog and a coat for you in about twenty minutes. For now, you're going to have to come inside and wait. Do you want something to eat or drink? I'll give you a jacket to wear."

Damian pulled the small rowboat inside the garage while he waited for Hannah to speak. Then he pushed a keypad in the back of the garage and she saw the room open into his lab.

Hannah walked in looking around at the various gadgets on counters and computer terminals and said, "What is this place?"

"This is the lower level of my house where I invent things." Pointing to his wave energy invention he said, "I'm trying to design a technology from waves that will provide electrical power to poor island countries."

Hannah nodded and said, "Makes sense as that may be their one natural resource."

So Damian thought, the girl had some intelligence about her. He continued "I'll save the explanations for another time; let's go upstairs."

He watched the girl to see if she would follow him and she did as she peered at his laboratory taking it all in.

Upstairs he took her into his kitchen and soon had a glass of milk and a turkey and cheese sandwich in front of her. She had a lightweight jacket of his on but she was drowning in it. To his great surprise his two cats had come inside at his arrival and as usual the one hopped up to beg for turkey while the other gave Hannah the evil eye.

"Hannah, the one on the chair is Bella and she's begging for turkey despite the fact that she had fresh fish about four hours ago. The cat on the floor giving you the suspicious look is Bailey and he's the harder one to win over. You are the first stranger who has visited my house that Bailey and Bella greeted."

Hannah reached out and gave a tiny piece of turkey to Bella, even though the kid herself was starving. Damian often thought you could judge another human being by their treatment of animals. He thought he would save questioning Hannah until Ariana arrived. He could see this was going to be a late night, his second in a row. He boiled water to make tea and then his cell phone buzzed with Ariana's number showing in the caller ID. He did a quick glance around his kitchen and didn't think the kid could get into any trouble for the few minutes he'd be gone. He handed her his TV remote and said, "I need to guide this boat in; I'll be back in five minutes, Feel free to turn on the TV."

He left her and went back downstairs and through his workshop and out the door to his dock. He could see a small boat approaching and relaxed a little. It was never good for an adult male to be in the company of a teenage girl even if she would have been the same age as his youngest child.

He waved to Ariana and her boat eased towards his island. He helped her tie it to the dock, as Miguel jumped out of the boat and headed for what he hoped was a great doggy adventure.

"Thanks, Ariana, for coming so quickly. I don't know what to do with a teenage girl except to get an adult woman to help."

"What's her story?"

"I was waiting for you to question her. Her name is Hannah and I fed her a sandwich and some milk, gave her a jacket of mine to wear. She has intelligence as she immediately understood the impact of one of my projects that I'm working on."

"This is quite a place, Damian, I had no idea you had this secret garage built inside your rock island. I may need to go back to calling you 'Manny' as you seem even more carved from this rock."

Damian winced at that and said "Let's go inside."

As he left the door to his workshop open, Miguel had already entered the house but was held back from the second story by Bailey blocking his way at the top of the stairs. Just as Hannah had done, Ariana walked through the workshop staring at everything wide-eyed quick on Damian's heels to reach his upper level. Damian reached the top of the stairs and picked up Bailey which allowed Miguel to proceed toward Hannah.

Ariana called out, "Hannah, he's a friendly dog, he just wants a piece of your sandwich, but don't give it to him."

"Why not?" the girl asked.

"Because I don't want to teach him bad manners," Ariana replied. "Besides you look like you need the food more than he does."

"What his name?"

"He's Miguel and I'm Ariana."

Hannah reached down to rub the dog's head. Damian thought it was time now that he softened the girl up with cats and a dog to find out her story.

"Hannah, I brought you some clothes that my niece left at my house. I wasn't sure what size you were, but now that I've seen you, you look about her size. Damian, do you have a shower she could use before she puts on some clean clothes? And perhaps a washing machine so we can get those clothes you have on clean."

Hannah looked at them, trying to gauge her personal safety. She really wanted to shower as she'd been on the run for a week, but she didn't know if she could trust the pair of adults. She looked down at their healthy and happy pets and decided she would trust them for the time being.

"I have a shower in my bathroom. I'm afraid I don't have any female smelling soap or shampoo, unless you brought some, Ariana."

"As a matter of fact I did, again thanks to my niece," Ariana replied reaching into the duffle bag she brought with her.

Damian directed the two women to the only bathroom in his house and found a clean towel for Hannah to use, then backed out of the room to let the two women finish their preparations.

Ariana returned a moment later to Damian's kitchen counter where he stood. It was as far away as he could be from the bathroom and still be inside his house. Miguel was guarding the bathroom door while the two cats were staking out their territory on his living room furniture.

"What do I do next with the girl?" Damian asked feeling overwhelmed between the lack of sleep and this sudden female invasion of his lair.

"I think she's been on the run from something for I guess a week. Let's try and get the story out of her and then I can take her home with me since I'm guessing this is a one bedroom house."

"I designed this house with only my occupancy in mind. There's no room for guests of any sort let alone a teenager. I'd be grateful if you would take her home with you. I have a friend who's a female retired detective and I thought about calling her, but I sense a story here and I'm not ready to turn her over to the authorities immediately, so you were my next solution."

"She's hardly said anything, but I see the intelligence spilling out that you were talking about. I'm guessing she's about fourteen, and I wonder where her parents are?"

"Can I get you some tea or something else to drink or perhaps some cookies?" Damian asked, recalling his manners.

"I'll take some tea and let's save the cookies to eat with Hannah. I think I just heard the water shut off. I was going to suggest she wash her clothes here, but it would delay us returning to my house. The question is how long will it take to get her story?"

"She may not feel secure in letting go of her only possessions, so let's wait and see if she talks."

"While we wait, why don't you tell me about this Bat-cave you built. I bet there are all kinds of special gadgets protecting it, though your jet ski hardly matches the Batmobile from the movies."

They heard the bathroom door open, and a cleaner Hannah in the clothes that Ariana brought, stood in the door frame. Her wet hair hanging in strands, she was yawning with exhaustion.

"Hannah, we're going to take you to Ariana's house tonight as she has a spare bedroom, but you need to talk with us. Do you need any medical care?" Damian asked.

Through another yawn, she said, "Medical care? Why would I need to go to a doctor?"

"Have you been hurt over the past few days or however long you've been looking for shelter?"

"No," she said slowly, "Why would I be hurt?"

"Okay, we needed to ask. Where are your parents and why aren't they looking for you?"

"They can't look for me, they're dead." Hannah said with a sob.

Damian looked over at Ariana to decide where to take the questioning next. Ariana went to the girl and hugged her, then put an arm around her shoulder to steer her to Damian's sofa.

"Hannah, what are you hiding from and how recently did your parents die?"

"They were killed last week, and the men that did it are after me."

"Did you tell the police that?" Damian asked. He couldn't recall a news story in the past week of a couple murdered and a teenage daughter missing.

Hannah was sobbing, reliving the terror of the men chasing her, and she finally said, "The men took them and said they were going to dump them into a lake. I've been running since and I won't talk to the police."

Damian looked at Ariana puzzled and then asked, "Why?"

"Because one of the men was a cop."

Damian looked at the sad child seated on the couch next to Ariana and exhaled a huge breath. It was approaching midnight, and Hannah was exhausted and it seemed like this was a long story to tell.

"Ariana, do you have an additional guest room that I can occupy?" Damian asked.

"Yes, why don't you pack an overnight bag? We'll head over to my house and settle Hannah in and then we'll all talk in the morning when we're not dead on our feet," Ariana said and then winced at her word choice.

He silently did as Ariana suggested and when he reappeared to take Hannah down to the boat, she was asleep with her head in Ariana's lap. He mouthed 'sorry' toward her, but she just shrugged and smiled. The child was so tired that when he picked her up she barely stirred and so Damian carried the featherweight child downstairs, through his workshop, and out onto the dock with Miguel at their heels. He settled her in to the cushions in the boat and covered her with a few blankets, again struck by how close this teenager was in age to what his youngest daughter would have been.

He locked his island up and soon they were crossing towards Ariana's home. The bay was deserted at this time of the night and the high speed straight path had them at her dock in little more than ten minutes. With Ariana in the lead, she led him into the house and up a flight of stairs to a guest bedroom where her niece stayed whenever she visited. The room was filled with pictures of the two of them.

After they tucked Hannah into bed, they left Miguel guarding her, as he would alarm Ariana if Hannah tried to sneak out in the morning.

Damian asked, "Do you need your boat covered or moved overnight? I can do that for you."

Ariana replied, "There's no rain forecasted for tomorrow, so I'll just leave it be for this one night. I brought your overnight duffle in along with her clothes. I feel like we should call the cops, but with her last revelation, I afraid to do so. Let's see what happens in the morning."

"I apologize for getting you involved in whatever is going on here. I'll admit my first thought was one of fear of being alone on my island with a teenage girl. Thanks, again."

"Damian, we all make our own choices and I could have chosen not to come just as you could have decided to turn your dinghy around and head back to the Richmond Marina, but there was something here with Hannah that we both felt compelled to help her with. It'll make sense in the morning after we all get some much needed rest."

Soon Damian was stretched out in a very comfortable guest bedroom, his mind still racing. It was time to close it down, he was very sleep deprived and once he got some sleep maybe his brain would work better. Finally, he drifted off.

CHAPTER 18

After a decent sleep, Damian and Ariana were in her kitchen the next morning sipping coffee and munching croissants. Damian felt much better as he'd actually slept soundly in Ariana's guest room. She'd checked on Hannah who was still sleeping. She let Miguel out to pee and then he resumed guard duty at her bedside. Hannah had been asleep nearly ten hours and it was mid-morning with the sun shining. He needed a ride back to his island, but he had hours in front of him figuring out Hannah. He wondered how Natalie was doing with getting the truck in the San Leandro junk yard. He'd checked his phone for messages, but all was quiet so far.

He and Ariana had discussed possible scenarios concerning Hannah including the fact that she was a runaway and her parents weren't really dead, but they'd both felt the truth of her story. Damian had searched the recent news and there was simply no mention of a couple being murdered and their teenager missing.

Ariana had left Hannah a note that they were in the kitchen and she should come down when she was ready, and a half an hour later, they heard sounds of movement and the click of dog paws on tile indicating the two might be heading their way.

As she saw Hannah tentatively approach, Ariana said, "Good morning Hannah, why don't you have a seat here," pointing to a seat between her and Damian. "I'll get you a chocolate croissant and orange juice. How does that sound for breakfast?"

Hannah nodded and sat down, clearly shy and unsure what to do or say to these adult strangers. At least she had the friendly dog to pat. Ariana placed the food and drink in front of her and Hannah looked around. The two adults must have already eaten and were drinking coffee. It was then that she felt stinging tears hit her eyes as she recalled her parents in almost this exact same position.

Ariana saw the flow of tears and guessed that the setting reminded Hannah of her family. She went over and just hugged the girl. When she sensed the girl had regained her composure, she walked her over to the breakfast bar stool and sat her down. Damian had watched the entire episode in silence, then asked, "Hannah, what's your last name?"

"Sherwood."

Damian nodded then typed away at his laptop. Hannah picked at her food in silence. He soon had information on her and her family.

"You live in Shepherd Canyon and attend the Mastley School and you're fourteen?" Damian asked.

Hannah nodded.

"Police were called by your school because you didn't show up to class and no one has seen your family. It says here that the police indicated that in a search of your house there was evidence that your family had left and moved to Bogota, Columbia. Hannah, do you have any connection to Columbia?"

"No, we weren't moving. My mom and I talked about my attending UC Berkeley and being able to live at home and commute to school. I won't be going to college for two years."

"Two years? Aren't you at least three years away from college?" Ariana asked.

"I skipped eighth grade and I'm doing advanced placement courses and I have straight As" Hannah replied and then added, "I've been tested and I have a very high IQ."

Damian thought that must have helped her survive on the streets for a week although IQ didn't necessarily translate to street smarts. Since she was so smart, it was time to be honest with Hannah. He was very smart himself and he always liked facts no matter how unpleasant.

"Hannah, I don't know what to do with you. I have a friend who is a retired detective from the San Jose police department. Maybe we should seek her help as there seems to be a problem with Shepherd Canyon police."

"No, please don't call her," Hannah replied in a panic, looking for the doors to Ariana's house to run.

Ariana frowned at Damian and put a hand on Hannah's shoulder to calm her and said, "Hannah, we don't want you running away; you need some adults you can trust and so you're stuck with Damian and I. Legally, Damian and I are in trouble as we have no right to take care of you and have a responsibility to notify the authorities, but I want to keep you safe. Are you sure your parents are dead and not just in hiding?"

"Yes, three men stormed the house. My parents built a safe room in our house to protect me and them. We even had drills on getting into the safe room as quickly as possible. I was up late reading and heard someone come through the front door, so I headed for the safe room that was in my bedroom - it was in the back of the closet. There are cameras and microphones throughout the house and monitors in the three safe rooms so we can watch and hear."

"Three safe rooms?" Damian asked. "Why were your parents so afraid that there would be a home invasion?"

"I don't know; the rooms were built when we moved into the house two years ago."

"Where did you live before that?" Ariana asked.

"New York City."

"Oh, so did I. So you ran into your safe room and watched the rest of the house on the monitors. What happened next?" Ariana asked gently.

Through sobs, Hannah said, "They walked into my parent's bedroom just as they were trying to get from their bed into their own safe room. They hit Dad in the back of the head and grabbed Mom by her hair." Hannah's sobbing was getting louder and her words harder to understand, but they knew they needed her to tell the full story.

"Then what happened?" Damian asked fearing the answer.

"They put a cloth over their faces and they stopped moving and just lay on the floor dead. They zipped Mom and Dad into sleeping bags and then carried them out of the house into a van."

Ariana handed Hannah a box of Kleenex and said, "And then the men drove away with your parents?"

"Sort of."

"Hannah what do you mean sort of?" Damian asked.

"They left one of them behind and he was supposed to find me. He searched the house and even opened the safe room in my parent's bedroom expecting to find me. When I wasn't there he stayed in the house for several days and even stayed in the house when the police came to the door. He welcomed them in and showed them an order that Mom had signed to move the house's furniture and they believed him."

The last sentence was said through a mixture of disbelief and sobs. Damian and Ariana looked at each other and silently agreed they could ask the girl no more questions, and Ariana went over to the girl to hug her for a while. The crying stopped eventually and Ariana had Hannah drinking orange juice. Hannah's final sentences came.

"I waited until the man was asleep and snuck out of the house. I was hungry and knew I needed to get far away. I thought I could hide at our boat at the marina, but just as I was about to sneak on board, some men came up from the lower level and cast off the lines to take off. It had taken me part of the night and all day to walk to the marina and just when I saw the boat leaving the dock I didn't know where to go or what to do so I climbed into your boat to rest a moment and fell asleep."

Damian nodded and went to work researching her parents on his laptop. Something very powerful was in play here, because it was as if, except for that mention of her school to the police, Hannah and her parents didn't exist.

CHAPTER 19

No further effort was made to get any more information from Hannah. Instead Ariana encouraged all three of them outside into the sun and Miguel was more than willing to distract. Soon Damian had Hannah using the drone to drop toys for Miguel in the water. It provided the perfect cover for Ariana and Damian to discuss next steps and to cheer up Hannah.

"She's a great kid and she has been through a very hard time," Ariana said.

"Yeah. I don't think her parents are necessarily dead which is good, but they have fallen off the face of the earth. I think we need to keep Hannah at your house until we can figure out what to do. I was thinking of starting by slipping into her home to see what clues there are."

"Me? What do I do with a teenager?"

"I don't have guest space at my house and besides I'm a guy," Damian replied as if that settled matters.

"Yes, but she needs to be in school, I don't have the legal right to care for her. What if she has a medical emergency, how to I explain her existence?"

"I can set up all the fake identification you and she'll need, remember, I'm a computer genius," Damian replied with a grin.

"Are we doing the right thing? Maybe we should call the police?"

"I'd hate for someone like her to get caught in the system, until the situation with her parents is straightened out. I can share her with you when you have to leave town. We'll just be surrogate parents until the real ones are found."

"How are you going to explain her to your friends?"

"Good question and I don't have all the answers yet, but let's ask her as well. She's a smart kid, let's explain to her what we're thinking and go from there."

Miguel looked tired and Hannah walked over to them and asked, "Are you done discussing me yet?"

As Damian said, the kid had intelligence and backbone; he started the conversation with Hannah about her future.

"Hannah, we're not sure that your parents are dead and you shouldn't be either, but someone has to care for you right now and keep you safe until we have answers about your parents. Like you, I'm a genius also. I can create paperwork so that it appears you're Ariana's daughter and I'm her back-up. You need to be in school, though not the one you were in. If you have a medical emergency, we need paperwork that gives us the legal right to take care of you. Our alternative is contact the police and keep this all proper and legal. What do you want to do?"

Hannah was quiet as she considered their offer. Her family and her future were so perfect a week ago. She wanted Damian to turn back the clock so that her parents had time to get into their safe room. Did she trust these strangers not to hurt her? Would they help her find her parents? Her intuition had never been wrong before. If she sensed someone was bad, she usually had evidence of their bad behavior within a few weeks. She didn't feel that there was anything too bad about these two people, even though she didn't so much as know their last names. Their pets were well cared for and that was always a good sign. She sighed not knowing what to do.

Damian had watched the girl and found himself guessing at what she was thinking and so he asked, "Would you like a computer so you can look us up and read about us?"

Hannah had pretty much made the decision to take a chance on these two strangers. But if she could do an internet search on them that would probably seal the deal for her. So she nodded her agreement.

They went back inside and before Hannah sat down at a computer, she asked, "You're sure you can create a secret identity for me? Do you know how to code?"

Damian laughed at her question and replied, "Hannah, I hold ten patents related to things I invented that required coding. When you want to learn, I can teach you. Is that what you want to do in the future?"

The tears suddenly welled up in her eyes over the word 'future'. For the past week, she'd concentrated on surviving and now she could devote a sliver of her personality to thinking about her future.

"Will you teach me regardless of my future? Can I look you up someday to help?"

Damian nodded, swallowing a lump over such a small request from someone who'd been through so much.

Hannah sat down at a computer and began looking the two of them up. Since Damian had looked Ariana up, he knew that Hannah should be able to form an opinion of Ariana based on what she found on the internet. He was curious to see what Hannah would find on him.

Thirty minutes later, she stopped typing and looking at Damian said, "Was your family really murdered seven years ago? Your daughter and I must have been about the same age at the time of her death."

"Yes."

Hannah continued to look at him solemnly, aware that he'd suffered as much as she had. Then she blinked and looked at Ariana and said, "You lost your husband to cancer three years ago and you don't have children. Right?"

"Yes," this time it was Ariana providing a single word, large meaning response to Hannah.

"If you'll have me, I'd like to stay with you. Will your niece mind if I stay in her room?"

"No, she'll just move to another when she visits."

"Will you take me back to my house so I can retrieve some things?"

"Hannah, I don't think that is safe. What exactly do you want?" Damian replied.

"Pictures. I had pictures in frames and pictures on my cell phone and I dropped it when I crossed a creek on the way to the marina. Can you get information off a wet phone?"

"Maybe, anything else besides the pictures? Is the creek close to your house?"

"Clothes and books can be replaced. What will happen to the house if my parents don't come back?"

"We'll have to do some research on that. In the near future, is the guy that was trying to find you still in the house? Longer term questions about electrical, water, and tax bills will need to be sorted out. At some point, law enforcement will need notification that the entire family is missing. We won't tell them that you're with us, but it would be good to have someone looking for your parents officially."

Hannah's shoulders looked weighted down by the view of her new future. So Damian said, "Hannah, I'll continue to search for your parents until we have an answer on their location. In the interim, we'll need a new name for you and a story so that we can enroll you in school. Do you want to be adopted by Ariana and I or would you rather be a relative that lost her parents in a car accident? What new name would you like? You could pick the maiden name of your mother or perhaps that of a grandparent, or maybe a nickname that your parents called you. You can think about it for a few days, but I think we should take you to be registered for school on Monday. I will be able to create all that you need by that date with your help. Just think about those questions and let me know when you've got answers."

Hannah nodded and then Ariana added, "We also need to change your appearance some and the easiest thing to do is hair and glasses, so give some thought as to whether you might want short blond hair and cool glasses to wear at your new school."

Hannah showed both fear and excitement with Ariana's comment. She'd get to start over at a new school and be anyone she wanted to be, but then she was reminded that there was someone looking for her that might want to kill or kidnap her.

"Hannah, Ariana and I have to make a few more arrangements for you and we need to have a private conversation. It's one of the few about your future that you'll be excluded from, okay?"

"Okay. I'll go sit in the kitchen until you're done."

Once she was out of earshot, Damian said to Ariana, "Are you up for this? I thrust this child on you less than twenty-four hours ago and now you'll be a full time parent. I'll be there to help and I'll look into modifying my home so she can stay there some times. I'll pay her bills. I don't know you well at all Ariana, other than you're a widow and a kind, occasionally reckless adult, but I think the two of us could make good surrogate parents until we have an answer on what happened to her own parents."

"I've enjoyed being an aunt, so I'll just slip into the role of doing it full time. Every other option I can think of puts that child in a worse position than she would have in my home. Damian, will you look at Hannah and see your younger child? After my initial attempt at trying to learn who you were, I never went back and looked you up after you told me your full name. I'm very sorry your wife and children were murdered."

"It's been seven years since their murders and just the other day I was thinking that if my oldest was alive she'd been preparing for college or a prom or something. Both of my children didn't get a lot of milestones with their lives cut short. I will think about my youngest at times with Hannah, but she's got a very different look and affect so other than the age, there's not many similarities. I hate to be crude, Ariana, but I researched you and I know that financially you can take care of Hannah, but so can I and I would like to set up a trust fund to pay for her expenses. You'll be doing the yeoman's work of caring for her day to day, at least let me take care of her major expenses.

"A final comment, if my wife and I had been murdered and our two children left in the wind, I would have been far happier for someone like you to care for them, than for them to go through all the proper legal channels. It had been an area of worry in our marriage as neither of us had family and so we looked at a few friends as possible parents, but we hadn't come to an agreement on what to do."

"Ok, we'll see how this goes and these are the raging teenage years. She may seem normal at the moment, but at some point her hormones will take over and you better be able to hang in there with me," Ariana demanded. "We're each going to be a single parent to this child."

"I guess I'll be making many mistakes from this day forward," Damian replied. "Speaking of being a parent, we have work to do and we need to go inside and talk to Hannah."

Ariana stopped suddenly and said, "We should probably look into Hannah's relatives, she may want to go to one of them instead of us."

"We'll check with the kid, but I would have thought she would have said something before now if that was the case."

They returned from a brightly lit living room and walked into the large open kitchen where Hannah sat at Damian's laptop with Miguel at her side.

"Hannah, you'll want to be careful contacting anyone from

your life in Shepard Canyon. You don't know who is watching or who might accidentally mention you in passing."

"I know. I posted a note on Mom and Dad's Facebook pages, so that they would know I'm still alive if they ever check. I used an avatar of my favorite cartoon character and just said, "The drill was cancelled until further notice as I performed well on the last one." Mom and Dad will know I mean the safe room drills and that I'm alive. With a name and location change, if they're alive, they'll have a hard time finding me, but I don't want them to wonder, I want them to look for me when they're able."

"Oh, sweetie," Ariana said as she gave the girl a hug.

"Hannah, I will look for them forever until we find them and I'm pretty good at finding information. I'm working with a retired detective on cold cases that date back almost thirty years and I've been able to find new leads for them so I'll work on your parents. I don't want you searching online as you could give away your location to the bad guys. I'll show you every week in my laboratory what new stuff I've done to find your parents, ok? Will you promise to leave the online world alone for now? I'll take you to my home on Sunday so you can see the work I've done to find your parents."

"Ok," Hannah said.

"Now we all have things to do today. Ariana, what's your schedule like today?" Damian knew that Ariana had an active schedule with her Silicon Valley start-ups and she was probably missing meetings.

"I told my contacts that I was taking a long week-end vacation and I'd be back in touch on Tuesday. That gives me time to set up Hannah's story and her new life. What do you need, Damian?"

"I was thinking that on your end, Hannah needs stuff - clothes, a cell phone, books, etc. I'll supply her with a tablet for games and school. I'm going to make its IP address bounce around the world so she'll be safe. I'll also provide you with a water gun that you'll not be able to take to school, but that both of you should keep with you at all times except at school."

Ariana smirked and said, "Water gun?"

"Before you laugh too hard, Ariana, let me tell you it's a modified gun. I found the perfect polymer to coat it with and so it's strong and has a considerable range. I fill the water chamber with a red chili mixture that disables your eyes for about four hours when hit with the stuff. My friend, the retired detective was fired upon by a gang thug and he missed, but she didn't and he's sitting in jail now. Would you like hot pink or lime green?"

"Hot pink" and "lime green" were chorused together by the two women.

"Hannah, I need your house address and the location of the creek where you dropped the cell phone."

"Is it safe to go inside Hannah's house?" Ariana asked.

"I've got infrared technology so I'll be able to see any heat sources before I enter. The difficulty will be in not alerting the neighbors. So you have any ideas for that Hannah?"

"You'll need Harry Potter's invisibility cloak," was her response after thinking about it for several seconds.

Damian thought of the bullet proof fabric he'd provided Natalie's family and decided that at night it would serve the purpose of invisibility. He pulled a Google Earth street view picture of Hannah's house up on his laptop and they discussed the house and where her pictures were located. Ariana, Miguel, and Hannah would escort Damian back to his island and he would go from there. Ariana's boat provided a comfortable ride and he thought about getting something similar for himself, but he could get to her house on the jet ski or more slowly in his rowboat with the small motor. Having a boat like hers would require a permanent dock and remove the look of his island being uninhabited, so he'd pass on a new boat. They dropped him off at his dock and as he waved good-bye he knew his life had changed forever. He went into his lab to gather some gadgets and while he was there he took a look around his lower level trying to decide where to build Hannah her own bedroom. He had space that wasn't in use, but there were no windows down here. Maybe her parents would be found later today and then building her a bedroom would become a moot point, but somehow he doubted that. He'd arranged to have Mike pick him up in a few hours. He wanted the sunshine of the day to look for her cell phone, but the cloak of darkness to visit Hannah's house.

CHAPTER 20

With his supplies sorted and ready to go for Mike's pick-up later, he went to look for Bailey and Bella. They were miffed he missed a second night on the island, but warmed up to Damian with the smell of fish. He stood looking out his kitchen window at the bay and thought, 'I've become a father again; how weird, okay maybe not a father but an uncle.' He'd protect Hannah as he hadn't been able to do for his daughters.

Then he thought, 'first order of business, Damian, is to get over your morose thoughts and move on to getting the child what she needs and trying to find her parents like you're trying to solve the cold cases.' He was grateful Natalie hadn't called him during this time that he was dealing with Hannah's situation.

He went back to the runs he was doing concerning who in the Aryan Brotherhood had put the original kill order out for Natalie. Going through seven years of some twenty thousand inmates and ex-inmates was challenging for his computer; it wouldn't have been something he could have done manually. Once he had the emails that were spoken in their code, he also had the computer go back and look at those emails from the same address written in plain English to assure there were no messages about Natalie. So far he hadn't figured out where the kill order had come from, but hopefully, he armed Natalie with enough of the Brotherhood's secrets that she'd get somewhere with their leadership. If not, he was ready to leak the first fifty or so emails to the black Guerrilla gang. He hoped he wouldn't have to do that as he didn't want to encourage a race riot in any of the state's prisons. It was time to check in with her.

"Hey, Damian, we were able to tow Avery's truck from the salvage yard down to our lab and the techs are going over it now. If they find evidence, it will be hard to prove the police did not plant the evidence."

"If the police don't have Debbie Altman's DNA or fingerprints, how could they plant evidence in the car?"

"The DA needs to hear that reflexive answer from you; he thinks because of the nearly thirty year delay in finding this car, we'll be accused of planting evidence. I wish Kevin had thought of the appropriate response when he spoke with her."

"The DNA you'll have for matching will be that of siblings. Close enough that you know you're dealing with close blood relatives, but not so close that you would have an exact match."

"I know, Damian, you're preaching to the choir, here."

"I can't find who ordered the hit on you for your meeting with the leaders of the Brotherhood, but I have fifty emails so derogatory and inflaming, that the prisons will have riots on their hands as soon as we post them," Damian said. "I hate to cause riots, but we must get them to back off you and your family."

"Maybe we should let the wardens know at the various prisons of the impending storm."

"They might react by turning off the email system to bide themselves some time and remove the inflaming emails if they have advanced notice. Most of these riots result in inmate deaths rather than guard deaths."

"I'm really torn on this one. Since so much drug use and

trafficking occurs inside prison, the guards have to be part of the distribution system; they just haven't been caught yet," Natalie paused a moment to think and then said, "It's my life and my family's that I'm fighting for, give me five of the fifty emails so I can take them with me and share with whomever I'm meeting."

"Will do."

"Eddie and I are looking forward to your meeting with Trevor and Haley this weekend. We really like her and you're like the final approval for him."

Damian had completely forgotten Trevor coming that weekend in the last twenty-four hours of solving Hannah's problems. He'd have to talk to Ariana about it. He planned to have the two of them over to his home after Trevor was there so he could work on Hannah's identity and get her approval for a small bedroom he could build her.

Instead he lied to Natalie, "I'd forgotten about the visit, in the wake of your shooting, but at least this is a safe place for him to relax. Do you and Eddie want to join them in a visit to my house this weekend? It's pretty safe here."

"Thanks for the offer but it's good for you to have some alone time with them for this first meeting. After that, you can invite us anytime."

"Okay I'll trust your opinion on the matter. How is everything working there? Have you experienced any problems with my technology or with any thugs?"

"Only the postman and our neighbor. Eddie filed a hold card at the post office and we put a sign up about stepping on the property, as it was dangerous. One of our neighbors with young children was outraged, but we explained that someone that I sent to jail was rumored to be looking for me, and we had set traps that would contain but not kill someone. She debated sending over her oldest for the day."

Damian chuckled at the image of the parent being pleased

with their child being caught up in a tree net for a few hours. "Maybe we overreacted, but it's better than being dead."

"I don't think we overreacted. We all especially appreciate the bullet proof fabric. I checked in with Andy and Sherman and they thought we did the right thing, so don't worry about it. Damian, thanks for your help with both the cold case and my own protection and I'll drop you a text if I hear anything new."

They ended the call and he wondered how Hannah and Ariana were doing with their shopping trip. What a complete flip of his life that he was suddenly worrying about people after spending nearly seven years in isolation not giving a rat's ass about anything or anyone. He laughed at himself and the stress he was feeling for Natalie and her family, and Hannah.

He moved into another area of his workshop containing lots of weird toys. He owned a forward looking infrared sensor. He used it to understand this rock of an island and the water flow around it. Tonight he was going to use it to see if there were any heat sources near Hannah's family home. He could sit several blocks away and yet still see any heat sources at her house. He would modify the technology so he could spot cameras that were connected to somewhere, be it the family's hidey holes or to the bad guys that took Hannah's parents. He had another device with him that would scramble all cameras while he was near or in the house.

This was all assuming that the coast was clear and the house empty. If he found heat sources, then he planned to wear a gas mask and fire a Halothane bomb at the heat source. Halothane was cheap and still in use in developing countries and veterinary practices as a quick acting sedative. The heat source should hit the ground in about fifteen seconds after breathing the stuff and stay down while Damian retrieved what he needed from the house. He wanted Hannah's stuff, any records or computer drives and any recording devices. He'd have his water gun as a weapon, but hopefully just be able to knock out the heat source, and scramble any security devices before his heat source notified anyone of Damian's intrusion.

Ariana dropped him a text with Hannah's new mobile number and just said the day was going well, and what time should they come tomorrow to work on Hannah's school records? Damian thought Trevor and Haley would be gone by three and so he had her plan for a four o'clock arrival. She knew he was having guests and if they wanted to keep Hannah's presence hidden until they had a good story in place, then it was better not to introduce her to anyone either of them knew closely. Fortunately Ariana's family and that of her dead husband's were all on the east coast.

He had an early dinner with the cats, sharing his chicken. They also were going to have their lives disrupted whenever Hannah stayed with them. The days were numbered as loners for all three of them. He cleaned the kitchen up and got ready to meet Mike down on the beach. He hoped to be back tonight, but he'd made no arrangement with Mike. Once at the harbor, he made plans with the harbormaster to borrow his boat. He'd leave it parked overnight at his lower level dock and take it back in the morning to do some grocery shopping then meet Trevor and Haley for his trip back home.

Plans in place, he turned his truck toward the creek where Hannah had dropped her phone. He had a fish net and some wellingtons to wade in, but he wasn't sure what kind of water he'd meet up with. Closer to the time that Hannah had crossed the creek, it might have been raging from a recent rain storm, or maybe she was wet and cold and the battery was dead anyway. Maybe she'd crossed in the dark and couldn't see anything in the water. Regardless, he'd do his best to find it. He parked in a county park and got out of his truck to begin walking the creek. How terrifying it had to be for a girl who had thought her parents were dead. Using the metal detector he began walking along the creek. Fortunately, no one seemed to be patronizing the park at this time of day to wonder what he was up to. After searching about three hundred yards of creek bed, his detector went off for the thirtieth time and there was Hannah's phone. It was a droid in a case of bright green, exactly as she described it. He picked it up took a picture and texted it to her new mobile phone for confirmation and Hannah confirmed that it appeared to be her phone. Great now all he had to do was try to save components that had been in the water for several days. He'd brought a bag of rice with him to start the drying process. After drying off the phone, he opened the inside and planned to toss the sections into the rice, but he stared at the extra piece inside. It was a tracker bug and he dropped it into a metal lined film pouch. He didn't know if it was working or who had put it there, Hannah's parents or the bad guys.

Now it was time to move on to the far more dangerous job of getting inside Hannah's home. He had the key and the code to shut the alarm off, but that was after he surveyed the property with an infrared scan. It was still daylight, so he couldn't try to get into the house yet, but he did do a drive-by to see what the neighborhood situation was. While all of his technology would work for a daytime invasion, he was hoping if there was an intruder in the house, he would have a harder time staying awake after dark. He'd checked the statistics on burglaries and most occurred in the daytime while the homeowner was at work, but as a novice he just felt better under cover of darkness.

His impression was one of million dollar and up homes on a quiet tree lined street. There were no cars in the driveway of Hannah's home. There was a mailbox close to the street end of the driveway. Elsewhere, there were no kids playing in the street. He pulled the truck underneath some trees along the front of a property upon which no house was built. He set up his scanner to look at heat sources in the house.

CHAPTER 21

There was one source inside the house and it was in motion in what was probably the kitchen. Hannah had drawn a floor plan of the house for him with directions of where he would find the pictures that she wanted. Since most security cameras worked by the concept of infrared waves, he had a different scanner that showed where all the active cameras in the house were located. There were a lot, and Damian wondered how men had ever creeped into the house without advance warning to Hannah's parents. They must have used a blocking device that also cut off the alarm or maybe there was a ten to twenty second delay to account for power failures that would be supplemented by a back-up generator after a short time. That short time would be enough for fast moving men to get into the house and up to the bedroom to take on the parents. Hannah had been awake and reading not awakened by a house alarm. She would have the added seconds to make it into her safe room and she was the secondary target after her parents. So what tools should he use to enter the home now?

He'd wait until complete darkness betting that the lights would be out in the rooms on the street side of the house. He'd take another drive through the neighborhood to see how illuminated it was, then he'd return and park his truck where it was, gathering his supplies to safely enter Hannah's house. He still wasn't sure what he would do with the man in the house. He had the means to incapacitate him, but how did he cut the alarms off?

Dah! He'd just use the code Hannah had given him and turn off the cameras that way. Sometimes he tried to over solve a problem by using technology when the answer was right there in front of his face. He watched the guy for a while longer and then drove away to a large retail store to use their restroom. It wouldn't do for him to pee his pants when he got surprised or scared during this operation. It was interesting acknowledging that he was going to be scared. Perhaps that would sharpen his senses or reflexes; he hoped so.

He drove past Hannah's house, this time in the dark of night. As he thought, the front was dark, he'd have little trouble being invisible in the darkness when he was ready to go in. He parked again on the empty block and gathered his stuff. He wanted to avoid dropping any DNA in the house, so he'd brought paper booties for his shoes, a balaclava for his face and a knitted beanie cap for his head, long pants and a turtleneck, and latex gloves. All items recently purchased at the department store, that way his DNA had less time to get on the clothing and he had no residue from his cats or the island. Over all that he put on a black cloth disposable suit. Thankfully, the temperature dropped into the fifties at night in this part of California or he'd drop his sweat all over the house. Someday, some police force would collect evidence at the crime scene of Hannah's house, and he wanted to be damn sure that his DNA wasn't there. He'd debated sealing up his clothing with clear spray shellac or flat paint, but he might die from the fumes before the night was out.

He brought a huge bag to collect anything for Hannah that he thought she might want beyond the family photos. He had his cell phone jammer, the infrared heat sensor, his water gun with special pepper spray, and the halothane homemade bomb to put whomever was in the kitchen asleep. The gas was odorless and colorless and he just needed to put the container near the heat source that he had viewed on his infrared detector. He hoped there were no squeaky boards that would give his presence away to the heat source. After gingerly moving through front yards in all black with the bulletproof fabric around him, he was soon on Hannah's doorstep disabling the alarm system. He also jammed cell phone reception to block the intruder from calling for help. He unscrewed the lightbulb illuminating the front porch and soon entered the house.

This was the first time in his life that he'd acted like a cat-burglar, and he could tell he wasn't cut out for this occupation as it felt wrong to break in and his heart was pounding and his body sweating with anxiety that the heat source might kill him before Damian was able to release the gas and make him go to sleep. It was why he carried the water gun in his hand and he knew he would be trigger-happy if anything didn't go as planned.

It was surprisingly easy to reach the kitchen. He heard no alarm bells go off anywhere in the house. The heat source hadn't moved but seemed to be sitting at a table and either asleep or doing something with a cell phone in front of his face. The stupid man was sitting with his back to the door and so Damian slipped on a gas mask, while he let the halothane disperse into the room. The man was soon snoring with his chin nearly resting on his chest. Damian bent down and picked up the homemade bomb and set it on the kitchen island next to the man. The substance might kill him if he had a heart arrhythmia or liver failure, but otherwise with any luck Damian would be well gone by the time he woke up from his evening nap. Damian moved quickly through the house grabbing pictures that Hannah had specified. He also opened her closets and chest of drawers and dumped as many items as he could into trash bags. Rather than carry three large bags back to his truck through the community, he would put the items at the curb and quickly fetch his truck and come back and load the items in the bed. He went into Hannah's safe room which appeared to be untouched and retrieved a hard drive that he hoped would have the footage of her parents' attack. Fifteen minutes later he had all that he thought was important in the bags. Putting his gas mask back on, he closed up the halothane smoke bomb and put it in to one of the bags and quickly departed the house. He put the bags at the curb and nearly sprinted for his truck. There'd been no action on the street during this entire entry into Hannah's house. Less than five minutes later, he discarded everything but the turtleneck and slacks into his truck and he was tossing the bags in the back and heading down the street without anyone noticing his movement. For the job he'd rented a dark blue truck and taken the plates off before he parked this last time. That way if anyone caught sight of the truck disappearing down the street, there were no identifying marks about the truck. He returned to the retail center parking lot and took another look at his infrared scanner. His heat source in the kitchen was likely starting to wake up since he could see the head bobbing on occasion, while the body was still seated. He changed back into his own clothing and parked the rental truck in the hotel parking lot next to the car rental agency and his own truck. He moved over his equipment and the bags of stuff he'd retrieved from the house. He would let Hannah go through her bags when she visited the next day. He'd been faster than he thought and could likely get a ride from Mike back to his island.

An hour later, he examined the tracker bug out of the phone having made sure that he drained the battery of the device back in the retail center parking lot. Last thing he wanted to do was give anyone a path to his island. He decided to start by asking Hannah if her parents ever mentioned that they had a tracking bug in her phone. A few texts later after he explained, she replied not to her knowledge. So either her parents had done it and not told her or someone else had got to her phone and planted the device. It wasn't that important at the moment and he might question her further later.

He moved on to the technology that he had pulled out of Hannah's safe room. Surely these criminals were not dumb enough to let themselves be photographed on camera? But that was assuming they knew of the second safe room or that they knew that any motion inside the house was recorded. He wouldn't know until he looked at what was stored on the tape. Looking at the tape he determined that it was only for the past thirty days. Even though the system only recorded motion, it ended up with a lot of data from security cameras. He checked the hard drive for software for the tracker bug but didn't find any. That didn't necessarily indicate that her parents hadn't put the tracker there, it just meant that the software wasn't on Hannah's unit.

Looking at the clock, he debated what to do next. He was very curious to look at the video, but he was tired and afraid that he lacked the focus to look at a lot of dull footage. He also wanted to know the date of her parent's abduction and it was too late to text the child at this hour. So he packed it in and started upstairs to his bedroom, then he thought of one more thing. He better do a quick search of all of the stuff that he'd brought from Hannah's house, he needed to make sure there were no other trackers in any of that stuff. If there was, he had to get his jet ski out and take the item s over to the Berkeley marina and drop them on a boat there. He hated to do that to some poor bloke that owned the boat, but he needed it off his island. Most cheap trackers just emitted a signal, but they didn't record where they'd been just where they were in real time unless they were being actively watched. He was an hour later getting to bed after he found a tracker in each purse of Hannah's, a hoodie that said UC Berkeley, and in the drive that he brought over. He gathered them up and took them over to the marina in his little dinghy. It was quieter than the jet ski and would take longer, but this was about stealth. He found the perfect vessel, a large fishing boat that advertised Salmon fishing in the ocean on its side and would surely be out on the water the next day, since it would be Saturday. He could have sent the devices to the bottom of the bay, but they might have mercury or lead in them which was bad for the bay's fish. So he brought duck-tape and taped them underneath a large pile of ropes and nets. Once he'd returned and had his island locked up tight he dropped into bed exhausted by the amount of adrenaline that he'd used up that day.

CHAPTER 22

Damian awoke a little later than usual when Bailey and Bella pounced on his bed. It was their stares that brought him to wakefulness.

"Okay guys you want some scratch time and then some of my breakfast, I suppose," and although they didn't understand humans they acknowledged his words by each coming closer to a hand. Three minutes of ear scratching and they had their fill for the time and released him to shower. Normally he'd get some exercise in the morning, but his schedule was so full with Trevor and Haley arriving in three hours and then Ariana and Hannah after that and he still had a hard drive to decode.

He was showered and shaved and dressed in blue jeans and a Golden State Warriors black polo shirt with their logo on it. Haley and Trevor were going to watch the game with him later as it was game two of the best of seven against the Portland Trailblazers and the Dubs were up by one game. He'd invited Natalie and Eddie, but they declined. He fixed eggs and bacon for himself and sardines for the cats. He was amazed they still wanted human food after all the other fish they caught, but then this was no work for them and it had a little seasoning. The island had no snakes or mice as neither could swim across the bay, but there were lots of birds which were off limits to the cats, and fish and crabs. So far the crabs were winning against the cats, as they spent so much time dancing away from the crab's claws that they couldn't kill or even harm them, but it was fun to watch.

With the kitchen and the rest of the house cleaned, supplies ready for snacks for his guests as well as beer and wine that he picked up yesterday along with his spy clothing, he finally went down to his lab setting his alarm as he went. He knew that he would forget about the time and leave Trevor and Haley to get blasted by the water spray alarm when he forgot to turn it off in anticipation of their visit. After spending years alone, he wasn't used to scheduling his day around other people and all of a sudden since the seventh anniversary of his family's death, his schedule was bustling such that he would have to plan an entire Saturday around other people's schedules.

Before he went down to his lab, he called Hannah to ask her more questions. While the phone rang, he tried to think of a polite way to converse with the teenager before getting to his questions. He'd have to ask Ariana how she communicated with her teenage niece; maybe you could get right to the heart of the question with this texting generation.

"Hi Damian, what's up?" Hannah asked.

"Today is Saturday. Can you tell me which date your parents were abducted?"

There was silence on the other end of the phone, he wished he could see her face to see if she was thinking, or perhaps trying to swallow around tears, or perhaps silently crying over the terror of watching her parents abducted and maybe murdered.

"Monday; my mom always liked to play this song called 'Manic Monday' on Monday, and so she played it earlier that day before she dropped me off at school."

"Thanks, Hannah, I have the hard drive from your safe room and it will go much faster if I can look at a specific date. When you visit later today, I'll give you all the stuff I grabbed from your closet and chest of drawers in case you want any of it."

"Thank you, Damian," and then the kid didn't say anything more. Damian wasn't sure how to end the conversation or even what was going on in the kid's head. So instead he asked, "Is Ariana near you?"

"Yes."

"Would you ask her to give me a call? I'll see you this evening for dinner," and they ended the call. He wished he wasn't so awkward dealing with this teenager. He knew so little about her other than the fact that she was smart and had a core of strength about her. He would have gladly mentioned the Warriors' game, but he didn't even know if she followed basketball or indeed any sports.

Seconds later his phone rang and he saw it was Ariana.

"I need lessons talking to a teenager. I don't know if I'm supposed to immediately say what's on my mind or if I'm supposed to ease into the conversation. I don't know if I'm making her cry or she's thinking or she's sullen like so many other teenagers. You're going to have to help me, Ariana."

He heard bubbling laughter on her end of the phone and then she replied, "Ha, I don't know a single adult that has that magic formula. You're on your own, Damian. I'm fighting for my own survival first. What time should we head over to your island?"

Damian had to unstick his grinding teeth before he could reply, "How about 4 o'clock? I have company here from about 12 to 3. That detective I mentioned has a son that's a friend and he's bringing his fiancée to my home for an introduction and to watch the Warriors game. He's an attorney and he could enumerate all of the illegal things we're doing to take care of Hannah, so it's better if your paths don't cross."

"You have a full schedule today! Tell you what, I'll bring dinner with me, and maybe we can eat down in your lab while we work on Hannah's identity," Ariana suggested.

"You're a woman after my own heart, I love being able to do two things at the same time."

"Three things, Damian."

"Three?"

"Yeah, you'll be getting to know Hannah at the same time."

That gave him pause and then he asked, "Is she being a good kid for you?"

"Too good, I'm wishing she would relax and give me a little teenage rebellion."

"Be careful what you wish for and I'll see you later," and so he settled into working on the camera footage.

Focusing on the date of Monday, Damian reviewed the footage. About 11 o'clock at night he saw the masked men enter Hannah's house in a very systematic fashion. They wore gloves and their faces were by no means identifiable. He assumed they were men, but he admitted to himself that was just a guess; he could be looking at a group of female ninjas that pulled this off. He saw Hannah's parents leap out of bed and make a run for their safe room, but they were caught by the masked men before they reached the room. Damian watched as each parent thrashed wildly until they went limp. Damian had to replay the footage several times before he realized the parents had each been injected with something. They were soon zipped up inside of bags and taken out of the house. The cameras had not shown where they were taken to or what kind of vehicle. Nor could he tell if they were dead or alive. Poor Hannah, watching this in terror, and then seeing what clearly was the men or women searching for her. They'd entered her bedroom, perhaps a minute after that of her parents, but it was enough time for Hannah to reach the hidey hole and lock the mechanism into place.

They searched the house for perhaps an hour looking for Hannah, but then they left leaving one person behind. It appeared as though Hannah had waited and watched the lone man for about thirty-six hours. She waited for him to fall asleep and then

Damian saw her exit the house. He also went back and studied the interaction between law enforcement and the moving company. He didn't have sound for the recording, but he could guess what was being said and he had to agree with Hannah, that someone from law enforcement was involved with her parent's kidnapping.

He leaned back in his chair and thought about what to do with the footage. Certainly he'd save it, but should he say something to Natalie or Trevor? He had no good answers and decided that no immediate decision was necessary. Having watched the abduction of her parents several times as well as the footage of the man left behind, he saw no opportunity for them to have left DNA in the house, so if he did say something to Natalie, the only evidence he had was the video recording to prove that it happened; but neither the people, their fingerprints, nor their DNA appeared to be left in the house from his amateur point of view. He decided he would share the footage later with Ariana since she was a smart woman and was implicated in their less than legal guardianship of Hannah to see if she agreed with his decision-making. He looked at his watch and realized that Trevor and Haley should be at the marina about to board the boat to his island. He put everything having to do with Hannah in a locked closet off of his laboratory. It wouldn't do to leave anything accidentally sitting around that Trevor might see.

CHAPTER 23

*D*amian stood on the edge of his island watching Mike's boat approach. He saw Trevor and a woman on board along with a few packages. He often had packages delivered to Mike who would store them until he had a reason to go out to the island unless Damian made arrangements to get them sooner. He'd made his way down to the beach where they would get off the boat and where the packages would be deposited. It seemed rather rude on his part to wait on the cliff's top rather than greet them down below.

Mike kept a lightweight ramp in his boat that he now slung from the boat to the beach. It was the easiest way to move people or packages off his boat. Introductions were made and then Haley and Trevor assisted Damian with moving packages off the boat and onto the sand. Within a few minutes, the ramp was back in the boat and Mike was waving goodbye having confirmed that he'd be return at three to take them back to the marina.

Once the boat was out of earshot, Trevor said, "Hey, Damian, Haley's an engineer and her company's experimenting with drone delivery. I bet she'd be good at operating your drone and depositing the packages on your doorstep."

Damian smiled and handed her the controls, "It's all yours."

Haley went to work while Trevor beamed with pride at her dexterity with the drone, moving the packages in record time. Damian said, "You're really good at that. On rare occasions, I haven't wanted to bother Mike with picking up something from me, and so my drone can reach the marina. However since it's over the water for much of the journey, I never feel comfortable, fearing I'm actually going to drop the package in the water, but with you at the controls I think I could relax."

"I've played a lot with drones at work and I'm developing the software that will allow a company to program an address and have the drone deliver it. The software directing the drone has to be smart enough not to hit anything in its way and to find an address. We're making progress, but we've had our share of drones smacking into walls," Haley said.

"Trevor didn't mention you are an engineer. I'll have to show you my lab as I have lots of projects underway there."

"Trevor told me you had wave technology here to make the island livable but intrude as little as possible on its environment. I hear there's a little zip line we can take instead of climbing up that hill," Haley said pointing to the cliff that Damian had descended in order to meet the boat.

"The zip line is the fastest and likely safest route to the top. That hill can be slippery and I'll admit I've left some skin behind. The game starts in ten minutes, so we best get going," Damian soon had all of them on top and they walked into his house.

Damian spent an enjoyable several hours with Trevor and Haley. He thought he would spend the whole time watching the clock wondering how soon he could escort them off the island, but he should have known better; they were great company. During halftime, he gave Haley a tour of his laboratory and had a great in-depth discussion about his wave energy technology. She perfectly recited the physics behind his theory but also understood his corrosive issues with water. She half-jokingly said that when he was ready to take on an engineer to help him, that she'd move to Berkeley and commute to his island daily to assist.

"Honey, how can we begin a life together if you want to live in Berkeley?" Trevor asked.

"You can quit your job with the public defender's office and do the same one for Alameda County. You've got a reputation, you won't have any trouble finding a job. I love the idea of using my engineering smarts to solve a problem for a Third World country."

Damian could tell that if he had offered her a job, she would seriously consider working for him. However he knew as long as Hannah was in his life, that he would need to keep people distant from his island. Of course he could set up a company close to the marina in a building and commute there every day, but he thought that some of his creativity came from living surrounded by water.

"Hey, didn't mean to cause discord between the two of you. Let's go back upstairs, grab a beer and sit down for the second half of the game."

The rest of the afternoon went off without a hitch with the Warriors winning. He was soon escorting his guests onto the boat and waving goodbye. He texted Ariana that the coast was clear, and they could visit at any time. It was early, but he wanted to give her that option. She texted back that she had a few more errands to run and that she and Hannah would be over in about an hour.

In the end, Damian decided to get a hard thirty minute run in on his treadmill since his exercise schedule had been so disrupted the last few days. That would also give him some time to think about all of the oranges he was juggling at the moment. He kept pen and pencil on the treadmill as he often thought of problems to solve and ways to solve problems that he had. He realized he hadn't thought of Greg Watson in the past few days and found himself wondering if anyone had followed-up with Natalie on what was going on with the search warrant by the Phoenix Police Department and the knife edge match from the medical examiner. He finished the run and wrote Natalie an email about the Greg Watson case and his pleasure in meeting Haley. He had just enough time to shower and catch a few fish for the cats and then he saw Ariana's boat approaching.

He opened his watercraft garage and extended the dock for Ariana to tie up the boat. He'd have to think about whether there was a better and more secretive way for her to park her boat at his house. For now, he welcomed the two women and the dog into his house. He'd brought the bags of Hannah's stuff out of the locked room so she could sort through it and see if she wanted to keep anything. Hannah looked older as she'd decided her new look would be radically different from the old. Her long brown hair was replaced by short black hair tipped with the shade of deep purple. Her eyebrows perhaps had also been dyed black and shaped. She had a flower tattoo on her upper arm and a ring of ivy around her ankle. She had heavy eye makeup on and a flawless complexion. Hannah was waiting for him to say something about her transformed looks.

"Hannah, I like your radically transformed look. I think it will help keep you safe. Are those tattoos permanent or temporary?"

"Temporary why?"

"If your parents are alive and able to return to you sometime in the future, I'm just keeping a list of sins that I will have committed as your temporary guardian. Permanent tattoos would have made my list because they are much harder to change than hair color. How do you feel about your look? Is it typical in your age group?"

All of a sudden she looked like a typical teenager when she gave him a look that said, 'you are such a dumb adult'. He felt so good getting that look.

"I had such an ugly hair color, but Mom wouldn't allow me to change it. I really like this new look and I think I'll fit in perfectly with kids at my new school on Monday. Ariana took me shopping to a few shops in the downtown area and I saw other kids with my look."

"There're a few more things she could do to change her appearance. She could get a couple of moles on her face as temporary tattoos as well as have a makeup artist show her how to make her eyes look more almond shaped. She has till the end of tomorrow to finish her modifications, because come Monday she's going to have to have her picture taken for her school ID."

"Actually, we should probably complete any changes to her face that we want her to have for the foreseeable future, as I need to take some pictures and age her backwards, so that there is a history to her new name. Hannah, have you decided what your new name will be?"

"I think so. My full name is Hannah Katherine Sherwood and I would like to keep the same initials. Since I love Harry Potter, my new first name is Hermione and the second could still be Katherine, right, and for the last name, how about if we chose Smith? Wouldn't Smith somewhat hide my identity since there are so many of them?"

"I can see now that I'll have to read Harry Potter again," Damian replied. "My oldest daughter was reading it and loved the story. Okay from this moment forward, we're going to call you Hermione. Smith is a good choice for the reasons you cited. Now the next question is how to make you related to Ariana."

"Or yourself. I could have ended up with you as my guardian, but because there's no school on the island, and Ariana is a good friend, she agreed to house me."

"Hmm, you may have a point there, Hermione, as I have no family to explain you to, whereas Ariana has lots of family."

Hannah giggled the first time that Damian called her by her name and she suspected it would take a while to get used to the new name.

"Ariana, what do you think?"

"There's a lot to be said for that explanation. I feel I might blow it sometime when I'm introducing Hermione to my family since I would constantly have to switch from my branch to that of my husband's and that might trip me up at some point. Describing her as your ward, but staying with me for school is much easier to explain and less likely for me to make mistakes with."

"Okay. After my family was murdered, I lost touch with everyone that we used to hang out with. I'll go back and build an identity based on one of those families as a model. I'll see where they are now and just use the same story for your background. I like the term guardian as that accounts for this coming out of the clear blue sky. Sorry, Hermione, but I'll have to kill your imaginary parents in a car crash."

"That's okay, it's all make-believe."

"What are your parents' first names?"

The teenager frowned in thought, then nodded, she understood the reason for Damian's question, "Jason and Amy."

Damian didn't want to kill imaginary parents with the same names as the kid's real parents.

"Okay, let me get your picture, then I need your vaccination records, any surgeries that you've had, and your school records. Do you think you could remember any of that?"

"Actually, if you get my phone working, there's a picture of my vaccine record and my transcript for grades 1-8. It also has my birth certificate. I had to have that information when I entered school and it seemed like they kept asking those questions, so I just kept a picture of it on my cell phone."

"That was brilliant, of course, assuming Damian can get your phone working again, but my money's on him being able to do that! We want to keep you in good health so before I forget, do you have any allergies - medications, food, bees?" Ariana asked.

"I'm allergic to raw tomatoes. My mouth gets real itchy, but if you cook the tomatoes like in pizza sauce or spaghetti then I'm fine and I've never liked ketchup but it doesn't seem to bother me on hamburgers."

Damian quickly researched raw tomato allergies and saw what Hermione was talking about. All three read the article and Ariana made a note to have the first pizza or spaghetti with Hermione near or inside a hospital just to be sure that this wasn't a full blown allergy.

Damian took her picture that he would use for various identifications and said, "It's a shame I didn't get a picture of you before your transformation that I could use for aging you backwards."

Ariana said, "I took a picture before her hair was cut; let me send it to you."

"Thanks, that will make this much easier since I won't have to spend time editing the picture back. I can do the rest of this on my own at a later time. Let's go upstairs and eat."

"Can you show me some of the things you're doing in your lab?" Hermione asked.

"Sure, over there I'm working on creating electricity through the power of wave action. Over there I monitor the various systems I have on this island - solar and wind generation and security. I should tell you, Ariana, that when you washed up on my shoreline, your phone didn't work because I have a jammer that blocked its action."

"What do you mean washed up on your island?" Hermione asked.

Ariana went on to explain her first encounter with Damian and her subsequent purchase of the tea and a drone. Hermione had her first real smile from the description of that entire adventure.

"Wow, you swam under the bay with scuba gear all the way to Damian's island? That's cool. Will you teach me to scuba?"

"Do you know how to swim?" Damian asked

"Of course I know how to swim. I competed on my school team."

"Did you win any races?" Damian asked with a small smile. He realized then that he'd seen medals and trophies in her room last night.

"I actually had hopes of swimming for Berkeley's team. They're really good. Missy Franklin swims for them although she quit, I think, so she could turn pro, whatever that means."

"So you want to swim for your new school," Ariana said.

"It's unlikely that I can mid-season. I was the holder of the season record in the 100 meter freestyle for my division."

"I bet you could at your new school. I'll find a way to get you a try-out with the coach at your new school, then you have to punch the speed button in the pool," Damian said.

Hermione looked doubtful that he could work such magic, so Damian moved the conversation on.

"I should have parts of your cell phone working by tomorrow morning. I think it will be dry by then. Do you want me to text or email the pictures to you?" Damian asked, then he had second thoughts and said "Forget that question. I don't want you walking around with pictures of your parents on your cell phone. That could cause a lot of questions. I'll set up an email address for you and send copies there."

Hermione nodded and then said with a catch in her throat, "How are my parents ever going to find me?"

"If we've done our job right, with the changes we've made to your identity and by putting you in my and Ariana's care, they won't find you. Right now, if your parents can find you then so can the bad guys. Hermione, I'll be searching for them every day and we might find them tomorrow or five years from now."

"Or never if they're dead." The teenager was definitely running low on inner strength at the moment and who could blame her.

"What if you don't want to take care of me anymore," she asked with the tears flowing.

"That's the great thing about having two of us; if one of us falters then the other can pick up the slack. Hermione, we will always be there for you," Damian said with quiet conviction, while Ariana hugged the girl.

"Let's go upstairs and eat dinner. We can discuss how I'm going to convince the coach at your new school to give you a mid-season try-out to the girl's swim team. I've got an idea."

With that, they headed upstairs and managed to catch the sunset in all of its purple and orange glory closing down the day and daylight on the west coast.

CHAPTER 24

Sunday proved to be a busy day.

The phone components dried out in the rice and he was able to extract pictures for Hannah, whoops, Hermione. He was having a hard time with the name change. Hannah just seemed to suit her better.

He had a Harry Potter audiobook playing in the background in hopes of refreshing his memory for common ground with Hermione and he also hoped that it would cement the new name in his head.

He searched for her swimming results at her old school, but couldn't find them published anywhere. He moved on to qualifying times so he'd sound intelligent when he spoke with the swimming coach. Both he and Ariana were escorting Hermione to school on Monday, ready to advocate on her behalf. He decided that he would indicate that Hermione lived with her parents on Norfolk Island, a tiny island that was a territory of Australia, and was home schooled. Her father was assisting in a nascent industry devoted to engines running on coconut oil. Her home school records would be hard to trace and she could fit in after a little testing in both academics and swimming. It would be a tough day of acting for her after the toughest week of her young life.

Hours later he had a plausible home school transcript, birth certificate, and vaccination record thanks to the photo on her cell phone. He sent it all over to Hermione and Ariana, with a plan to meet them at Ariana's house the next day at seven so they could arrive at the high school by eight. The poor kid was entering a new high school in the middle of the semester. Oh well, at least she was smart and athletic; hopefully that would make the transition easier.

He put his new ward aside for the moment and spent some time in the lab working on his latest innovations. Then he checked the release dates of prisoners convicted of felonies and felt as though it had been a previous life when he last checked to make sure no-one was released early.

Finally back to the two cold cases and the attack on Natalie. The wheels of justice moved slowly. The man that took a shot at Natalie had been arraigned on attempted murder charges. He refused to say anything during questioning according to her. The detectives studied the exterior tapes trying to decide if she was a random hit or if he'd purposely targeted her but they couldn't tell. No one else was around Natalie at the time of the attack, so she could have been the first one to enter the parking lot; just plain bad luck. The cameras didn't show much of the direction he'd come from so the police had no recording of him sitting in a car waiting for someone in particular to arrive or if he had just decided to go after the first person he saw. Damian was sure Natalie was the target given the fact that he was the son of the only person she had to kill in the line of duty.

The medical examiner had finally gotten back to Detective Shimoda and the knife could have created Barbara Watson's fatal wounds, but without her body he was reluctant to say that it was the knife used in the crime. According to Natalie's explanation, that left all kinds of holes for the defense to shoot through, no pun intended. So they were back to square one as far as solving the cold case. He went back and read the Barbara Watson case. The crime scene unit at the time collected fingerprints from around the area where the bones were found as well as on the clothing. It wouldn't do them any good to just find Mr. Watson's DNA on her clothing. All he had to say was he did the laundry. But if his DNA matched anything they pulled off the ground or foliage then they would have something that the DA would take notice of.

Then he thought of another roadblock. He wasn't aware that they had Mr. Watson's DNA; all they had was his fingerprints. So how could they get his DNA? How about the knife? Damian pulled the report and saw that they swabbed the knife as well as took fingerprints off of it.

Okay, then they never ran the knife as DNA wasn't a technology widely in use at the time the body was found. So the police could match the knife to the victim on a DNA match and then with the husband's fingerprints matching perhaps that would be sufficient suspicion to get a court order for a DNA sample. He discussed his thoughts with Natalie who agreed with his reasoning. They had reached their wit's end and were thinking of bringing Greg Watson in for questioning and hoping that they would be lucky and he would confess. A weak strategy at best, but the only one open to them as they couldn't get Mr. Watson's DNA without his knowledge or permission unless he was charged with a crime. He was living a quiet life in Arizona without a hint of criminal activity. He wouldn't give his DNA voluntarily unless he was completely innocent and knew that. The defense could also say there was good reason for his prints to be on the knife as he used it for cooking.

All right, time to put aside this case and return to Debbie Altman. Did he have any brilliant thoughts about that case other than the belief that John Avery committed the murder? Maybe he should study the Aryan Brotherhood a little more or maybe the truck they picked up from the salvage yard might have some evidence in it. Maybe it would help to call Natalie about the case. He looked at the time and briefly wondered what she would be doing on a Sunday afternoon.

"Hey Natalie, how's the protection system going?"

"Really good. We have everything sorted out and we're not getting annoying false alarms, yet we feel protected."

"Good. That's how the system should work. Have you met with the Brotherhood yet?"

"No. My approach has been a voluntary request for a meeting rather than a law enforcement meeting since I don't want law enforcement to know about the email cache. It's taking longer, but I think the leadership will meet out of boredom if nothing else. I think it could take as long as two weeks to arrange this meeting, so hopefully your safeguards work until the meeting gets set-up."

"They should work for another year or so unless your neighborhood boys spring all the traps and I make no guarantees about curious eight year old boys. I was thinking about Debbie Altman and the lack of evidence since her body was never recovered. Did the crime scene folks collect fingerprints from her apartment? I mean you don't have her DNA or her fingerprints, but do the CSIs collect evidence from a missing person's apartment thinking they might have her DNA or fingerprints for a later match?"

"They likely sampled her toothbrush or hairbrush if there was one. If there was a dirty clothes hamper then underwear would have been taken."

"Is that evidence still available? Has a DNA analysis been done on it? Could we use it to match what they find in the truck?"

"Let me check on the answers to your questions. The evidence should still be here and I doubt that DNA testing has been done since the DNA backlog is so large and we don't tend to randomly submit cold cases for analysis."

"Could we send a sample from the old evidence and new evidence retrieved from the truck to a private lab for testing, and then if it comes back as matching, send it through the official channels for testing? I would think that if the state lab knew another lab confirmed a relationship that they might be quicker with the results."

"I don't know how they operate as far as priorities, but keep in mind that several investigative journalists have reviewed the DNA backlog and they all agree that waits are too long or they haven't been tested at all. There's a backlog of something like a hundred thousand cases across the state and some of that is due to the fact that if you get arrested, the police take a DNA sample. So there's a huge backlog related to just incoming prisoners. They're also behind processing rape kits by shocking numbers. It blows my mind that we don't commit the financial resources to process lab results. Can you imagine going to your doctor, having blood drawn, and then the blood sits there for several years because your doctor's office doesn't have enough staff or machines? That's the current state of DNA testing."

"So why don't you use private labs?" Damian asked.

"Because in the budget it's one more officer on the street versus spending on DNA analysis. The average taxpayer will never feel the impact of DNA analysis, but they do like to see their men and women in blue."

"So it's not like a private lab analysis can't be used for court?"

"No, I believe that some California cities have already contracted with private labs and certainly the defense often sends evidence to them. I'll ask Kevin to ask his Lieutenant about sending these samples to a private lab as this is not a fishing expedition but rather we have some strong connections. I'm guessing the testing might run five grand which will be quite a hit to his budget."

"Natalie, that sounds like it isn't going to happen. You know, I lack the patience to be a cop. You're expected to solve cases but you don't have 100% of everything you need to do the job. It's like we tell you to solve a crime without a camera to take pictures of a crime scene."

"Damian, it's really not that bad. It's rare that DNA is the only indicator to solve a crime and we're hampered in this case because it's a cold case and no citizen is in immediate peril, but look this entire case might never have been solved if they hadn't hired me and if I hadn't invited you into the case."

"Well I don't like that we can't solve this case with all the modern tools available immediately. The victims' families deserve answers. I have some acquaintances in the DNA industry. I'm going to talk to them to see if there's a cheap and time saving alternative to what you're suggesting."

"That's fine, Damian, just remember you and I can't commit the resources of the SJPD to solve this crime. Any solution you come up with has to be blessed by the hierarchy."

"Can I send you my dental bill for the teeth grinding that you're causing me?"

Natalie laughed, "I hear your frustration loud and clear. Just remember that most cases are not solved by DNA alone. Usually it takes good detective work to lead us to a suspect and DNA confirms what we think."

"True. Okay, I'll quit whining and let you go about getting the evidence and then get it tested."

"Thanks Damian, I really do appreciate your help. As detectives, we don't have the experience that you do in analyzing huge databases or even mixing and matching databases whereas you can do it in your sleep. I'll get back to you when I have some news."

CHAPTER 25

*D*amian's worries about Hermione had him sleeping restlessly all night. He wondered if Ariana and Hermione had also been restless. He worried about the background he'd created for the kid and the potential for things to go wrong if the three of them didn't have their stories straight or all the answers required.

If they got her settled in school for the time being, then Damian's focus would shift into figuring out her parent's situation. Were they dead or alive? Why were they looking for the kid? Who were the bad guys? Why were they after the Sherwoods? Given the safe rooms, her parents knew about some threat to the family, but where was it coming from? Were they in witness protection, or something?

He dressed carefully wanting to appear to be a respectable guardian in appearance at least. Then he thought of the emergency measures that he and Ariana had taken in the last seventy-two hours and decided that they were off to a great start. The kid was fed, provided with the appropriate tools, disguised, and not at all traumatized since coming into their care. With that thought, Damian's confidence returned and he was excited to outsmart the school and the swim coach; however he could sense Hermione had a few worries. He used the little dinghy to head over to Ariana's, his paperwork in hand.

As he was pulling into her dock, she met him with a thermal cup of ginger tea. A good choice as they had a stressful day ahead.

"Thanks, Ariana. Before the day takes off, I want to say that you and I are going to make great parents and thanks for being my partner in crime."

"You're welcome and I hope her real parents, if they're alive, agree with our decision not to contact the police. If they're dead, we'll be seeing this thing through for many years to come. Mostly I'm looking at this situation in one of two ways - either I'm excited to shape a young person's mind or life, or I'm thinking the bottom line is she is safe with us until we can figure out what is going on, and those are both good motives."

"Yeah I was tossing and turning last night thinking of any loopholes in the paperwork or in our story and I think we have all the bases covered, although we should do another walk-through with Hermione. Is she nervous to go to school?"

"My guess is she loves school, but navigating this new world of hers takes quite a bit of mental energy on her part. I'm going to have to figure out some activity that allows her to be her and thus relaxes her."

"We'll talk about that with her or maybe something at school will pull her in, let's see what the day brings."

They had reached the door to the house and entered it to find Hermione sitting at the kitchen counter waiting for some signal from the two of them perhaps that they'd changed their minds as guardians or about school or something.

"Hey, Hermione, we thought we would practice asking questions of each other to make sure we had our stories straight. We don't want to blow our cover on the first day," Damian said.

Thirty minutes later the three of them felt solid with the story and ready to face school officials. They got in Ariana's SUV and headed toward the high school. There was a fair amount of activity around the school, so they found a visitor parking spot and the three of them followed directions to the principal's office which seemed like a good place to start. It was very rare for a kid to enter in the middle of the semester, but fortunately there had been enough students that they weren't thrown into complete chaos.

By mid-day Hermione was completely enrolled and accepted into all of the appropriate classes. Her empty backpack was now straining with books and she with assignments. Hermione could have been worried, but instead she appeared to be excited to compete against a new group of students. Their final hurdle was expected at two, when she had a private try-out with the swim coach. Damian was most worried about this as there was nothing he could do to pave the way for her and since he had never seen her swim, he could only hope she would do well in this arena as well. He remembered the trophies back in her parent's house and tried to be confident.

He and Ariana sat in the bleachers surrounding the pool watching the coach put her through the paces. Then he had her swim a few different lengths and strokes and then brought the session to an end and walked over to talk to them while Hermione went and changed.

"She's quite a swimmer. I've never in my twenty years of coaching had a mid-season walk-on that passed my testing, so congrats to your daughter. She'll need to be at swim practice three times a week, with meets after school or on weekends. There's just enough meets left that she'll have time to qualify for sectionals if she performs well," said the coach. He then handed them a sheet that repeated what he'd gone over with them and left. The first meet was in four days.

They sat alone waiting for Hermione to return.

"So, did I make the team?" she asked.

"Yes," chorused Ariana and Damian at the same time with the same prideful grins on their faces.

She relaxed and threw her fist in the air and then fist bumped the two of them.

"You have two meets to qualify for sectionals and one of those is this Thursday," Ariana said. "So the treadmill is going on high speed for you sweetie. I hope you can handle it between the new classes and the swim workouts and meets. You did really well today at both the testing for classes and the pool. Let's head to my favorite café for ice cream and we'll sit down and plan the week."

"I can't help you swim faster, but if you need help with your homework, just ask," Damian said.

Later over ice cream, they discussed her classes and swim schedule and worked out a plan. Ariana would ferry her to school and back unless she had a meeting regarding one of her companies, then Damian would step in and provide the transportation and escort home and stay with her until Ariana arrived. It would create quite a hole in his schedule as he would have to head to the Richmond Marina, get his truck, and then go over the bridge and into Marin County to pick the kid up for a five minute ride, but he felt it was important for her peace of mind to know that one of her guardians was always close-by.

It was a little smothering for a fourteen year old; but in time either her parents would return or she would push them away as a part of growing up. This week, Ariana had cleared her schedule so the first time Damian would hang with them was Thursday at the swim meet although he did intend to keep up with her through texting.

He had a laundry list of items to work on in regards to her parents. Who were they, what to do about the house - should he pay the utilities and taxes to keep it someday for Hermione? If her parents were dead, it was her inheritance. The utility bills question he would answer immediately by paying their bills, the longer term what to do with the house could wait. First he needed to make sure the parents owned the house. They could have been renters and in that case, the only inheritance to Hermione was the contents.

After the ice cream, Ariana stopped to grab some groceries and then the three of them sat at her kitchen counter going over books, subjects to be studied, and assignments due. They discussed nutrition and training. They worked out a complete schedule for the remainder of the week accounting for swim practice and the meet, assignments due and food to power her through the day. Tomorrow would be the real test for Hermione as she entered all her classes as the only new kid and she wouldn't have Ariana and Damian paving the way for her.

It was clear that Hermione had a handle on organizing herself for school work. Ariana and Damian admitted to fumbling around as neither had been in school for over two decades. Heck, they had constant reminders of how difficult it was to be a parent even to a highly cooperative kid. They realized that at least they lucked out on the kid and Damian thought it would be a real pleasure caring for Hermione until her parents returned or perhaps the remainder of his life. He was excited to help her succeed and decided to invite himself to dinner tomorrow to hear how her first day went.

Damian reached his island late; thankfully he kept a little fish in the freezer for rainy days or other days when the fish were not biting. His cats lined up while he was at the stove cooking it for them. It suddenly occurred to him that he could just filet the fish and serve it to them raw as that was how they ate things in the wild. Maybe he'd try that next time. After five years of making them fish dinner perhaps they'd developed a taste for cooked fish over raw.

His mind was going a thousand directions, yet he was tired and excited too. He felt like his sleep had been disrupted for the past week between dealing with Natalie's and Hermione's problems. He also felt very satisfied that he'd served others well this week. His late wife and daughters would have been proud of everything he did this past week, he thought, and let out a great sigh at that thought. Maybe he would put on some music and grab a beer to watch the gradual darkening of the sky.

One moment he was relaxed and thinking about what he'd need to build a guest room on his lower level, then a thought struck him and he reached for his cell phone to text Ariana. He'd never asked her about her security set-up but had assumed she had a top of the line system. She had given both him and Hermione keys so they could come and go as they pleased, but Damian couldn't recall seeing her set a security system. He would fix that tomorrow if need be. He could install the same underwater sensors on her beach as he did with the island to protect her house from a water invasion. Ariana texted back that she had a security system but rarely used it, but he'd be pleased to know that she'd turned it on after getting his text.

Advanced warning was what had allowed Hermione to escape the kidnappers twice. It hadn't saved her parents, but the kid was quicker and that's what they needed to build into Ariana's home. He would survey her property tomorrow and look for a way to build an invisible fence around the perimeter. It was interesting that she hadn't asked for a safe room to be built for her. Okay, time to put those thoughts to rest if he was ever going to get some sleep.

CHAPTER 26

The next morning, Damian tried to establish his old routine: working out in his gym and spending some time with his wave technology. He'd figured out how to collect the energy, but he wasn't satisfied with his storage idea. Batteries were the common storage solution, but he wanted something different. He was experimenting with salt and hydrogen as were other researchers around the world. Given that he was aiming to help third world countries with his technology, all of them were located in tropical climates. Sure there were islands like Ireland or New Zealand that didn't have tropical climates, but they weren't impoverished countries. So he needed a storage solution that worked in hot climates. He'd convert the energy into something for storage and again back at the time of usage. Enough of that invention, it was time to move on to something else.

He wanted to solve the DNA problem now that he understood how large the backlogs were, the cost of performing the test, and the time involved. Maybe if he could fix the processing of some specimens, he could solve part of the backlog. He started by going to the U.S. Patent Office and read the patents on a few machines designed to read DNA. Some took as little as twenty minutes to read and others up to ten days yet they were all in the 99.9% accuracy range so why would you use an analyzer that took a long time? He decided then that his next engineering project was to significantly speed up DNA analysis and he worked out a plan to approach the problem.

Then it was time to move on to Hermione's parents. He had their pictures from the phone he recovered. He also had facial recognition software that he ran the pictures through and he couldn't say he was surprised that no matches came back. Either they had work done on their facial features or someone had managed to wipe their identities off of all systems. The house had been purchased about three to five years prior by a company that went from the Cayman Islands to Iceland, on to Russia and Damian had to give up tracing who actually owned the company or even when the Sherwoods had moved in. He guessed based on the 'Hannah Sherwood' pictures in her school yearbook that they had been at that location perhaps three years. Next he wormed his way into the utilities and found the same corporation paying the bills. He would check again in a week to see if that continued. He'd need to talk to Hermione over several conversations to see if she could drop any random information about her parents. He'd check their facial recognition and the fingerprints daily for any new entries. He had grabbed the toothbrushes from her parent's bedroom when he visited the house and dusted them in his own laboratory. He could only guess that the larger fingerprints actually matched her father. He wondered if they were in some witness protection program and his matching their fingerprints would alert whoever was monitoring the Sherwood family; nothing like a heavy dose of paranoia to worry about as he searched for the identity and location of Hermione's parents.

Okay now to move back to Natalie's cases. He looked up at the clock and realized he would have to head over to Ariana's house soon as Hermione would be finished with both school and swim practice. Since he only had a few minutes, he took a look at the emails over the last few days between Aryan Brotherhood members. He was curious as to whether there was any conversation about Natalie and if so, between what members? He was also curious as to whether they changed their language again. Both questions were negative.

It was time to head across the bay. He thought about the boat he had to use and if he should purchase some kind of faster, but compact boat he could stay dry in. He'd looked on line and found a few models that would keep him dry and still fit in his watercraft garage. He paid a retainer to Mike for his parking spot and unlimited transportation and delivery from the Richmond Marina, but in Hermione's case he was heading the opposite direction and he would be traveling there several times a week.

After the slow trip across the bay, he pulled into the dock at Ariana's house. Miguel came out to greet him and gave him this look as if to say, 'follow me inside', and so he did.

"Hello ladies, how was your day?"

'We're just talking about it," Ariana said with a smile. "Would you like some iced tea or lemonade?"

"Iced tea would be great," Damian replied as he pulled out a stool at the counter.

"We're just chatting about the name 'Hermione'; it was apparently a big hit and from the start, teachers and students alike expected our Hermione to be smart and she was!" Ariana said beaming with pride.

"I listened to the first Harry Potter book while I was working on your identity on Sunday, and while you may be as smart as that Hermione, I don't recall her being gifted athletically unless that happens in one of the later books."

"She's not the best flyer on a broomstick, but she's great at disapparating, so she has a way to get there."

"It's all about making your way in this world," Damian noted. "How about swim practice? Was it good to get in the pool again?"

"I was worried what would happen to my hair color. I had visions of black and purple dye leaking out from my swim cap as I swam, but then I remembered that it hadn't happened yesterday. The other kids weren't excited to have another swimmer as they are all a competitive bunch and I beat some of them in time trials. I know that I might knock someone out of qualifying for sectionals, but they should all be competitive enough to want to beat my time rather than beating me on a personal level."

"That's a very mature way of looking at the situation, Hermione, but not everyone is that analytical, so be careful of hurt feelings; they may be masked as other things like bullying," Ariana cautioned.

"I know. I already had that conversation with one of the girls on the team. She backed off when I challenged her to swim harder to beat me, but I have a feeling I'll hear more of that from her."

"Did you tell the coach about her?" Ariana asked.

"Of course not! I can handle my own problems without snitching to the coach on the first day. Gosh, I'll never make friends if I do that!" Hermione said with perfect teenage angst and eye rolling.

Damian and Ariana's eyes met briefly as they delighted in seeing normal behavior for one her age.

Damian had a small panic attack on the way over wondering how he was going to communicate with Hermione. He had planned a few questions in his head if the conversation stalled but it was going fine.

"So tell me about your classes; are they at all challenging; do you need any help with schoolwork?" Damian asked.

"There are a lot of smart kids at this school and the teachers must have had word of my test scores, because they asked me questions in class on materials from the books. It was fun."

Again Damian and Ariana caught themselves grinning. How

lucky were they that they were guardians to a kid who said school was fun.

"I caught a couple of kids talking about me behind my back in Spanish and then Chinese, and once I answered both back in their own language they stopped doing it, but I'm sure they'll find another way to torment me, it's the way of teenagers."

Ariana had to speak on that note, "Kiddo, you're far too wise for your years. Congrats for speaking those languages by the way, I only know a smattering of words in each language. How about you, Damian, do you speak a second language?"

"Latin and German because they're convenient to science. With the Latin background I can sometimes decipher Spanish, French, or Italian, but I'm not fluent to speak. Where did you learn those languages?" Perhaps this would be his first clue about her parents.

"When I was growing up, we lived in both China and Columbia. I was home-schooled but it was easy to pick up the language when we went shopping or anywhere outdoors."

"Why were you living there?" Damian asked.

Hermione gave him an evasive look and said, "How would I know why we lived in a particular country?"

Perhaps she was used to hiding this information from strangers so he asked, "Do you know if you lived there because your father or mother had a job there? Who home-schooled you?"

"Dad worked for a drug company and mom home-schooled me."

"Does your father still work for a drug company?"

"I don't think so."

Jeez getting information from the kid about her parents was like pulling teeth. "Listen Hermione, I'm trying to help by finding your parents, but I don't know who they even are yet. There's no fingerprint match for them."

"Fingerprint match? How did you get their fingerprints?" Ariana asked.

"I took their toothbrushes when I invaded the house a few days ago."

"Wow." Ariana said. "You're a little scary. Not only do you have the ability to collect fingerprints, but you also know how to hack into databases looking for a match."

"Once you learn the finesse of hacking, you can pretty well tackle any database. So back to your parents," Damian said looking at Hermione. "What can you tell me about them to help me identify who they are and where they might be?"

There was still silence from the girl and so Damian sighed and said, "I can see you don't trust me yet. When you're ready, answer my questions, okay?"

Hermione nodded, glad to have the spotlight off of her parents. Her parents had spent years teaching her to trust no-one and reveal no personal information about herself and while on one level she really trusted these adults, she couldn't ignore the lifetime of warnings from her parents.

"So all in all, this was a good first day in this new life of ours, would you agree?" Ariana asked smoothing over the tense silence.

"Yes and I realize that this new coach and pool are going to be good for me; they're much more competitive. At my old school, there weren't as many swimmers and I can't recall the coach working on technique for getting off the starting platform. He worked on every swimmer's technique and he cut about half a second off my start time through better positioning."

"Is half a second a lot?" Ariana asked.

"It's the difference between first and last place in a short race like fifty meters, so yes it's a big deal."

"Is that one of your races?" Damian asked.

"It was at my old school, but it won't be this year at this school as I'm too slow. I'm also fourteen and some of the swimmers are seniors and they're seventeen or eighteen so they have a lot more muscle than I do."

"From a physics point of view, they may be larger but they

have more resistance against them in the water. So don't sell yourself short simply on size," Damian noted.

"I won't, but I'm realistic too."

They moved on to having dinner and playing with Miguel outside. Damian checked in with Hermione on her homework in detail and decided that there was nothing he could lend a hand to there. It was close to sunset and he preferred traversing the bay in daylight so he departed with plans to show up at her meet on Thursday. It was away at another high school, so he'd drive to the school in northern Marin County.

As he was tooling along he marveled over how different his schedule had been over the last two weeks compared to the past seven years. He'd doubled the people close to him in one week. Likely the only two people that tracked him to care if he was dead or alive had been Natalie and Trevor, now perhaps Ariana and Hermione would search for him if he didn't show up somewhere on schedule.

With a smile he pulled out his phone to scan his email and saw he had an update from Natalie concerning the Debbie Altman case.

The DNA was sent out for testing. Collecting trace evidence from a vehicle around for over thirty years was painful for the CSIs. So many people had touched this car. They also collected fingerprints and found matches for John Avery on the typical areas of the car - the rear view mirror, gear shift, driver side door frame, and the latch for the truck gate. It takes the FBI computers a little over two hours to match latent prints. We also got a match for both Debbie Altman and the missing Santa Cruz County woman as they had their prints on file for their driver's licenses before their disappearances.

It would be great if the trace came back as blood and included DNA, but I'm rarely that lucky as a detective; whoops ex-detective. The trace may take 2-3 months to come back, but we have enough to require him to be interviewed by a judge and depending on what he says we may have enough to hold him pending the trace being analyzed by the FBI.

Unfortunately, simply having the fingerprints is not enough to slap him with a murder charge.

Okay, this was a good news-bad news thing. They were much further along with the evidence, but it wasn't nearly enough to get a murder charge against the man. Damian was now a man with a moral dilemma. He had the financial resources to pay for the samples to be processed through a private lab rather than waiting for the police. He felt bad for the families that had no answer for such a long time. He promised himself he would work on a new way to process DNA. At the start of assisting Natalie with these cold cases he remembered that he had looked at DNA processing times and had come to the conclusion that he couldn't do much to shorten the length to less than sixty hours. What he hadn't known about was the huge backlogs everywhere in the state and the nation. He needed to look again at the process and see if there was anything he could change from being performed by humans to be completed by machinery. As he recalled the largest amount of time of the testing process is spent extracting DNA from whatever it might be sitting upon. So if he could invent an extraction device that would greatly reduce the largest piece of human processing time.

Soon he was hitting the remote for his watercraft garage and the dock was folding out toward him. He had his dinghy inside and the garage closed. He stopped at his workbench and made some notes about the DNA processing and then proceeded upstairs to his kitchen. The cats must have heard the garage open and close as they were waiting at his front door to come in. He spent some time giving each of them attention, then prepared their dinner. They scampered outside again and would come in later just as Damian was going to bed.

Grabbing a cup of tea, he leaned back on his sofa and puzzled Hermione. She knew some secrets about her parents, but years of training had her keeping her mouth shut. Perhaps that was why the man was waiting in her house to catch her. He could only hope that in time, she would learn to trust Ariana and himself. Despite moving around and being paranoid about safety, her parents had managed to raise a kind, smart and strong teenager and so he was on their side if he ever met up with them; but he didn't even know if they were alive. He would assume they were and keep the girl safe until their return. He sighed, stood up and stretched, let the cats back in and headed for bed.

CHAPTER 27

Natalie carried a folder of emails; it was the only thing she carried into San Quentin prison. Her purse, including her neat little water gun was sitting in her car in the parking lot. She'd actually never been inside San Quentin and she was the first to admit that it was intimidating. She knew that some of the most dangerous and evil men called the prison home. Before she walked inside, she took one look to the south and east, but couldn't see Red Rock Island.

She arranged to visit Damian after her visit to the Aryan Brotherhood leader, Barry Silverstein. She'd interviewed some terrible murder suspects in her time as a detective, but the man she'd made the appointment with might be the decision maker behind nearly 18% of all prison murders. By her definition, that was a very bad person. If Mr. Silverstein refused to take her off of their hit list, which she thought was the probable outcome, she'd stop by Damian's and watch as he released the AB's translated email to the Black Guerrillas. It would be an ugly day in the California prisons.

After multiple security checks, Natalie was shown into a visitor area filled with picnic tables and chairs. She would have to keep her voice low so that other inmates and their visitors would be unable to hear her conversation. She watched men and their wives or girlfriends talking and in some cases children were visiting their father. How depressing to spend your childhood visiting your father here or perhaps your mother in another prison.

Natalie watched a man in his 50 or 60s approach. He had on the requisite jailhouse blue denim shirt and jeans, with a wife-beater t-shirt underneath. Tattoos covered one arm in a sleeve, as well as his neck. She'd bet that if he took his shirt off, his back would be tatted up as well. As he approached, he assessed the other inmates as well as Natalie before sitting down.

The face of evil stared at her waiting for her to speak. Natalie thought 'may as well get right to the point.'

"Hello Barry, I'm Natalie Severino and your organization has put my name into your Aryan Brotherhood kill hat and I want it taken back out."

He tilted his head and just smirked at her, saying nothing.

Natalie waited him out a while to see if he would say something, but he just sat there trying to intimidate her.

"So, there will be consequences if you decline to remove my name."

She got an eyebrow raise from that, but still silence.

She pulled the first document and said, "This is an email from you to a fellow AB leader at Soledad. I have your original document as well as a translation of what you sent. Go ahead and look at it to validate the translation," Natalie said as she held the document out to him.

He declined to hold the paper and instead quickly glanced at the document. The smirk disappeared once he finished.

"Where did you get that?"

"Doesn't matter; I have it and more correspondence. All of it translated from the AB code into English. Are you still refusing to remove my name from your kill hat?"

He didn't answer, just stood there glaring at her and started to turn away to leave.

She called out to him, "I haven't told you how the Black Guerrillas are involved in this discussion."

He halted and turned around and returned to the table, looming over Natalie and said with menace, "What did you just say?"

"I thought you might need some incentive to pull my name out of your kill hat and so did some research into who your enemies are in this prison. I have five emails, that'll I'll be sending to the Black Guerrillas if you fail to remove my name. Have you changed your mind?"

He leaned closer still to Natalie and in a rich vocabulary filled with expletives indicated he would not. Natalie just shrugged and stood up to leave not making any other contact with the prisoner. She was out in her car shortly heading back across the bridge to Richmond. She met Mike at the marina and was soon on her way to Red Rock Island. Damian was waiting for her arrival and soon she was entering his house.

Walking over to his kitchen sink she said, "I feel like I need to wash my hands after touching things inside San Quentin."

Damian was leaning against the counter and said, "Bad vibes huh?"

"I should be immune to it as lots of criminals I arrested over my decades long career eventually ended up at San Quentin. I guess it's the atmosphere. In the visitor's room there were other men meeting with their families and by family I mean the wife and kids were there. If I felt unclean from being in that room, I wonder what those children feel like."

"Probably half of them are scared of their fathers and the other half believes their fathers are innocent."

"Yeah, right."

"Think about it; how many guys are appealing their convictions? It seems to go on for decades. Occasionally, a convict is found innocent after DNA testing so they can hang their hat on that as well."

"Anyhow, I spent less than five minutes in the presence of Barry Silverstein. He called me a few names that I haven't heard in years when I mentioned sharing their emails with the Black Guerrillas. So I'm here to watch you deliver on my threat."

"Let's go down to my laboratory and we can do just that."

Natalie nodded feeling better. Between the wind blowing against her on the boat ride here and washing her hands, she felt she had left the gunk of the prison behind her.

She sat next to Damian as he pulled up the five emails that they planned to forward to the Black Guerrillas. They were specifically targeting that gang's members named in the emails; whether they were leaders of the gang remained to be seen but they were sure they would be quickly notified.

"Are you ready for me to hit the send button?" Damian asked.

"I haven't thought of any other way to handle the problem; I'm just bothered by the violence these emails are likely to incite. That goes against my law enforcement training."

"Natalie, you warned the guy, he's choosing to ignore your warning or maybe he doesn't care; regardless you were upfront and honest about the consequences of ignoring your request to be taken off their hit list."

"Yeah right, go ahead and hit send."

Thirty minutes later, Damian was watching Mike's boat heading back to the marina with Natalie aboard. It would be interesting to see if violence did break out. Unlike Natalie, he thought there were no innocents in San Quentin and if a few of them got hurt or killed as a result of the emails, he simply didn't care.

Natalie got back in her car and headed back to San Jose. She was concentrating on the traffic and worrying about the impact of those emails on the guards at San Quentin. She didn't notice a pickup truck several cars back and to be fair there were five lanes of traffic and many white trucks on the road.

Inside the truck were two men who tailed Natalie on the orders of Mr. Silverstein from San Quentin to the Richmond marina. Mr. Silverstein wanted to know who had hacked into their emails and decoded their language. He knew it wasn't Natalie, and he figured she was heading towards her partner in these email leaks. The two men had watched her get into a boat and return about ninety minutes later. They were unable to see where the boat went. They took a picture of the boat and its driver so they could return later and ask questions. When they followed her onto her street and did a drive-by of her house, they were puzzled by the signage on the front yard with dire warnings about staying off the grass. There was another car in the area assigned to watch this house and so they turned around and headed back to the Richmond marina to find out where the retired detective had gone in the boat.

They casually questioned a few of the boat owners and soon elicited the direction the female detective went. They regrouped with other Brotherhood members to plan an attack on Red Rock Island.

CHAPTER 28

Damian monitored activity in San Quentin over the next couple of days and it seemed as though a particular cell block had more fights. He was unable to tell if these were fights between the Brotherhood and the Black Guerrillas. He hoped Mr. Silverstein was regretting his denial of Natalie's request. Damian and Natalie had agreed to wait seventy-two hours before releasing another blast of Brotherhood emails to the Black Guerrillas. They wanted to give the AB leadership an opportunity to reconsider Natalie's request. Their daily fights with the Black Guerrillas were a distraction from the main activities of the gang which was managing the income they made on illicit drugs as well as protection money. The Brotherhood's operations closely aligned with the Mafia.

Thursday he drove over to the high school hosting Hermione's swim meet. He and Ariana cheered her on for the three races she swam in. For a kid that had been running away from some very bad people a week ago, she performed well enough to earn third-place at the meet. While she was disappointed with her third-place finish, Damian was pleased given that the kid had only had three days of swim practice prior to the meet.

Friday evening they were going to Damian's house. He wanted to show her his plans for the addition of a guest bedroom and he had a cute little fast and lightweight watercraft to also show the two of them. The boat strictly seated two people, but he planned to take them each for a ride to show off his new toy. He had a simple meal planned of fish, potatoes, and broccoli. He had cheesecake for dessert to celebrate the one week anniversary of when she'd arrived in their lives and to congratulate her on a good first week at a new high school.

Sunset was still about two hours off, but it had been foggy all day so the daylight had seemed darker all day. The two women were inside the house preparing a salad while Damian ignited the barbecue to heat it up for the fish. He looked north and noted a boat that seemed to be on a direct course with his island. Usually, unwelcome visitors arrived in the morning with hopes of hiking the island. He'd never had a trespasser this late in the day. Something made him uneasy about the boat. The barbecue could wait and heat the extra time it would take for him to get binoculars and check out the incoming boat. He kept a pair outside in his toolshed for whenever he had the urge to look at something on the bay. He focused in on the boat, and noted three Caucasian men aboard. All heavily tattooed. He'd bet the royalties of his last invention that the men were from the Aryan Brotherhood. He put the binoculars down and hustled inside.

"Ariana and Hermione, there's a boat that appears to be heading right for this island out on the bay. I told you about the work I'm doing with the retired detective. We did something earlier this week to purposely anger and put pressure on the Aryan Brotherhood prison gang at San Quentin. I believe the guys in the boat may represent that gang. I have security and some homemade weapons but I'll need your help with operating a few of my weapon systems. Dinner is going to be delayed. Okay?"

The two women snapped to attention; all thoughts of food

gone. Ariana said, "Tell us what we need to do to defend you and this island."

Hermione looked pale and scared. She'd been chased by bad men two times in the past couple of weeks.

"I have equipment and cameras down in my lab for us to use. I'm going to try to get the cats inside as it looks like the men are holding automatic weapons."

He went back to the front door and was lucky when the two cats, probably smelling the barbecue smoke came running when he called.

"I built the house with materials designed to withstand a siege. Automatic weapons will have no impact on us. One thing I never planned for was an open watercraft garage and a guest boat sitting at the dock. Your boat could sustain some damage, but whoever they are will still be unable to enter the house through that garage. I can only hope that if they stay on the present course, they'll fail to see the dock and your boat as it's on the opposite side of their approach, so let's keep our fingers crossed."

"How are we going to fight them, Damian?" Hermione asked.

"When their boat gets closer, I have a series of nets under the water that I can release which will hopefully clog up their propeller. I also have a small unmanned submarine I can launch that will drill a small hole in their boat. I want the boat to sink but not close to the island where they might try to swim ashore here."

"What other weapons do you have?" Ariana asked, somewhat alarmed. The fact that men were approaching with semi-automatic weapons scared her but at the same time she'd never shot a gun herself and this wasn't the time to find out if she could hit the side of a barn when firing a gun.

"I have water cannons in the cliffs of Red Rock Island; they just need to be fired at any one approaching. I have used them before when unwelcome visitors have ignored the private property signs. Those guns are filled with water. For these men that are approaching, I'm going to add concentrated pepper juice to

RED ROCK ISLAND

the water so that it will hurt them when it drips down their face. There is a unit of measure called the Scoville Rating that rates the spiciness of chili peppers. The pepper spray that is used by the police is about 500,000 units of heat. I sourced the Carolina Reaper, which is considered to be the hottest pepper in the world with a heat rating of 855,000 to 2,200,000. So it will disarm and bring great pain to any human that touches it. In addition to the water cannons in the cliffs, they're also under the sand of the two small beaches of this island. I want you two to stay inside and operate the water cannons. I'm going to hang over the cliff edge with a high powered water gun filled with pepper spray. I also have a slingshot that I'm going to use to place this messy fishy substance on their boat and that will cause birds to attack them. When I see their boat turnaround to head back to wherever it came from, that's when I'm going to drill a small hole in their hull in hopes that the boat will sink before it reaches shore but well after the time it leaves this island."

They nodded their agreement and Damian showed them how to fire the water cannons. He was lucky in one regard that they were here as it would've been very difficult for one person to watch all of the monitors and he should've thought of that at the time he designed it. Of course, on the other hand, he wished both women were safe at Ariana's home and not in the middle of his war!

They did a Three Musketeers, one for all and all for one cheer, and then they manned their battle stations. Damian exited the house wearing a combat helmet and body armor carrying his high powered long-range pepper spray and gun. He also had his remote control to operate the unmanned submarine that would drill a hole in their hull.

Lying on his belly, he observed that a direct hit by one of the water cannons disabled two of the men with the pepper juice. A third man, who'd avoided the spray, clearly was in a quandary of what to do. He stopped the boat's forward progress and threw both men into the bay clearly with the hope that the water would get the substance off their faces. Damian guessed that it would take about six hours for them to recover their eyesight. In the interim, the only guy not blinded was constantly looking over his shoulder for fear that the juice would hit him and at the same time he was trying to help the two men in the water as one of them could be heard saying 'I can't swim.'

Damian launched the smelly fishy gob and landed it on the front of the boat. Soon a lot of birds were swarming the boat adding further confusion for the one man who could see. Damian could see that he'd given up on his mission and was just trying to pull his two friends back into the boat so they could head back to whatever marina they'd come from. Damian drilled a hole just as the man pulled the second guy into the boat. Depending on how far away they were going, the one able-bodied man might end up towing his two blind friends to shore. Oh well that was his problem not Damian's. Soon the boat was speeding back to where it came from and Damian entered the house and went down to his lab.

"Good job ladies! Were you able to see all of the action from the monitors?"

"Yeah, we cheered when the two men jumped into the bay with their faces on fire. What's going to happen now?" Ariana asked.

"Depending on how far they're going, they may make it to shore; or the one guy with vision may end up towing the two blinded men to shore. I heard one of them say he didn't know how to swim. So now the guy can't see and can't swim. I'd be sympathetic, but they were on a straight course for this island with semi-automatic weapons to join us for dinner."

"Are you going to call the police?" Ariana asked.

"The trouble is that this island is owned by three counties and so first I would have to figure out which county sheriff has a boat to get out to this island. I suppose I could call the Coast Guard since they used to have a ship signal station on this island, but I don't know if they would respond. This is the first time I've been attacked since I bought the property, so I guess I would have to figure that question out because unfortunately I think the men will be back."

"Why are they mad at you, Damian?" Hermione asked. The kid seemed to be feeling an adrenaline rush from the battle and was confident with her ability to defend this house.

"They're mad at me because I hacked into their emails and I shared the content of those emails with their rival prison gang."

"Why did you do that?" Hermione asked.

"I've mentioned the retired detective to you. She was the one I would have talked to about the incident at your house. She killed the man that murdered my family and now the prison gang wants revenge for that killing. So she met with the prison gang leaders at San Quentin Prison and threatened to share their private emails with the opposing gang if they refused to remove her name from their hit list. They refused, so we did and now they're retaliating."

"Maybe you should move into Ariana's house," Hermione suggested biting her lip, worried about Damian.

"But then I would bring those bad guys near you and I think that's a very bad idea. Besides they could really damage my island if it was deserted."

"Damian, I think you need to call the police," Ariana urged. "Those are very bad people and they're raising the stakes with each encounter. It's not going to stop until both you and your detective are dead."

"Yeah, I know but I had to do something to try and help Natalie. The other problem is that I committed a crime getting the information by hacking into their private emails."

"It's a messy situation. What are you going to do tonight? I think Hermione and I will leave while your dock is safe, but those men are going to come back. Probably tonight."

"Yeah I know. I'm going to call Natalie and see what she suggests. She may have a relationship with one of the three Sheriffs' departments. If I don't get the help I need there, then I'll call the Coast Guard."

"What happens if they come in scuba equipment or by helicopter?" Ariana asked.

"I have sensors in the water; that's how I detected you when you washed up on this island. As for a helicopter attack, I have a couple of spring-loaded nets that I can fire at the rotor blades of the helicopter which will bring it down, but I'm in way over my head if I need to do that."

Ariana looked worried; conflicted between staying and helping to defend Damian's house or going and keeping Hermione, her boat, and herself, safe. She looked at the amount of daylight and her watch to assess the time.

"We have a few minutes right now, why don't you call your cop friend and we'll listen in on the conversation."

Damian nodded and did just that.

"Hey, Natalie, my house was just attacked by what I believe to be three members of the Aryan Brotherhood and I need some help."

"What? How did they know where you lived?" Natalie asked and then answered her own question, "I must've picked up a tail coming out of the prison and they followed me to the Richmond Marina. It wouldn't be too hard getting information out of some of those boat owners."

"So I have three counties that each claim part of Red Rock Island as their territory. Do you have any friends in the Contra Costa, San Francisco, or Marin County Sheriff's office? I need some help. If I do say so myself I did a great job defending against the first wave of crooks, but they'll be back and I need some help repelling these people."

"What did you do to the three people that sent them scurrying away?"

"I power-washed them with Carolina Reaper chili juice. Two of the men are blind for the time being but that will go away in a day or so. Their boat may sink on the way back to the marina and if that's the case, the one guy with sight will have to guide the other two men to the shore and one of them can't swim."

Natalie sighed and said, "I do love your style, Damian."

"I called you because I think they're going to be back and I need some law enforcement help," Damian reiterated. "Who can I call to get someone out here? I do have the men approaching by boat on video and you can clearly see their guns."

"That's a good question, Damian. My first instinct is to connect you to the San Francisco Police Department but they're so far away across the water that they would take too long to come to your rescue. Let me do some research on Contra Costa Sheriff and I'll call you back with the name shortly."

After the phone call ended, Damian looked at Ariana and Hermione to say, "You ladies better get going across the bay. Natalie will help me defend this island and while I think the bad guys will be back, I don't think it will be tonight."

Ariana stood there thinking for a moment and Damian could see the wheels turning in her head.

"You know, Damian, I do believe you can defend this island by yourself, and it would be good for Hermione if we don't expose her to any further risks, so we'll be going. If you need help day or night, call and I can be here in fifteen minutes at full speed. If your cops aren't going to help you, you can always count on me."

"And me," Hermione said.

The support of these two women was causing huge fissures in the ice around Damian's heart. Before he could understand his own behavior, he had enveloped them both in a hug. Moments later he let go and said, "Let's go," as he lead the way downstairs and to the dock.

Moments later he could see both the sun setting on the west and the retreat of Ariana's boat towards her home. He heard his cell phone trill and pulled it out of his pocket to answer Natalie's call.

"Did you find someone?"

"Yeah. I spoke with a friend who is a Santa Clara deputy who has a friend working in the Contra Costa Sheriff's department and fortunately he's on duty and on his way along with a deputy from their Marine patrol. They'll know the location of your island and will be there in about twenty minutes. I gave them your cell phone so they can make arrangements to get up to your house."

"Thanks Natalie. I don't think the Brotherhood will be back tonight, but it doesn't hurt to have back-up ready when I need it."

CHAPTER 29

After ending his call with Natalie, Damian thought about how to greet the Marine patrol. Should he reveal the existence of his dock and watercraft garage or should he invite them up via the zip line. While the plans for his house had been approved by the three counties, the watercraft garage was on no blueprint; not that the deputies would know that. He decided not to mention the garage because if the island was under attack, he would not want to open the garage, and possibly let the intruder know of access to the lower level of his home. He wanted help to come from the beach.

He took his own zip line down to the beach and awaited a phone call from Sheriff. The beach was on the opposite side of the island from where their boat was coming from. Again his cell phone rang and he answered it to find a lot of wind noise and the sheriff on the line.

"This is Deputy Shawn Peterson, Natalie Severino gave us your information and we can see your island and are approaching from the Richmond-San Rafael Bridge. Do you have a dock?"

"Do you have the ability to park your boat on or close to the sand?" Damian replied not answering the question about a dock. That way he avoided lying to the deputy.

"We can anchor close to shore and use a ramp to walk on to your sand. Where's the beach located?"

"It's on the opposite side of the island from the direction you're approaching. I'm standing on the sand ready to assist in your approach."

Damian could hear the noise of the motor boat approaching and hoped it was the sheriff rather than another boat filled with Brotherhood members. He'd taken off his body armor and was vulnerable to attack on his sandy beach. He heaved a sigh of relief as he saw the word 'Sheriff' painted on the side of the boat.

The deputy maneuvered the boat close and anchored it. Damian assisted with putting a ramp on the sand and tying the boat to two hitches that he'd installed just for this purpose. Within minutes, the two deputies stepped from the ramp onto the beach and shook Damian's hand as introductions were performed.

"I've always wanted to see this island, but it's your private property and I haven't had an official reason to visit."

Damian explained in detail the attack earlier that evening, and offered to show the deputies his recording. He'd looked at it before they arrived to make sure he hadn't seen anything in the video that he didn't want the deputies to view. He offered them the choice of hiking up the hillside or riding his zip line. After answering their questions about the safety, function and design of the zip line, they chose that option.

Once on top, they surveyed the perimeter of the island with the one deputy actually filming it. Then they entered his house and walked down to the lab. Damian pulled the footage up and explained his pepper juice water guns. He decided not to mention the submarine punching a hole in the bottom of the boat as he might've violated some law with that tactic.

"This is an extraordinary set-up you have here. Most people

don't have this level of 'weapons' to protect themselves. What made you put this security in place?" asked Deputy Peterson.

"Two reasons. I am an inventor so it's part experimentation."

"And the other reason?"

"My wife and two little girls were murdered seven years ago in San Jose by a convict that was mistakenly released by Soledad Prison. It's how I know Natalie; she killed my family's killer during the manhunt for him."

"I'm sorry, man. I get it," replied the deputy. "Was he a member of the Aryan Brotherhood?"

"Yes," better to let the officer think that was the reason for the gang's anger against him.

"So you think they'll be back?"

"Don't you?"

The two deputies gave it some thought. Considering their training about gang behavior, they agreed they would keep coming back until the job was done.

"Yes."

"So, suggestions on how to survive this group?" Damian asked.

"You appear to be doing a great job on your own. Certainly call us and we can have help here in about 10-15 minutes via helicopter. I'd like to take a copy of the video with me as it's enough to issue an arrest warrant and we should check with urgent care and hospital emergency departments to see if they sought medical care for their eyes.

Damian thought, 'that is if the boat didn't sink and drown them,' which was his hoped for outcome.

"I was lucky tonight. I was lighting my barbecue when I noticed the boat and used my binoculars to observe their brandishing of automatic weapons. They could have just as easily taken me by surprise which is to say they could have gotten on the beach intending to climb the hill, but I use water cannons to persuade unlawful visitors to head back to their boat. Those cannons aren't loaded with pepper juice; it's just water, so it probably wouldn't impede them. My house is made with bullet proof materials but they could do a lot of damage here."

"I don't know what else to tell you. You got good defenses here and we're going to try and find them and take them off the streets, but my experience with gang members is that they're like picnic ants, you kill one and ten more are waiting to invade your food. I am going to brief the Sheriff about your set-up here and the actions of this gang. We'll see if we can trace the boat they had, but there are many places to rent a boat up and down the Bay and Delta. We'll have an all-points bulletin, but they could easily attack this island before we find them as a result of an APB. Is there anything else you can think of to suggest we do?" asked Deputy Peterson. This guy had done a lot to protect his island, but he was facing a criminal enterprise with unlimited guns and gang members ready to die for the cause.

"When I called you I frankly thought there wasn't anything you could do to help as my distance and isolation makes your response times slow. But issuing an APB is helpful as well as just establishing contact so that if I call for help, someone will actually respond to this island rather than think it is a prank call."

"We'll add a blurb to the daily report to get the word out as you're correct, some dispatchers and deputies might think this location is a prank call. We'll also let you know if we catch your intruders."

They headed outside and as it was now dark and the path treacherous all three headed down on Damian's zip line. Damian untied the lines that were holding the boat to his island and waved off the two men.

Upon returning to the house, he relayed his conversation with the deputies to Ariana.

"How's Hermione doing? I would hate to cause the kid more nightmares than she is already having."

"I think she's a strong kid and will be okay. I, on the other hand will be having nightmares for a while. Goodness, being attacked by gang members with automatic weapons. I must say I love your weapons; they completely stopped the attack without killing or seriously harming them. It was very disabling."

"I could install it on your beachfront." Damian offered.

"No thanks. If I need that kind of protection, I'll just need to move to a new city."

"I've had peace and quiet for seven years, but thugs are thugs and they don't quit until they're dead."

"On that piece of pessimism, I'll say goodnight and good luck. Keep us posted."

"Will do."

CHAPTER 30

Damian had a peaceful night with no intruders attacking his island. He decided to hack again into their email system to see if there was any communication about the event at his island, although when he thought back to other emails it seemed likely that they communicated some other way about activities on the outside of the prison. He certainly hadn't found who or when Natalie's name was placed in the hat so on second thought, why waste his time.

He began running on his treadmill to think about the people and problems in his life. They were rather like his inventions; he never knew the outcome of any tweak he applied to a design until he tried it. Sometimes he was spot on and other times he missed by a mile. He had to be grateful that all three women in his life, Natalie, Ariana, and Hermione were not drama queens.

Then a new thought hit him, the police report of last night. His personal privacy was so important to him and now there was a public record that he owned this island because of the police report. This morning, he would devote his time to figuring out how to erase his existence from the Sheriff's database. He would give them twenty-four hours to get the word out about his island

and the problems there, but then he'd make sure he erased his name from their database or at least substituted the corporate name that the property was listed under.

His cell phone rang and he saw that it was Natalie.

"Was Deputy Peterson helpful?"

"More than I expected since he put a bulletin out to arrest the guys in the video and he notified his dispatch that if I ever call it's not a prank. The thought of being a one-man army with no re-enforcements is daunting in light of the vast number of thugs that belong to the Brotherhood."

"What did he think of your pepper spray water cannons?"

"I think he rather liked the idea of disabling the enemy without causing permanent serious harm or death."

"You have a unique need because of your island status, but I admit if I could cheaply add it to the sides of my house to keep criminals out, I would. Of course that just moves the problem elsewhere, but at least my home would be safe. Guess it is rather like Medieval Times, when they threw boiling oil over the castle walls, except I surmise a fair number of them died from their burns."

"Thanks, Natalie, for that vision. Though, I'll admit that the men probably looked much the same after being doused in my pepper spray as they would if hot oil had reached their eyes."

"Back at you, Damian, thanks for that horrible vision. What should we do about the Brotherhood? Should I try meeting with the guy again or should you release a few more emails today?"

"Natalie, I hate to be horribly pessimistic, but I'm no longer sure under what condition the Brotherhood will take your name out of the hat. I almost think we need to incite a riot where all the leaders are killed. How's that for lowering myself to their level of scumbag?"

"It's called fighting fire with fire. I feel like I need to talk to someone who understands this gang's behavior. If this is indeed hopeless, what are my options?"

"I wonder what the Black Guerrillas would say about the Aryan Brotherhood? Maybe we need to partner with them to get them to back down."

"I'm going to talk to the department and see if they have any ideas. I'm sorry I dragged you into this mess."

"From the day they murdered my family, I've been at your side fighting these domestic terrorists. You didn't drag me into this fight; this is where I want to be. Why don't you talk to your gang experts and get back to me as to whether we should release any more emails?"

"Will do."

After they ended the call, Damian did a search on successes against violent gangs. The only tactic that seemed to work was changing their sentences from life imprisonment to being condemned on death row. Even if he went back and looked at the violent gangs from the 1920s, they were stopped by putting the gang members in jail for tax evasion. Today's prisoners had so much more contact with the outside world that they could run criminal enterprises from behind prison bars.

He thought about the situation some more and decided he had nothing to lose by stirring the pot so to speak. So he released another five emails to the Black Guerrillas. He wanted to send them anonymously to the Justice Department so they would go after the gang members for racketeering. He dropped Natalie a text asking her what she thought of that strategy while she waited for an answer from her gang experts.

Natalie didn't respond right away and so he changed tactics completely doing some more research on Hermione's parents. He couldn't identify them with fingerprints and he could think of ways to avoid having your fingerprints on file. So how about facial recognition? He went back and slowed down the video from their house to see if there were frames that he could use for facial recognition. He didn't have such a technology yet, but first he wanted to find out if he had a decent facial photo. Then Damian smacked himself up the side of his head, 'what was he thinking?' Hermione's recovered phone had pictures he could use.

He pulled up the file with her images and started going through the pictures, then he had to smile. Her parents were masters at making sure their faces were never caught on camera as a full frontal. Without fail, each picture had their faces turned to one side or the other. The few full frontal shots were in costume, presumably Halloween. Next he went online to see if any of their monthly utility bills had been paid and he was excited to see that they had. Then he noticed they were on an auto pay scheme so that would continue as long as there was money in their bank account. Maybe he could track the bank account to see if money was being deposited it to it.

Banks were some of the hardest to hack into after a Russian group of mobsters stole an estimated $100M after hacking into over one-hundred banks worldwide. Then Damian saw another path he might take. He banked at the same institution as the Sherwoods, so maybe he could enter through his account. He was thinking about that when his alarm system sounded.

Crap! He was hoping to have more time before the idiots came back. He moved over and checked his monitors to see where they were. They were trolling close to the island and were planning on landing on his beach. He tried Shawn Peterson first and then thought he'd move on to dispatch if he didn't answer his phone.

"Peterson."

"Hi, it's Damian Green and the Brotherhood are back. They're surveying my beach to land there."

"Let me order our copter then I'll call you back."

Damian sat at his computer screen firing his water cannons at the approaching boat and men. He also sent his drone around to drop some of the excess purple smoke bombs he had from setting up Natalie's house as well as the green ink bombs. He moved the ink from the device he used for Natalie's house into a water balloon. After he'd been attacked the previous night, and once the cops left, he rigged up his drone to assist with dropping the bombs. It might make a mess out his beach sand, so he hoped he could drop it on them before they reached the shore.

Peterson called back and said the helicopter would be arriving in about ten minutes. He was traveling by land and would be much slower. Damian gave him directions to the Richmond Marina while Peterson's partner called the Harbor Master to ensure a boat ride upon their arrival. Damian had set the phone down to chat by speakerphone while he operated the drone by headset and the water cannons by a joystick.

"I'm firing water cannons at the boat, but I don't have them loaded with pepper juice and they'll realize that sooner or later. I'm about to drop green ink water balloons on the men and I'm putting purple smoke bombs on the sand which will block their view. Your helicopter can land on top on my island or just follow the boat if they give up and head back to shore."

Peterson's partner relayed that information to the approaching helicopter.

Damian debated getting the submarine out, but his hands and eyes were occupied operating the cannons and the drone.

Over the noise the men didn't hear the drone as he had it sweep in from the back. They were wearing what looked to be ski goggles to protect their eyes. Three on the boat were hit by the green dye balloons and they were soon covered in green ink. Two other men wearing raincoats had stepped onto his beach.

He moved the first drone quickly away from the boat and back around his island as he didn't want them shooting it. A second drone dropped purple smoke bombs on both the boat and the sand. Sadly, it became a casualty of automatic gun fire. He had secondary water cannons that would soon go off from the cliff adding to the barrage on the sand, but this landing party was in a different boat with more men and based on the raincoats and goggles, they came prepared for pepper juice.

Peterson said "Copter has your island in view and sees smoke. They want you to confirm that nothing is on fire."

"It's just smoke bombs on the sand. Warn your Copter that the men have automatic weapons as before. They've successfully shot down one of my drones and are working on the water cannons, but that's just wasted ammo."

"They plan to hover over the boat and give them a message from the air."

Damian checked his boundary cameras and could see the copter's approach. He relaxed a little knowing that re-enforcements had arrived. He landed the working drone as he didn't want it near the copter. Within a minute the copter was in place over the bay and was using a PA system to address the boaters. Damian didn't have speakers outside and decided that was the next security enhancement he would install. In a small portion of his brain, he wondered how long this little war would go on. Were the men back because of yesterday's action or this morning's second release of emails? The boat pulled away leaving the two men on Damian's island while the copter pursued the boat. Great thought Damian, there went my back-up.

"Damian, the copter's going after the boat. We have a boat approaching your island from the Delta; it's about fifteen minutes away. My partner and I made good time and we're pulling into the Richmond marina. We've arranged with the harbormaster to borrow a boat so I hope we'll be out there in about five minutes."

"There's a few more smoke bombs I can drop on them and the water cannons should make it hard to climb the hillside to my house."

"Is there a second beach we can dock the boat at on your island?"

Damian debating revealing the location of the dock but decided he needed a few secrets still. He didn't know why that was important but it was.

"There's a second beach, that's harder to navigate, but doable. It'll give you cover; just come in slow and be careful as there are rocks in that area. I'll text you a quick diagram of what to avoid. It's around the corner from the beach you landed on yesterday." Damian drew two quick images of his island and texted them to the Deputy.

He could hear the wind noise in the background and then Peterson said, "Got it. Are they making any progress scaling your hill?"

"Not so far. It's tricky under the best of circumstances and with the water pelting them; they're stuck on the sand. The water is coming from the bay so I can keep the cannons on for a long time. You'll be able to land, peer over the hillside and then I can turn them off when you're ready to move. They've fired a lot of bullets at my hillside so hopefully they'll be out of ammo soon."

"If you can, aim the cannon at the gun as water in time will cause the gun to fail."

"I didn't think of that! Thanks, will do."

Damian studied the two men's movement and moved his water guns accordingly. Soon enough one of their guns failed to operate. Awesome! Now he was down to just one serious thug.

He could see through his security cameras, Deputy Peterson approaching his second smaller beach looking over the front bow of the boat watching for the rocks that Damian had drawn on his map. They drove the boat right up onto the beach and hopped off, taking cover. Damian sent Peterson a picture of the thugs on his other beach. They nodded and moved forward with the hillside providing cover.

Peterson texted Damian to shut off the water as they were in position.

The water noise ceased and then Peterson called out, "This is the police, put down your guns and put your hands in the air."

The two men scrambled to take cover. The one man was wielding his non-working gun like a piece of pipe. The other took aim and fired at where Peterson's voice had sounded from.

Damian could see that Peterson and his partner had combat helmets on along with body armor, but they were vulnerable in the face, legs, and arms. They normally didn't carry riot gear in their car.

Expecting a confrontation and knowing their own back-up boat was still about twelve minutes away, they requested the assistance of another airborne unit and help arrived in the form of two copters from neighboring municipalities. The two men were debating something among them whether it was death by cop, surrender, or perhaps swimming to escape, Damian couldn't tell. He hoped the men would just dive in the bay and take this problem away from his island and his home. He spared a thought for his cats and figured they were huddled in one of the tiny caves on the far side of the island.

One of the copters was preparing to land on Damian's front lawn, and that was when the two suspects dove into the water, planning on swimming to shore and away from police. The two copters just stayed above the water adding wind turbulence to the difficulty of the swim. The water temperature was sixty-one degrees and unless they were high on Meth, the cold would soon get to them. Then Damian noticed they had stripped off their street clothes to wet-suits underneath, a mask and snorkel must've been hidden on their person as that suddenly appeared as well. They disappeared below the surface and were not seen again.

Damian doubted they drowned, but he wouldn't place it past them if they had buried a scuba set-up underwater to facilitate their escape. He was tempted to send out his unmanned submarine, but decided he would let the police deal with it. The two copters were watching the surface as the police cruiser arrived from the Delta.

What a flaming mess and his privacy was now shot! Ugh. He wished he had an underwater torpedo that he could fire across the bay at San Quentin. He was fed up with the Aryan Brotherhood and the mess they were making of his island and his privacy. He pounded his fist against a boxing training bag he had in his gym and let out a primordial scream, took a deep breath, before heading upstairs to exit his house.

He walked outside to the noise of the two copters close by. Since they couldn't hear him down on the beach, he texted Peterson that he was coming down on his zip line and not to shoot him. Wouldn't that be ironic; to be shot on your own private island. Peterson texted back that he would make sure they held their fire.

CHAPTER 31

Nearly eight hours later, he was fed up with the world and law enforcement in particular. Crime Scene techs had collected ammo and fingerprints from his beach, they wanted copies of his video and had been down in his lab to understand his technology. He was proud of it for all of about ten minutes, and then he wished they would get out of his lab and off his island. Worst still was the picnic ants; he knew the Aryan Brotherhood would be back. They had their endless ants to spoil your picnic, and with each attack, there would be more of them. He needed to talk to some gang psychologist on what to do. He couldn't go through one of these attacks every couple of days.

Finally, when it was over and everyone had left his island, he debated what to do. He could call Ariana and let her know about the second attack and then invite himself over; he decided that he needed something else that night. So he got in his new, fast, two seater boat having made arrangements to dock it near Pete's bar. Thirty minutes later he was inside at the bar chatting with Pete, a cheeseburger underway in the kitchen.

Damian had sought out Pete with the thought that this was where he always came to lighten his mood and he was at a loss to understand why this bar gave him that experience. He looked around and thought about it and decided it was because he fit in. There were people of every ethnicity in the bar as well as a few of every interest there. There were men huddled over whisky and beer that he thought he'd seen before in the bar. The Warriors playoff game was on the TVs and that was attracting a younger crowd of both sexes. He bet the final group stopped here on the way home from work because it was peaceful. It wasn't quiet at all, but you could fall into the zone of your own choosing and stay there until it was time to leave.

When Pete returned with his food, he asked, "You seem to have a little of everything here Pete. How many regulars do you have here and how many nights a week do they stop by?"

"Well, there's you, Damian, and you stop by about once a month."

"Touché, but go on."

Pete went on to name about half the people in the bar and their frequency. There were a few patrons that he didn't recognize but as Damian had thought they were regulars of all sorts - daily weekly, monthly, and others like himself that were irregular regulars.

"So what's your problem at the moment, Damian?" Pete asked.

Damian looked at Pete's face and said, "What do you mean, what's my problem?"

"Usually when you come here, you have some problem in the back of your mind that you're trying to figure out. Once in a while it seems to me you're here because you're sick of your own company. Based on the way you're watching the bar patrons, I would say it's the former rather than the later."

"You're very wise, Pete."

"I have to be, I'm a bartender. I solve many people's problems. So what's yours today? Maybe I can offer the 'Dummies guide to astrophysics' solution to your problem."

Damian laughed and said, "It's not astrophysics and I don't think you'd believe me if I told you."

"Try me. I've heard some pretty wild yarns in my two decades as a bartender; some of them actually true."

Damian laughed again and said, "The Aryan Brotherhood has invaded my island twice and are trying to kill me."

"That might be as wild a yarn as I've heard and if it was anyone other than you, I'd cut off your alcohol and refer you to a good psychologist. What did you do to make them mad?"

"Hacked into their email system and shared it with the Black Guerrillas."

"Damian, you're a man of intriguing qualities. I'm sure you had a reason to do that. Have the prisons had any riots yet?"

"Not that I can tell."

"Hmm…. I know an ex-Brotherhood guy. He's an irregular regular, just like you. How about if I speak with him on some options?"

"Hey Pete, thanks for your help in more ways than you know. I debated where to head tonight and found myself beating a path to your door. Thanks for believing my story."

"I owe you a lot. Your software saves me money and allows me to keep good staff that can't steal from me, why wouldn't I want to repay you in a minuscule way? My only problem is the guy is like you; he comes in on a non-routine basis and I don't have his phone number."

"Except you have my phone number."

"Yeah I do," then Pete paused and watched the doorway. "Damian, after your horrible day, life is about to get better; he just walked in the door. Imagine that, two irregular regular guys visiting my bar on the same night. Let me wave him over here."

Pete stood up and waved a guy over. Damian didn't want to make the man uncomfortable so he didn't turn around on his bar stool and look at the doorway, but man, he was flooded with curiosity as to what the guy looked like. He was impressed with

Pete for getting to know the guy. Perhaps a minute later, he invited Damian and the man into a back room.

Damian had finished his cheeseburger and was working on his second beer, so he picked up the glass and followed Pete to his office. Damian had been there before when he installed his computer system.

He eyed the other man in front of him. He was Caucasian, since you had to be to belong the Aryan Brotherhood. Damian guessed him to be late 40s early 50s, but then he'd likely lived a hard life first in prison and second by participating in the gang's activities. He had various scars on his face and neck; some he guessed were from knife wounds, others perhaps tattoo removal. His arms were covered and he was medium build, clean shaven, with a short brown nondescript haircut. He looked like your average longshoreman from the nearby Port of Oakland, the second busiest port on the West Coast.

Pete performed introductions and they shook hands. He dropped random facts about each of them as part of the introduction. Damian was a genius who designed the computerized system for his bar saving his business. Angus Walsh worked nearby at the Port doing logistics. Then Pete got down to business after taking Angus' order for dinner.

"Damian, here has your old gang trying to kill him. Got any suggestions on how to avoid death for him?"

Angus' reply was quick and grim, "Good luck with that man; they're a bad lot."

"Aren't you the master of an understatement."

Pete left the two men to talk and to get Angus' food order underway.

"Who'd you piss off? You don't look like their normal target."

"What do you mean?"

"You don't look like an ex-con, and Pete says you're a genius. Geniuses don't hang out with the Brotherhood."

"I don't know about that, you strike me as very smart as you managed to leave the gang alive. How did you do it?"

"I was sentenced to Soledad in the late 1980s for a rape and murder that I didn't commit. I was so mad and enraged with the world that I joined the gang. The Innocence Project took my case on about five years ago, and I was exonerated and released. Once it looked like my case would go somewhere, I started studying how to get out of the gang. After twenty years of violence, I was sick of them anyway."

"So, how did you do it?" Damian asked. "My understanding is that you have a credo that the only way to leave the gang is to die."

"That's true. The leadership are usually serving either life sentences or thirty years or more. When you're looking at thirty years, tacking on another ten just doesn't impact you; so what if you kill another prisoner?"

"How did you avoid killing another prisoner? I thought that was your initiation into the gang."

"I always made sure, I was the biggest screw-up in regards to attempted murder. Someday I believed I would be found innocent as I knew I hadn't done the crime I was convicted of. I wasn't going to give them a real crime that I did commit. I misunderstood instructions for nearly every crime and acted slow so they thought it was my IQ. However, I have a photographic memory, so just about an hour before my release, I threatened the gang leaders at Soledad."

"With what?"

"I wrote down every derogatory statement they ever made about their followers in Soledad and their leaders at other prisons. I showed them a copy of the document and a copy of the instructions to my attorney to release it if I should die of anything but natural causes."

"The Art of War," Damian suggested.

"Exactly. I read a copy of the book and knew that the only way to keep the gang from killing me is to creditably threaten the leadership with its own members."

"Wish I thought of that. I tried using their enemies, the Black Guerrillas, as my counter-threat."

"Bet that didn't work, mate," replied Angus with a smirk.

"No, not by a long shot. I feel like the entire gang outside of prison is trying to siege my home and kill me."

"How did you use the Black Guerrillas against them?"

Damian weighted his answer and decided to ask a different question to see if he could get the measure of the man. He was halfway to trusting Angus, but he wasn't willing to spill his guts. While Angus had given him his strategy, it wasn't an illegal activity whereas it was a violation of federal law to hack into email.

"What have you done with your life since you left Soledad?"

"I should be on Broadway getting a Tony for my acting ability. I was always reading books in prison 'trying to correct' my low IQ. When other inmates were around, I'd hold the book upside down or never move a page to give the impression I couldn't read. In reality I earned a couple of degrees while I was behind bars and a small company in Oakland took a risk and hired me to do their logistics."

"Congrats, Angus, that's a great story," Damian said. Then thinking about it grimaced and said, "Sorry wrong response. Spending all those years in Soledad is a terrible story. I guess what I'm trying to say, is that it's amazing that the prison never dragged you down."

"Yeah, I'm a regular miracle man," replied Angus grimly.

Damian wasn't willing to reveal his secrets still, but he was inching closer to trusting the man.

"Hey, can I have your contact information? I'd like to get my ducks in order then talk gang strategy with you some more."

"Want to go a Google search on me huh?"

Damian reddened but said, "A Soledad convict was accidentally released early and killed my wife and two little girls seven years ago, so yeah that's exactly what I'm going to do."

"Sorry man, I remember the incident at the time. My fellow convicts cheered the mistake made that sprung the guy early and cared little that your family was killed. Here's my contact information, feel free to contact me in the future." Angus said writing his information on a cocktail napkin.

Pete opened the door and entered with Angus' food, but was waved back into the bar.

"Thanks Pete, but we're done talking here; I'll eat my burger at the bar" and Angus stood up to follow Pete out of the office.

CHAPTER 32

Damian was approaching his island having left Pete's bar a short time ago. He'd checked his security system repeatedly through the evening and there had been no more breaches. He did a slow circle around the island with night vision goggles on and saw his cats, but no other movement in the darkness. He circled around to the watercraft garage, opened the door, and folded out the dock.

An hour later, he searched out everything he could find on Angus Walsh and it all seemed legit. He didn't like the coincidence of the man walking into Pete's bar just when he was looking for help, but he was everything he said he was.

Could he be living the non-gang life in disguise? Could Damian have gotten the same acting job that Angus mentioned in regards to the gang? Could Angus be the gang's leader on the outside? Damian studied the guy's finances and thought that if he was, he was sure hiding the money from criminal enterprise well. Of course that could be on an all cash basis and perhaps it was buried under another name. Maybe he'd hack into the prison system for his fingerprints then see if there was any match at any time with another crime. Then he'd follow the guy from home to work, and then anonymously call him at work to see if he could handle a logistics problem. He would also ask Natalie to do a little research on the guy; sometimes she had invaluable word of mouth resources.

It was late, but he was having a hard time relaxing; probably no surprise after his day. It wasn't every day that an average Joe had an attempt on his life by a notorious prison gang, and lived to tell about it. The score was presently prison gang zero, Damian eight men defeated. He was very curious to know if the first three made it ashore alive. He sure hoped not. He dropped an email to Natalie summarizing his day and his question about Angus. To his great surprise, he heard his phone ring, and noted the caller ID said it was Natalie.

"You're awake late!"

"Back at you! I saw your email arrive and decided to call you. If we're both sleepless, we may as well get some work done. I haven't heard anything about the idiots after you or me. It's frustrating being on the outside of law enforcement now."

"Gee whiz I thought you might at least have the inside scoop."

"So you would hope. Tell me more about Angus Walsh."

Damian explained how he met him and added, "Trevor can tell you about Pete and his bar. He did some small legal work for him and I designed his alcohol dispensing system. He had great wait staff but he was always having to fire them as they couldn't seem to stop giving away free booze. Pete will do anything for Trevor or I as a result. So Pete is above suspicion for introducing me to Angus. I'm also not surprised that he made friends with Angus and knows his story as he did the same with me. I'm simply bothered by the timing of his walking in the bar."

"I don't blame you, Damian, as it was highly convenient, but you've done your research on him and he's everything he said he was. Give me a few hours to check with my sources, you do the fingerprint search, and then let's sit down and chat with the man."

"Exactly what I was thinking. Perhaps there are another couple of email accounts that the leadership uses that I could access. Then we try his tactic of exposing their thoughts and behavior to the gang."

"Sounds like a plan. Have you found anything else on my unsolved cases?"

"I thought I provided you with some really good leads."

"You've provided me with nearly all the information on the case. I'm stuck on the DNA analysis delay. Do you have any ideas on how to get around that?"

"When we first started the cold cases, I looked at the process and decided there wasn't much I could do to speed things up. By design, testing is supposed to take about between fifty and sixty hours and there were good reasons for those times. However, I didn't realize there was such a shortage of human beings for the human side of the processing. So I was thinking about designing equipment that can automate that, but that is at least two years off from getting FDA or FBI approval to process specimens if I had a nearly finished product today. I'm back to the private lab suggestion. It's about eight thousand dollars per trace specimen. How many specimens did they get out of the car?"

'I'll ask in the morning but I would think there would be a lot. Hairs alone in a thirty year car have to be forty to fifty and with a pet add another fifty."

"What if we prioritize the hair to Debbie color's and require a hair follicle to be attached to the strand and asked the crime lab to prioritize that first. Would that reduce the turnaround time for results?"

"It would and it might reduce the numbers sufficiently enough that the department might be willing to send it to a private lab. I'll contact the crime scene folks in the morning and see if I can find an inventory of all the specimens."

"If you get me all of the fingerprints collected, I can at least run those for you," Damian offered.

"Sounds like a plan. Let's both hope we can get some sleep now."

After they disconnected the call, Damian went back to look at Barbara Watson. The Medical Examiner could not confirm that the knife with Mr. Watson's fingerprints was the one that killed her. Where was it postulated that she was killed? Her home, somewhere else? Stabbing someone was not a quiet affair unless you drugged them first. He pulled up the file on Mrs. Watson to see what was said regarding the details of her death. The police report stated she wasn't murdered at the scene where her body was located. Inside the file was a list of alternatives. Damian read it and thought it felt like a brain-storming session to him rather than actual suspicion of possible murder sites. He yawned and realized his adrenaline rush had finally ended. He crawled into bed soon after much to the dismay of his two cats that had staked their own territory out on his bed.

CHAPTER 33

He awoke late the next morning to the delightful news that the Warriors had pulled out a final two minute surge and victory in their play-off series. Now for the final game, they were returning home to determine who would advance to the NBA finals. Damian visited a few different news sites to read up on the game. He visited the Warriors site contemplating buying tickets for the final game. At least if he was inside Oracle Arena, the Brotherhood would be unable to kill him. Then he looked up Hermione's swim schedule and realized there was a swim meet that night. He'd take a pass on the tickets and content himself with checking the score of the game on his phone.

The phone rang and he saw that it was Ariana.

"Happy Sunday morning," she said. "Would you like to join me in giving Hermione her first scuba diving lesson?"

"Given your penchant for forgetting your air tank pressure, count me in if only to save you two. What time?"

"Why don't you come over for lunch and we'll start after that. I downloaded the guide from the PADI website used by dive instructors to teach novices. It's for ten years old and up, so I thought we start there, then go out to my pool to practice with the tank and regulator, and then if she's doing good, we'll go out in the bay. If she likes scuba diving, then I'll enroll her after school ends with an official PADI instructor so she can get certified."

"Sounds like an excellent plan. I'll bring over my equipment. Do you have lots of air in your tanks or do you need me to bring over extra gas?"

There was a pause and then Damian could hear the chagrin in her voice, "I actually haven't looked at the gas level of my tanks since my adventure going to your island. I can run out here and get the tanks refilled."

Damian had been checking the internet as they talked and said, "The dive shop closest to you is closed today. I'll bring over my own gas."

"Will the gas cylinder fit in your boat?"

"Yes and when it's full it weighs about sixty pounds. I just have to make sure I don't bounce on the water and break off the regulator. If that happens it will turn into a torpedo and go through my boat into the bay and I'll be swimming ashore."

"I'd worry about you doing that, but I'm sure if that happened you find a way to repair the boat and resume your journey here."

"Thanks for the faith in my engineering abilities," Damian said with a laugh not at all sure he could repair that large a hole while the boat was upside down and he was treading water in the bay.

"I assume the Brotherhood didn't bother you yesterday."

Damian paused debating whether to tell her, but since they were co-parenting Hermione, he supposed he should say something in case she ended up with sole possession of the kid.

"Actually, I guess I should have called you last night. They attacked around mid-day. I had help from two different police agencies."

"Oh my gosh Damian, you should have called and updated me. Did the police catch them?"

"I don't know and no. A boat came over with five presumably gang members. Two got on my island and three drove away with a copter chasing them. I didn't hear if they found them, but I don't know why they wouldn't have, but they didn't call me to let me know."

"How about the two guys on your island?" Ariana asked urgently. "Surely they caught them?"

"No actually they didn't. Apparently they had wet suits on under their clothes and carried mini-scuba units and masks. You've probably seen them; you can carry them on your shoulder in case your unit fails. They're good for like five minutes of breathing. They dove into the water and disappeared. They must have come by earlier and buried a regular scuba set near some landmark under water as we never saw them again."

"Maybe they bled to death and a shark ate them."

"If only I could be so lucky. Anyway, I'm safe and I'll tell you more about my evening later. I'm completely unharmed."

"You live a dangerous life. We need to do some planning on what I'm going to do if you fail to defend yourself. We have Hermione now and I don't have your expertise to create identities. If either us of us dies, the other person has to completely assume care and legal guardianship of her and we need to make sure all of our ducks are in order."

"Ah, good point, Ariana. I'll think about your issue and you do also and we'll talk to make sure it's all set up. Do you want me to come over about noon?"

"Yeah, we'll see you then."

They ended the call and Damian thought 'whoops' he should have thought of the very issue that Ariana brought up. They had taken control of the teenager without any legal approval. If Ariana died, he needed a legitimate legal course to care for her. Likewise if he died, Ariana needed enough of a paper trail that her right to the kid would never be challenged by anyone other than Hermione's real parents.

He went down to his lab to pack his scuba supplies and air canisters thinking about what he'd done to create Hermione's background to get her into school. He felt really good about the set-up and didn't think there was anything more he could do. He would leave the kid perhaps half of his large estate. Ariana could easily cover the kid's expenses including college, but perhaps that half of his estate would give her the financial freedom to do whatever she wanted.

He turned back to the location for Barbara Watson and dropped Natalie a note asking her if she could tell from the police report if they used Luminol on her house or car. Some of the police abbreviations were hard to decipher, so he couldn't always understand a report.

He then sat in front of his computer terminals and put some thought into how he would increase his security. He had cameras around his island looking out onto the water. Perhaps if he put some kind of facial or object recognition software in place, it would sense the approach of the men that had attacked his island. Trouble was he doubted that the same ones would be back. He studied the men on board the boat and those that made it ashore.

They were so convinced that they could conquer his island that they failed to try and hide their identity. He would have thought that they would at least wear balaclavas. He studied their images and wondered what he could program into the alarm system? Search for white and heavily tattooed individuals that were on a direct course for his island. Looking at the film of both attacks, the men were indeed Caucasian. Most of them you could see had many tattoos. Not one of them had a naked arm free of tattoos. It was a vague description but better than nothing. He bet he'd get a lot of false alarms. How many sailors out in San Francisco bay had tattoos? A lot he'd guess. He would set the alarm to ring at a distance of one-hundred yards and see how many alarms he got. If the bells were going off hourly that would drive him nuts and he would reduce the range. So far they had strictly gone for daytime attacks. Maybe he would have to add some night vision lens to the camera at night for better detection in the dark.

He was out of time so he set his system, made sure the cats kibble and water bowls were full, then took off for Ariana's house. He decided to take a fast and circuitous route around Alcatraz Island. He hadn't seen anyone following him on the water and they didn't know where his watercraft garage was so in theory they were watching the wrong side of his island, but it never paid to be careless with his, Ariana's, and Hermione's security.

Despite his detour he was soon pulling up to Ariana's dock. The little two seater was a joy to drive and ever so quick. Miguel greeted him as he pulled up, ball in mouth. He flung the ball up on the sand as it wasn't time yet for him to get wet. He pulled a chair up at the island to watch Ariana put the final touches on their meal. Hermione was watching and duplicating Ariana's motions where possible. They both seemed relaxed and content.

"How's it going? Need any help with your homework?"

Hermione rolled her eyes and replied, "I do my homework while I'm sitting in class."

"Really, how do you listen to the teacher and respond if you're concentrating on homework?"

"You must be really old or not as smart as I am when you attended school. I can do all three at once. I've always gotten good grades for class participation."

"I think it's that I'm old. I grew up in foster care so no one paid attention to whether my homework was done, but I guess I probably did what you're doing."

"Wow, you grew up in foster care. That sucks!"

Then as though a switch had been turned on, out of nowhere it seemed, Hermione sobbed, "Oh my gosh, I'm in foster care. I'm an orphan just like you Damian."

Ariana and Damian hugged the girl as a unit. Ariana was tearing up and Damian thought great I'm hugging two water pots.

"You know, I never got to stay with anyone as smart and cool as Ariana. I stayed with one boring couple after another. I was never an only child in a household. Your situation may be temporary or it may be permanent until you leave for college if we don't find your parents by then. They could be looking for you right now, but we done such a good job creating a new identity that you'll be hard to find. Let's hope they see your Facebook post to know that you're alive."

They could feel her rub her face on Damian's shirt to dry her tears and then she leaned back a little embarrassed.

Ariana saw the look and said, "Sweetie, you've had an amazing week adapting to a new school and swim coach. At your age you are also raging with hormones so I'm surprised you haven't been overwhelmed by your situation before now. Now let's finish making lunch and we'll sit down and eat and listen to Damian describe his second go round with those terrible thugs."

Soon they were all munching on a delicious salad filled with four kinds of greens, nuts, strawberries, chicken, and numerous other colorful things. It was topped with a creamy goddess dressing and very delicious. They washed the food down with a variety of iced teas. Dessert was chocolate chip cookies that Hermione baked.

Once Damian took the first bite from the cookie, Hermione said "Tell us about the thugs. Did you blast them with the water cannons again?"

CHAPTER 34

"Sort of. This time there were five of them and they pulled up to my beach, which is on the other side of the island from the water cannons you were firing. The two that came onto my island were prepared; they were wearing dive masks expecting to be shot with pepper juice, but I don't have that loaded into the cannons on that side of the island; it's just straight bay water."

"Did they get up your hillside?" Ariana asked.

"This time I called the police as five guys with assault weapons is a little much for me to take on. They sent a boat and a copter and two officers went to the Richmond Marina and caught a second boat. The copter chased the boat containing three men and I was left with the two men on my beach for about ten minutes before the boat from the Richmond Marina arrived."

"What happened next?" asked Hermione "Weren't you scared?"

"Two bad guys with assault weapons? You bet I was scared! I put security enhancements into my house, but it was with the thought of a single guy with a gun; not a party of five with automatic weapons. Plus I was worried for my cats, hoping they had the common sense to take cover in one of the many small caves on the hillsides, but it wasn't as if I could go outside and yell for them to come in.

"The deputy suggested I aim the water cannon at the assault weapon rather than the men's faces to cause their gun to fail so I did that and it worked with one of the guns. I also dropped homemade green ink bombs on the guys in the boat and purple smoke bombs on the beach to block their vision."

Hermione clapped her hands while Ariana gave Damian a high five as she asked, "Why green ink?"

"I developed this heavily staining lime green ink that I filled a water balloon with and had my drone drop it on the guys in the boat until the poor drone was shot down, but the guys won't get the ink off of themselves likely for a month or so. That makes them easier to capture when they're wearing the evidence."

"This sounds very funny but it's not since you could have been killed," Ariana remarked in a serious tone.

"If it makes you feel better, I paused for about two seconds to laugh at the guy with green ink on his face. I was musing earlier that they obviously thought they would be successful at killing me as they arrived with no disguises on their faces. That just made them easy targets for me and my green ink water balloons."

"I don't need to go to the movies anymore," Hermione observed. "I'll just call you up and ask you about your day."

Damian chuckled.

Ariana asked, "So backup arrived to help you with the two goons left on your island?"

"Yes the deputies beached their boat on the skinny shoreline in the cove next to the one containing the two men. About the same time a second police boat arrived as well as two copters from neighboring municipalities."

"So they were arrested and hauled away to jail?" Hermione asked.

"No, although I didn't realize it at the time, the masks the guys on shore were wearing were diving masks. They pulled their clothes off and dove into the water in wetsuits. Just as they went under I noticed they had one of those mini tanks that allows you to breathe for about five minutes underwater. We never saw them again so we think they left scuba tanks underwater, swam down to pick them up and escape."

"Wow!" said Hermione.

"How about the guys in the boat with the green ink? Did they at least capture them?" Ariana asked.

"I just got word on my way over here, that they headed straight out to the ocean and the copter pilot had to let them go when he became worried about having enough fuel to return to land."

"That sucks," declared Hermione.

"Yeah that's pretty much my feeling. All those bullets, all that effort, and the police have nothing to show for it. Their crime scene team stayed behind on my island for nearly eight hours collecting evidence, but I haven't heard of any identification of any of the five men so far."

"You must've had a hard time sleeping last night. I know I would've worried that the men would come back and yet been exhausted, from the adrenaline rush from earlier in the day."

"Yeah that pretty well sums up my evening. I needed to chill out and debated coming over here, but in case I was somehow being watched at that time I didn't want to lead anyone to you guys. So I went to my favorite bar in Oakland where they make the best cheeseburgers in the world."

"You should've come here; we could've played a game to take your mind off the day," Ariana suggested.

"We could've played Destiny on Xbox. I'm really good at it and you would've had to concentrate hard on the game rather than the problems you're having with these people if you wanted to beat me."

"Ladies, thank you for your support, but it turns out I made a good choice in going to Pete's. I met an ex-gang member there. I asked him how he had left the gang alive. Natalie, my friend the detective, is checking his story out but everything I could find on the guy says he's legit."

"What was his advice?" asked Ariana.

"The strategy that Natalie and I used against the brotherhood was to share some of their more explosive emails with the Black Guerrillas who are their natural enemy inside the prison walls."

"Sounds reasonable, but given the attacks on your island, I would say your strategy is not working," Ariana commented.

"You'd be right about that; it's not working. Angus Walsh is the ex-gang member and he was sent to prison for a murder he claimed he never committed. After DNA testing and twenty years in prison, he was exonerated and released. He knew the gang would expect him to work for them on the outside and he wanted to cut all ties. The Brotherhood is hard to run from as they generally have a branch in every prison in the United States. They get their income from drug trafficking on the outside."

"So what was his suggestion?" Hermione asked.

"The guy strikes me as having an above-average intelligence and he indicated that he had a photographic memory. So photographic that he could remember every conversation of his adult life and a good part of his life when he was a child. He pretended to be illiterate and slow while in prison and so the gang leadership relaxed while they were in his presence and said things they shouldn't have. He collected all their comments about other brotherhood members both in prison and out and threatened to share it with them if he was harmed. Their leadership would not have survived such a betrayal."

"So how can you use it on these guys that are after you?" Ariana asked.

"I was going to talk to Angus at length, but first I wanted it confirmed by Natalie that he was who he said he was. I'd hate for the gang to be setting me up for a big fall"

"Okay, makes sense. You think you'll have an answer soon?"

"Yes, I would expect one today."

"Good! Let's go teach Hermione scuba diving in the meantime!"

Ariana had the girl read the course as though she was going to be certified. While both Damian and Ariana were certified, they were not instructors and therefore could not certify Hermione. If the kid liked what she did today, then they would get her certified and take her somewhere special.

In less than half an hour, Hermione mastered using the scuba equipment in Ariana's pool. They moved on to the bay and practice on the shore with the distraction of the waves. They'd had to put Miguel inside as the dog wanted to participate in this experience. Once they were comfortable that Hermione was operating the equipment as it was supposed to be operated, they took her farther out to explore the bay. Damian was tempted to put a diver's flag on the water to inform nearby boaters that they were underwater, but they were moving all over the place and the flag wouldn't really indicate where they were in the water.

After some time passed, Damian indicated that it was time to return to Ariana's house. Without diversions along the way, the return trip was much faster than the one going out. Damian thought it a terrible place to scuba dive as there was so much junk on the floor of the bay and none of it interesting.

They surfaced and began walking up the beach.

"So what do you think? Would you like to get certified?" Ariana asked.

"Yeah, I would. I've seen pictures of how beautiful it can be, just not here. There was a lot of pollution down there."

"Awesome," exclaimed Damian. "Ariana, do you want to sign her up or should I? I've a friend who's an instructor and he taught me."

"Why don't you take the lead on this one? You're a more careful diver and so it's better to learn your habits rather than mine."

"That's for sure. I don't want her to learn your carelessness for scuba diving," Damian agreed.

"Are you ever going to let go of my mistake?" Ariana asked.

"No, but the tea you sent me is softening my memory," he replied.

Hermione clapped her hands in glee and laughed. "I wish I'd been there to see it. Sounds pretty funny when you described it last time."

"I told you the story so you remember not to be dumb like Ariana and run out of air. If she'd been far below water, it would have been dangerous to come up quickly and if she tried the long swim back to her house, she risked being run over by a ferry."

"I would tell you not to call me names, but you're right I was stupid. Of course now that I know why my cell phone didn't work, I feel like you contributed to my problems," Ariana added in her defense. "If I'd known I only had to get back in the water and swim out about fifty yards to make use of my cellphone, I wouldn't have needed your help."

"So what happened?"

"I filled her air tank and she swam back home."

"Once I got home, I tried to learn who Manny was."

"Manny?" asked Hermione in confusion.

"Manny, as in Man of the Island"

"I had to tell her my name then if only to get away from that horrible nickname."

Ariana and Damian smiled at each other as the kid had never laughed so much in their presence and that could only be healthy for her. If all they had to do was repeat the story then they would keep it going as long as they could.

"When I couldn't figure out who he was, yet I still wanted to thank him, I ordered that drone that you use to drop balls for Miguel. I got the idea from Damian as he used his drone to send me a cup of tea and to move my air tank up the cliff. I practiced for three days and then drove her to his island with two boxes of tea for him. Two, in case I dropped one in the bay."

"Did you drop it in the bay?" Hermione asked appalled at the thought that Ariana was such a poor operator.

"Nope, got it on the first try. I put a camera on the bottom of it so I could see where I was going."

"Ariana parked her boat beyond my security sensors, so I had no idea she'd left me a present until I opened my front door to go fishing for Bella and Bailey and there was the package on the doorstep."

"So you bent down and opened it and called Ariana?" Hermione said thinking she knew where the story was going.

"Actually no. I did a quick calculation of how much damage a box this size could do if it was filled with explosives. You see, I've owned that island for nearly seven years and lived on it for a little more than six and I've not had a single package delivered to my doorstep in all that time."

"Wow," Hermione said filled with new respect over the ingenuity of Ariana's gift.

"Then I saw it addressed to 'The Man on The Island' and somehow I knew it was safe to open."

"So the moral of the story," Ariana said, "Is to thank a tech guy by using tech to get his attention!"

"That's a really great story. How soon did that happen before you met me?"

"One or two weeks," Ariana replied.

"And yet you answered Damian's call when I appeared in his boat. Thank you," the girl said suddenly serious and wanting the adults to know she appreciated their efforts on her behalf, knowing she could have ended up in a lot of hell holes.

"I took a gamble calling Ariana, because she was only one of two females in my life and when you appeared in my dinghy, I wanted a female presence for many reasons. The other female lives farther away and she's a retired cop and somehow I didn't want a cop in the picture at the exact moment I made the call to Ariana. I'd stopped by her house for lemonade one day when I was out on my jet-ski. So Hermione, the lesson here is although I hadn't had much interaction with Ariana, and I did do a background check, but I trusted my gut that she was the individual you see standing before you today."

"So background check my friends as a foundation, but then run on my gut as a means of determining whether we should be friends," Hermione summarized.

"It's a little harsh," Ariana protested, and then added, "For however long you need to live with me, there's a part of your past you can't tell your friends about, no matter how good a friend they are. I and Damian could go to jail for failing to notify authorities that your parents were kidnapped and that we've temporarily adopted you. Likewise, Damian would be in trouble for creating your false identity to hide your background. We believe we are doing it in your best interests, but that's not the way that the police look at. Got it kiddo?"

"It was much the same for me with my parents except it was their background I would never reveal, not my own. Although I tend to hide the locations we have lived in."

"Hermione, you still haven't told us much about your parents and I haven't found anything on them yet. So it would be very helpful if you would share some information about them."

"No, maybe some time in the future."

"Okay," Damian said with a sigh. "I'll see you ladies tomorrow at the swim meet unless you need me for anything else."

"I'm good," replied Ariana.

"Me too," muttered Hermione. She felt bad for not telling Damian more about her parents, but never trusting strangers ever, had been drilled into her by her parents.

Damian was approaching his island when the island alarm bell rang his phone. He was glad he was in the fast two seater, rather than the kayak if there was trouble ahead.

CHAPTER 35

Damian brought the boat to a halt and paused to study the alarm. It was his house alarm. Damn, these guys didn't give up and they must have come by copter. He called Deputy Peterson again rather than dispatch as the description by even his own standard, was far-fetched.

"Deputy Peterson."

"Hi, this is Damian Green. I'm sitting in the bay in a boat and my house alarm is going off. I checked the cameras, and this time the gang used a copter to attack my home. They're trying to break down the front door as we speak."

"I'm going to put you on hold and see if we can get our copter dispatched to your island."

Damian sat on hold with his speakerphone function while watching the men try to bust into his front door. They even fired bullets at it and to his surprise and pleasure the materials he'd used were repelling their efforts. The presidential motorcade had the same glass in their car as he had in his windows.

Damian heard the click and the deputy was back, "Copter's on its way and the boys from the Coast Guard and SFPD are also in the air. It will be about ten minutes for all of them. Stay where you are in the bay, do not get close to your island."

"Actually, I'm a sitting duck out here, so I'm heading the opposite direction to San Francisco just to make sure there's plenty of distance."

"Good idea. I'm going to use my cell phone to broadcast our conversation to the responding copters, so you're being recorded."

"Okay."

The Deputy introduced himself and Damian not sure who was listening to the transmission. He then asked Damian to describe what he could see.

"Six men with automatic weapons, axes, and sledgehammers are attacking my house. I should tell you that the construction of the house consists of the same glass and metal used for the Presidential limousine so it's holding up well to their beating. They have not succeeded in entering my home or otherwise damage it."

"Wow," was all the deputy could say.

"There is not room for a second copter to land," Damian said trying to give the pilots what he thought would be useful.

"Can you describe the suspects?"

"Six males, Caucasian, some visible tattoos, wearing jeans and t-shirts; all have guns into the back of their jeans and some are holding automatic weapons while others laid them down to swing their various tools at my house. Now they're having a conversation in a circle I'm guessing trying to decide what to do next."

"What's the ETA on any copter?" Deputy Peterson asked to the airwaves.

Apparently he could hear the answer on the other end as he soon said to Damian, "Nearest copter has an ETA of less than three minutes. They have a visual on your island. What are the suspects doing now?"

"Looks like they've reached a decision and are going to leave. They're picking up their weapons and tools and heading back to the copter."

"That's not much time, they've been at it maybe five, seven minutes. I wonder why they're giving up so soon?"

"My guess is they have your response time programmed into this operation and frankly it appears that they didn't succeed at all. Why sit there hammering a house with bullets and hammers if they don't see progress? They've piled back into the copter and are lifting off. Should I crash the copter?"

"No," came the immediate response.

"Okay it's departing my island. Can the approaching copter see the copter that just lifted into the air?"

There was silence for a short time and then the deputy asked, "Yes the copter has been spotted by all three responding copters. Just to verify its blue and white, correct."

"Yes."

Now Damian could see a total of four copters in the air. He sent up a silent plea for them not to come his way. The last thing he wanted was to be a sitting duck when a copter fight took place overhead.

Then to Damian's surprise the copter filled with thugs headed for San Quentin. He smiled at the idea that they might land in the prison yard. He had no binoculars in the boat so he could see approximately where it headed, but not where it touched down.

His line was still open with the deputy so he asked, "Did the copter land inside of San Quentin?"

"No. It appears to have landed on a very large water storage tank on the hill behind the prison. The men are running down a ladder on the side of the tank and running for cover with guns slung around their backs."

"Do you think it is safe for me to go home?"

"No, we're sending a boat to that area and I'll arrive at the Marina shortly."

"Are there one or two of you?"

"I don't understand your question."

"I have a fast two seater boat and I could pick you up."

"There's two of us, but could you ferry us one at a time?"

"Sure be there soon."

Minutes later, Damian greeted the deputy at the dock and he hopped aboard the boat. Eyeing it he asked, "Where do you dock and store this thing on your island?"

A reasonable question Damian thought, "I have a watercraft garage and a dock that folds out on the opposite side of the island from the beach."

"Of course you do, but you didn't tell us about its existence because?...."

"I value my privacy. I saw no need to tell you about the garage."

"What if you were attacked there and we needed to defend it?"

"You won't be able to find it, nor will the thugs, so I'm not worried about an attack coming from that angle."

"Were you going to tell me about the garage or park this thing next to your beach?"

"Perhaps I was thinking about that question as I picked you up. I guess I shouldn't have volunteered to be your chauffeur if I didn't want to reveal my secret entrance."

"I am a trained investigator you know. I wondered about that question when I was here before. You're obviously rich and what an annoyance to always call the marina for a ride. I figured you had some mini-helicopter hidden somewhere that you used."

"I actually looked into something like that. You know a man escaped East Germany when the Berlin Wall was up on a single lawn mower engine so the short distance to the marina would be a piece of cake. Sadly there's a high failure rate on those devices, so I think I would ruin a lot of clothes dropping into the bay," Damian said and then pointing to the cliff he said, "See an entrance anywhere?"

He paused giving the deputy time to look and then he shook his head and said, "No".

Damian hit the remote and the door opened and with a second push of the button, the dock came folding out.

"Pretty cool. You're sort of Q from James Bond."

"I've never killed anyone, Q makes lots of weapons for James that serve to kill his opponents. That's against my core."

"Good to know," said the deputy. "That means I won't have to arrest you for that someday."

Damian hated leaving the cop to roam in his private space, but he brought this on himself by agreeing to ferry both deputies. He was back ten minutes later with the second deputy who introduced herself as Susie Sanchez. He replayed the video of the gang's attempt to break into his house, then they went outside to look at the damage. There were lots of cartridge shells lying on the ground and a few dings in the walls of his house but those walls withstood the violence of the thugs. He felt very satisfied in his choice of materials. He'd read up on how to repair the few dents.

"This is very impressive, both the strength of your house materials and the number of weapons they came armed with. Why are they so mad at you?" asked Deputy Sanchez. "I've seen this kind of violence before when it's one gang against the other but never against a private citizen nor frankly one of your wealth unless drugs are involved. Are they?"

"No. I'm working with a retired homicide detective from SJPD; she was on their hit list so the two of us took counter measures, which rather than removing her name from the hit list served to make her and me bigger targets. After she met with a certain inmate at San Quentin she stopped by to see me on her return to San Jose. She must have been followed to the marina by gang members waiting outside the prison."

"There's obviously a couple of stories within that explanation," replied Sanchez.

"Yeah there are," Damian replied changing the subject. "What happened to the men in the copter chase today? I'd love to hear that they're sitting in your jail."

"I was arranging for the crime scene techs to return to your island. Let me check with dispatch to get a status update."

Deputy Peterson photographed the scene and Damian stood looking into the distance at San Quentin. Deputy Sanchez finished her call and said, "The helicopter pilot was held at gunpoint to fly the guys and while they were on the ground, one of the thugs stayed in the copter with his gun. Total of seven men; three died in a shoot-out, one fell when climbing down the water tower and the other three are being searched for in the neighborhood."

"Crap that means they'll be back. Natalie and I are going to have to do something radical to stop these guys."

"Natalie?" asked Sanchez.

"The retired cop."

"I advise you against doing anything rash. Fighting violence with violence rarely yields your objective," advised Sanchez piously.

"Trust me we're not resorting to violence; this is going to a bloodless effort to overthrow their leadership. What are your next steps here?"

"Like yesterday, the crime scene techs will review your video footage to determine where evidence is on your property," replied Deputy Peterson. "They'll also be over at the water tower so it's going to be a long day collecting evidence from all these sources. Since there are multiple agencies involved, there are boundaries that will need to be established by all involved today. They're our criminals but they strayed into Marin County so they have some jurisdiction for what happened at the water tower. Whomever discharged their weapons at the suspect will have to undergo a police review. It's likely very confused at the moment given all of the moving parts."

"Could you guys collect the evidence so I'll have my island to myself sooner?

"No, it's best for prosecuting these guys if the crime scene techs do it."

"Aren't the charges stemming from trying to escape in the copter and firing on police far worse than the 'vandalism' they did here? I'd be happy if my island and myself stayed out of any police case."

"Sorry, you called 9-1-1, once you did that, it became public record. I suppose you could ask the DA not to prosecute on your behalf."

"Can you give me the contact person for that? I'll deal with these thugs in my own way, I just wanted you guys here to keep me from being killed and to run them off my island which you've done and so I'm done."

The deputies provided him the name of a contact in the DA's office so he could call the next day.

"I don't think there is anything else for us to do here. Will you give us a ride back to the Marina?" asked Deputy Peterson.

"Sure," Damian thought anything to get them off his island. "I'm ready to go when you are."

Less than half an hour later, he had the island all to himself and he went in search of Bella and Bailey. The island wasn't big, but he was too big to scale the cliffs like the cats could do. Ten minutes of calling and they came running. Poor things had their lives upturned. After six years of no island visitors other than Natalie, his sanctuary had become a three ring circus the last few days.

He savored a cup of tea sitting at his kitchen counter, looking outside to the bay with the sounds of his cats chowing down the fish stew he'd made them. Peace at last.

CHAPTER 36

Natalie was on the phone with Detective Shimoda and she did a little happy dance when he indicated that the crime scene techs had gone back through the hair samples to find those with follicles attached. After all the time and people in and out of the car, there were just three samples with the follicles attached. One hair was thought to be a dog or cat. The state lab was putting a push on the remaining two. Debbie Altman had been a natural redhead, so the DNA in her hair was not damaged by peroxide. They would have the results back in about two days as the specimen preparation with hair was much quicker than dragging DNA out of someone's fabric. If it came back positive, the ADA indicated it was enough to arrest John Avery and hold him for more testing.

As for Barbara Watson, the police were bringing Greg Watson in for an official interview to talk with him regarding his wife's cold case. Natalie and Detective Shimoda were flying down to Phoenix for a joint interview with the local police department which was supplying a police psychologist for observation and analysis on Wednesday. Finally some progress on these cold cases!

They still didn't have enough information on either suspect to convince a jury, but they were moving closer. She felt one of the two would confess during the interview process. She'd never talked to either, one on one, so she didn't know why she had that feeling that one of them would confess, but she did and she was looking forward to it.

She spent some time detailing the questions that she and the detective would ask. It was important to work through the flow as on rare occasion it would trip up a suspect. She looked back on Damian's question about the luminol results from the Watson house. She confirmed what he suspected, their house was never checked for blood as she started out as a missing person and years later when her remains were finally identified, they didn't go back and check the house as Mr. Watson was not a suspect at the time.

She looked up the property records for the county to see if she could find the owner. Even some thirty years after murder they could use luminol to find blood traces. If she could walk into the interview with information that blood was found in his house it might be enough to flip him into a confession. Natalie had two days to convince the owner and Detective Shimoda to allow her to have the house tested with luminol. She could eventually get a court order, but that would take time. The owner of the house might not want it confirmed as they had to notify potential real estate buyers in California that a death had occurred in the house.

Natalie contacted the property owner and thought all of her luck was raining down on her in one day. The man used it as a rental and he was between renters at the moment so she could send in the crime scene team as long as they would clean up after themselves. Natalie knew the crime scene folks didn't clean up after they examined a scene, so she would hire a cleaning service to clean up. If it led to solving this case, she'd submit it as an expense and see where she got with that.

An hour later, she met two CSI techs at the scene anxious to see what they could find. Detective Shimoda was detained elsewhere and couldn't be on scene with them. When they sprayed

Luminol it only showed areas where there was blood for thirty seconds. Then the biochemical process ended and so a tech had to take photos quickly after spraying. Mrs. Watson was stabbed to death, so if it occurred in the home, there would be copious amounts of blood likely in several rooms as the body was moved to a vehicle for transportation and dumping.

It was a nice home, about 2500 square feet with two stories and four bedrooms on a quiet street in the Almaden Valley region of San Jose. No wonder the owner wanted to keep it for a rental; she bet he was charging about five to six thousand a month to rent. Natalie also bet that the cleaning service would be a little more expensive than she expected given the size of the home.

They discussed which room to start in and Natalie was in favor of the kitchen. The knife with Greg Watson's prints on it was a kitchen knife and so if they had a domestic dispute that turned into a crime of passion, then it might have started in the kitchen. Natalie discussed the house's layout with the techs theorizing where she might have been stabbed and then discussing what would have happened next to dispose of the body.

She took a guess on where a knife block or knife drawer might be and started the techs there. The kitchen slowly lit up ever so briefly as the luminol did its thing. There were patches of quick phosphoresce but that was a reaction to bleach or other cleaning chemicals. Blood had a much slower reaction to the stuff. Just finding Barbara Watson's blood in the kitchen wasn't enough to throw suspicion on Mr. Watson. A small amount might be from little nicks that might routinely occur in a kitchen. They needed to find copious amounts of blood like that from a stab wound. They also needed to find enough to sample, not an easy task after nearly thirty years. Over that time period, the house likely had new flooring as tastes changed and flooring wore out. They might find a splatter pattern on a wall, but blood was nearly impossible to get out of drywall.

Several hours later, they had it. Natalie was wrong; the murder hadn't occurred in the kitchen, it occurred in the master bathroom. It was in the plaster and the tile grout. It was like the classic scene from Psycho with a woman stabbed in the shower. Keeping her fingers crossed, Natalie pulled up the carpet next to the shower enclosure and the plywood had a large old black stain. Bingo, now she had something to question Mr. Watson with in advance of DNA test results being available. She really wanted to high five the CSI techs, but all that would do was contaminate the scene with their DNA. She called Detective Shimoda to discuss their findings and since he was wrapping things up at headquarters, he decided to stop by the house and look at what they found. Someone had been murdered in the house, it was just too early to confirm that it was Barbara Watson.

She dropped an email to Damian updating him on what they were finding at the prior Watson home. His response described what had happened at his house the previous afternoon, asking if she found anything unusual about Angus Walsh. He was fed up with the attacks on his house and ready to cause outright civil war within the gang by releasing all of the emails to all of its members. Hopefully that would cause the current leadership to be overthrown and in the midst of the gang chaos for them to forget about him and Natalie. He really wanted to discuss the idea with Angus, but he needed to be able to trust that he wouldn't tell the gang of the pending email release. Natalie hadn't heard back from her sources; she would see what she could do to light a fire under her 'friends' in the next hour or so. She described the attack on his house and the urgent need for an answer, then she went back to work on the Watson's former house just as the detective arrived.

"So we likely have a murder in this house; we just don't know whose murder," Shimoda said.

"Yeah, since it was a cooking knife, my money was on the kitchen, but it's more like the Psycho movie set with a large amount of blood in the master bathroom in the sub-flooring.

Wood's a good surface to get blood samples from so we'll have the results in a few weeks to validate if it's a match for Barbara."

The detective walked through house and then stopped to observe the work of the techs. Several decades of the plywood's life had passed and it still looked like it had a lot of blood imbedded in it.

"Too bad we can't test how long the blood's been there."

"Perhaps someday we'll have that analyzer. It will be long after I'm done investigating cold cases."

Natalie and the detective discussed their approach with Mr. Watson, given the information they we're seeing in the house. After formulating a progression of questions they left the house along with the techs, now finished with collecting evidence from the house. Natalie mentioned to the detective on the way out, "Do you think the department would pay to clean the house since the owner was cooperative; we didn't have to get a warrant which in theory saved the department time and money?"

"Let me check on that and I'll get back to you."

"Thanks, I know the owner has a renter ready to move in within the next few days, so we'll need an answer soon," Natalie said making up this last piece of fiction.

"I'll get an answer soon," and the detective waved as he got in his car.

Natalie did another check on her email, hoping her friends had come through on Angus and finally they had. Just as Damian said, every comment checked out on the guy and he seemed legitimate. She decided to call Damian and see what his next steps were.

"Hey, did you find any information on Angus Walsh?"

"Yeah, that's why I'm calling. He seems to be everything he says he is according to my sources. What are your next steps?"

"I was going to contact him to arrange a meeting tonight at Pete's in Oakland. Can you join us?"

"I thought that might be your plan and yes, I'll meet you there. What's the address?"

"You've never been to Pete's? Don't have dinner; you can grab it there as he makes the best cheeseburgers!" Damian said after he gave her the address; then he ended the call.

He then tried to contact Angus and was pleased when he responded to his email and they set a meeting time of eight. He knew what he wanted to do; he just wanted confirmation that he had his thoughts in the correct order. Oh well, it was time to speed across to the marina and grab his truck to head to Hermione's swim meet. He'd go from an after meet celebration to his meeting with Angus. He shook his head at the extremes he was experiencing; from high school swimming, to an ex-member of a notorious jailhouse gang.

CHAPTER 37

Damian was sitting in the bleachers next to Ariana waiting for Hermione's heat. She was swimming three different races and there were two semi-final races that dumped the winners into a final.

"Have you met any of the other students' parents?" asked Damian in a soft voice.

"Yes, but none of the swimming parents. Usually it's at Starbucks, where all the cool kids go to start their day."

"Sounds like you mean all the rich kids go there. I don't recall drinking $4 and $5 lattes at their age."

"Yeah, me too, in part because back then there wasn't a Starbucks on every corner and if you went to the corner store, then you were harassed by the neighborhood gossip who managed to tell everyone your business. It just wasn't cool to hang out there.

"Here she comes," Ariana murmured.

Hermione lined up on the starting block with seven other girls. They took their sprint positions bending at the hips and with a starter's horn they were off. The color of their swim caps helping to distinguish the swimmers. Ariana and Damian found themselves standing and cheering their kid on. After several laps the group separated and it appeared she would come in second. Good enough to advance to the final heat. She exited the pool and gave them a shy wave and found four thumbs up in return. It was all her surrogate parents could do to stop themselves from embarrassing the girl by calling out her praises. She swam her other semi-finals to advance to those finals as well.

"I hope she has something left in the tank," Damian said. "Although the kid doesn't look like she's dragging at all."

"She told me before the meet that she was aiming just to advance in the semi-finals, and she wanted to place in the finals. The kid has goals," said Ariana proudly.

"She sure does. Kudos to her for so quickly handling this terrible situation with her parents and fitting into this new life we've built for her," Damian replied. "Kudos to you for taking on a strange child in a twenty-four seven role. You're doing an awesome job."

"You're not so bad yourself; she feels your support on a different level than mine and I know that if I have anything crop up I can count on you to take care of her in my absence. I haven't tested you yet, but it's just in your core."

"I was thinking of taking a short vacation to Mexico after she's scuba certified. We could take her diving every day in warm water with something better to see than murky San Francisco Bay."

"We could celebrate her end of school and teach her the new skill of scuba. I like that idea."

"Give me some dates that work for you and I'll arrange to rent a house or condo for the three of us. We could take Miguel as well. I'll use a private charter jet and he can just ride in the cabin with us."

"That sounds like an awesome idea. She can get certified in a day. Let's have a conversation with her after the meet on that idea and let's find out what she's done previous summers to entertain herself. We don't need to tell her about scuba diving or Cozumel yet"

"Good idea," Damian said and then they focused on Hermione as she stepped up for the second race.

After she came out of the locker room with her hair in the process of drying they congratulated her on the meet. She'd placed on two of the three events including first place on one of them. Not a bad start. They headed over to a restaurant to chat. As this was an away meet, the team members and their parents were not having a post meet group dinner.

"Awesome job in the pool, kiddo," Ariana said. "I competed in field hockey and never once played on a team that placed.

"I changed high schools frequently in foster care and never stayed in a school long enough to join a sports team. Congrats,"

"What high school sport would you have played?" asked Hermione.

"I'm not a great team player so it would have had to be an individual sport like swimming, track and field, or tennis, perhaps. I'm not tall enough for basketball, and not wide enough for football. I could have done the running for soccer, but I'm not coordinated with my feet. So maybe I wouldn't have even made a team," Damian said, finishing his thought processes. "Kiddo, I'm content to live out my high school athletic dreams through you."

Hermione just smiled, happy with the world for a few moments and her place in it. Then, as usual, she got the wistful look that made Damian think she was at that moment remembering her parents. Soon they broke up for the night. Ariana had asked if he had any more attacks on his house and he lied and said no. There was no point in having the two of them worrying about him needlessly.

Soon he was on his way to Oakland for the meeting with Angus and Natalie. He was going to arrive half an hour before the two of them which was good as he wanted the right table in the bar. If need be, he'd get Pete's help getting it. There was a table in a dark corner that would allow them to have their backs to the wall and they wouldn't have to worry about anyone overhearing their conversation unless they were standing in front of the table. When he arrived he told Pete of his request for the table and he watched as Pete smoothly moved the couple there to another part of the bar. Damian took a seat and withdrew his computer tablet. He had it connected to his own WI-FI spot so he didn't have to worry about someone hacking into his tablet. He had the perfect microbrewery beer and his thoughts and data were organized and ready to go, he just needed Natalie and Angus to walk in the door.

They walked in together apparently having met in the parking lot. Natalie would have known him from the criminal background check; it would have included a photo. Damian stood up and waved them over.

"I see you two have met perhaps in the parking lot?"

"Yeah," was all they both said.

"Pete will be over to take your order in a minute," Damian said. "Before we get started, is there anything you want to know?"

"So you both did checks on me and my story was the truth?" asked Angus.

Damian thought that it was a weird question and replied, "Angus, I told you I was going to check your background. Are you upset that I did?"

"No, I just wondered if the government expunged my record to the degree that they said they would when I was exonerated."

"The story that you told Damian is what I found when I looked at every available law enforcement source," Natalie said.

"Good - I'm happy to hear my record was expunged like promised," Angus replied. "Okay we can move on. How can I help?"

Damian refreshed Angus and Natalie on the current series of attacks.

"What happened to the guys in the copter?" asked Angus.

"Three got away and the rest of them are dead. The pilot that was hijacked is in critical condition as the gang shot him."

"My ever so violent 'friends'", Angus commented holding his hands in quotations around the word friends.

"Angus, congrats to you for surviving their system and despite the grave injustice done to you, getting your life back on track," Natalie said with evident sincerity. "I don't know that I have the strength of character to survive and thrive as you have."

"I was raised Catholic and you can choose to believe that it's all bunk, or you can gain huge amounts of emotional solace by deciding that God has a greater purpose for you. It didn't take me long after my conviction to choose the latter path. An added benefit was that the guys left me alone when I was praying. So it was a win-win all the way around."

"We all deal with the devastating hits to our lives in different ways," Damian relied. "When my family was murdered, I decided there was no God that could allow the taking of two young lives and my wife. Rather than devoting myself to God, I devoted myself to making sure the mistake was never made again; to each his own way of dealing with tragedy. Let's move on to the happier topic of how do we take the leadership of the Aryan Brotherhood down?"

"With the intent of causing so much internal disorganization that when new leadership takes over, Damian and I are no longer targets," Natalie added.

"You obviously have a plan, so what is it?" Angus asked.

"I've been able to access the AB's email systems and to decode the coded language through all of its iterations," Damian replied.

"I don't know whether to say 'wow' or 'cool'," Angus said.

"It's how I got the emails to send to the Black Guerrillas, but that didn't do us any good. It just brought the gang in a unified manner after me and to a lesser degree Natalie. This time I thought I would decode the emails and share it in a blast to all the members of the AB. That way anytime a leader spoke derogatorily of another member, it would now get circulated. Do you think that would cause the leadership to be toppled?"

"Do you have an example of some of the emails?" Angus asked.

Damian soon had an example of a few emails explaining his reasoning for selecting them and his data strategy with all of them.

Angus leaned back in his chair and appeared to be thinking. Natalie and Damian looked each other in the eye for a moment and then waited patiently for his thoughts.

"You have done research on the gang and so you know there's a council at each prison that operates the gang. There's communication with leaders at Pelican Bay. So basically you can't do anything just to target the guys at San Quentin, you've got to go at all of the prisons at once. You need to create so much chaos that the leaders can't respond to all of it in time. They have stolen cellphones in parts of the system, but often communication is slow because it's done via small writing on toilet paper or by moving materials down a cell block with a fishing line. So slow communication will hamper the leaders' responses across the prison system."

"If we take on the entire system, then it might result in the death of innocent prison guards from rioting," Natalie said with deep concern.

"First off, there are no innocent prison guards. They move cellphones, narcotics, and messages. Second we're not talking about whole prison riots, we're talking about just one of five major prison gangs involved in a civil war," replied Angus. "The gangs like to handle their dirty laundry internally so it might be a quiet coup d'état."

Natalie contemplated his statement and while she was former law enforcement herself, she knew that drugs were rife in prison. She hadn't known much about that topic until the state made a move a few years back to early release some prisoners and send others back to the county jail they came from. There were many addicts among those two groups of prisoners and how else could they get the drugs unless they were smuggled in by the guards?

She would like to think that it was a just a few bad guards, but she acknowledged that it was more than a few.

"So do I have agreement that we're going to do the entire system? Do we need to worry about other states as part of this coup or is the Brotherhood managed as an empire in California?"

"There is some tie to other states, but the leaders are selected from their own state membership, not a national organization. Members targeted to be killed or harassed are decided upon at the local level. Your problem seems to cover two prisons, San Quentin and Soledad. I think you could start with overturning the leadership in those locations and see if that ends your problem."

"Did you ever see names removed from the kill list, yet they were still killed?"

"Very rarely. That goes against the leaders of the gang and there would be consequences for making your own rules."

"How did other people get their name off of the kill or harass list?" Natalie asked.

"The only way I know to get your name off the list is to pay your debt," Angus replied.

"But we don't have a debt here," Natalie protested.

"Yes you do; you killed one of the Brotherhood. So you have a debt that can't be erased except by erasing you," Angus said. Looking over at Damian he added, "You also have a debt. You're Natalie's family and since you aided her, then you're on the list. Likely they would have also put you on the list for calling the cops when they 'visited' your island. If you topple the leadership, the new leaders may be grateful to you for allowing them the opportunity to run the gang. I think they'll more likely feel that way than seek revenge for causing the civil war."

Natalie and Damian just stared at Angus dismayed at the gang's logic laid out for them; knowing there was no logic they could counter with. All they could do was to topple the leadership.

CHAPTER 38

"Okay I'm ready to do a release. I'll need a little time to write the algorithm for all of the guys at Soledad and San Quentin, but the email strike will go out perhaps one in the morning. That way the guys with the illegal cellphones will have all night to stew if they're checking their in-box."

"I can take a list of the names and tell you if you left anyone out or if you included anyone from a rival gang. I'm eighteen months out of date, but I'll mostly be accurate."

"Have you thought of inciting the gang?" asked Natalie.

"Isn't just sending the email prodding the gang into action?" replied Damian.

"You could be more brutal by adding a standard line to all of the email distributed," she suggested.

"Wow, Natalie. You're all in to this operation; so much that you want me to stir the pot further," Damian stated amazed.

"Yeah, well we only have once chance to get this right. So perhaps it's in our best interests to fan the flames in the direction we want them to go."

"Not a bad idea, Natalie. I'm trying to think if using the gang's creed on them will do that," Angus said rubbing his chin in thought.

After pausing in thought for a while, he decided it wouldn't work.

"I don't like the creed for this; instead, how about mentioning family? One of the ideas that the gang preaches is that the Brotherhood is your family now inside of prison. They'll take care of you inside and outside of prison. I think if there are disrespectful emails circulated, then that takes away the illusion of family."

"Okay let's work on that language," Damian said. "Also, I was just targeting in-prison members, but it sounds like I need to add Brotherhood members on the outside as well."

Angus and Natalie agreed with that strategy.

"That's going to require several more hours of computer work to figure out who those people are. We better finish up here so I can get working."

"You know tomorrow is a national holiday so I'm off work. I don't know how to hack but I'm pretty quick with data," Angus said. "Can I help you get it done faster?"

"Ditto for me, Damian; can I help even without the technical skills?"

Damian's mind moved at lightning speed considering and discarding thoughts. His gut reaction was not to invite Angus to his home. Ever since Ariana washed up on his shore, he'd had an endless round of visitors on his island, so he was inclined to say "no" to both of them. But he was back to Natalie's comment that they had only one shot to get this right, so if he wanted the attacks on his island to stop, he might need to enlist the help of these unlikely partners.

"Okay. I don't like strangers on my island. Up to a month ago, Natalie was my only visitor across the years that I lived there; so Angus understand it's not you personally when I say I don't want you there. However, I need to get it right and the more eyes the better. I'll leave right now and the two of you can park your cars at the Richmond marina and I'll come for you there."

"I don't have a car I walked to the bar, so I'll have to ride over with Natalie."

"I thought you two met in the parking lot," Damian said.

"We did. I walked down the street and through the parking lot to the door."

"Okay, I'll see if anyone can give you the boat ride at this time of night, otherwise I'll move you myself out to the island."

They broke up their meeting and departed. It was close to ten at night and he knew Mike was normally an 'early to bed early to rise' kind of guy. Perhaps the harbormaster knew of someone. Natalie hadn't seen his dock and for some reason, he wanted to keep a part of his island a secret, even from his closest friend. He would feel better about letting them on his island if they had to come by boat and zip line. A ride was arranged and he relayed the information to Natalie. A short time later he was watching a boat approach in the dark with lights on the bow and stern. The guy said he would return for Natalie and Angus even if it was three in the morning.

The zip line had them on top in short order and they entered Damian's house. He paused in his kitchen to make them all a cup of tea and they went down to his lab. Several hours later, Damian was ready to hit the send button. He checked in with Natalie and Angus one more time before hitting the send key. With their nods, soon there would be thousands of emails being sent out to Aryan Brotherhood members both inside and out of Soledad and San Quentin.

"When do you think conversations will start? You said communication was slow, do you think this civil war will begin today or some other day in the future?" Damian asked.

"I would guess tomorrow because guys on the inside will be slow to receive email if they don't have an illegal phone. They'll have to pay to use a kiosk. Guys on the outside will know just as soon as they open their email," Angus replied.

"Let's hope this works. Meanwhile I'll arrange transport back to the marina for you guys," Damian said.

Within half an hour, Damian had his privacy back. He didn't know how else he would have finished the night's work without the two of them there, but he hoped that within forty-eight hours he would have his life back. He yawned and headed to his bed to sleep hoping for a vastly different world upon awakening.

CHAPTER 39

*D*amian and Natalie did an across the telephone high five and he sent Angus a gift certificate that gave him the next year's tab at Pete's free, Damian would pick it up. In three days of upheaval for the Aryan Brotherhood, new leadership was elected and the slate was wiped clean for all names in both the kill and harass list according to Angus' inside contact to the gang.

Natalie came back from Phoenix with a confession in hand from Mr. Watson regarding his ex-wife's death. She texted Damian before she left Phoenix, with Detective Shimoda and Greg Watson. She followed up with an email later that read,

The blood at the crime scene had been too much for him to ignore and he cracked when he saw the pictures of the master bathroom blood stains; the memories of the murder were too vivid in his head. The couple had been having arguments off and on for a year and she'd been unfaithful to their marriage. He thought to threaten her with a knife during an argument they were having in the kitchen. She said she was in love with the other man, he'd been chopping vegetables for a dinner salad. She walked away from the argument by stating that she was going upstairs to take a shower. Without realizing it, he followed her upstairs with the knife in his hand.

They argued some more upstairs and he said he was waving the knife back and forth as an extension of his hand. He wasn't threatening her with the knife rather he moved his hands a lot when he talked. While his hands were in motion she charged him with her hands in front as though to shove him backwards out of the bathroom. She tripped on a rug on the floor and fell onto the knife and died instantly. He thought it went straight through her heart. He didn't know what to do, he just knew if he called the police that they wouldn't believe him that it was an accident. We likely wouldn't have believed him. So rather than take his chances with the police, he waited until it was dark and then took her body out to the dump site in a garbage bag. He went back home and cleaned up the mess, then called the police and filed a missing person report. He then backed his car into a post at a high speed crushing the trunk and causing the car to be totaled. He thought there might be blood evidence that leaked out from the bag. He replaced the bathroom floor linoleum with tile that apparently another owner replaced with laminate wood flooring which was what we pulled up to see the stained plywood. So we were lucky. If the tile was still down we wouldn't have found the stain.

He waited for the discovery of his actions or her body for years and it didn't come until the utility workers discovered her remains so many years later. He'll serve some time for this mostly for the cover-up, but I would guess the DA will have a hard time getting twelve jurors to agree on a guilty verdict. The department is very pleased with this first case and they know I have a second one that's close to being solved. I'd love to share the spotlight with you Damian, are you sure you don't want to be recognized? I'm sure there's a way we can cover up your computer hacking.

No, Damian thought, I absolutely don't want recognition that I had anything to do with these cases. It was bad enough that the Brotherhood had entered his life without also having a police department and the media there too. He replied,

I don't want recognition and if you let my name slip out, I'll never lend you a hand again. I've very sure I don't want any recognition. Do

you need me to stop by your house and dismantle the booby traps? I can send Eddie instructions on how to do that as well?

Natalie indicated that Eddie would make an attempt to dismantle the stuff, which was great in Damian's mind as the commute to San Jose could be brutal. When he had time, he'd look at commuting in his zippy new two seater boat to the Redwood City Marina. That had to be a faster commute than driving, but for the time being he had no need to journey south.

He now had one cold case solved and the Brotherhood off his island. The second cold case was waiting DNA analysis which Natalie might get the following week. It was time to return to his everyday life and a list of things he'd been ignoring. He made an appointment with his friend to get Hermione certified in scuba diving. He booked a house in Cozumel, located on a beach that they could walk out in their scuba gear to dive. He arranged a charter jet to get them there a week after school ended. Which was two weeks away. They had one more swim meet and then if Hermione did well, she would also go onto the regional swim meet. He sent the details to Ariana and they agreed to tell Hermione of the planned vacation after her swim meet that night.

Finally, he got back to his work on the wave technology. He was stuck on how to store the energy efficiently, safely and cheaply. He was still convinced that the answer would be found in salt or hydrogen; he just hadn't figured it out yet. After another couple of hours, he wasn't any closer to an answer. So then he moved on to DNA analysis. It would take two to three years of work to get federal and law enforcement approval for anything he invented in this area. That was a depressing thought, but maybe if he figured out something that worked, it would serve to prioritize certain specimens for the police; move them ahead in the official DNA lab until he got approval and a patent for this invention. He started by using a dry-erase board to describe his needs. It would need to process a wide variety of surfaces from clothing to wood to metal. He continued to detail his needs lost in thought about the perfect analyzer. He was startled by his phone alarm and looked at the time. He was due at Hermione's swim meet soon. He'd have to leave the island in the next ten minutes to make it to Ariana's house in time for the two of them to commute together to the meet. He'd skipped lunch, so he grabbed a few snacks on his way out of the house and was soon speeding across the bay.

Ariana waved to him from the house when he arrived. He tied up his boat and walked over to where she was standing.

"I thought for a minute that you were going to be late; let's go," and she turned to head toward her garage.

"Can I grab some bottled water before we go? I was lost in an invention most of the day, missed lunch, and ate a few snacks on the way over here, but now I'm parched."

Ariana grabbed a bottle for each of them as she often found herself thirsty cheering on Hermione.

"So what were you working on?"

"DNA testing."

"Don't they have that already?" asked Ariana puzzled.

"They do, but it's a pretty screwed up system. At a minimum, it takes fifty-six hours to process each piece of trace evidence. It's why rape kits are backlogged as long as two years in some states, which I find unconscionable."

"So what's the bottle neck? What's your plan to fix it?" she asked while driving.

"From my research, the problem is extracting trace evidence from surfaces; it's done in a very labor intensive manner. Imagine a shirt comes in with three blood stains. A tech will spend several days extracting the evidence in a sterile environment. If the item is old and covered in dirt, that makes it more difficult. Or if it is wood, it will absorb evidence differently than cotton."

"Got it," Ariana said. "So you want to make a device that senses what the surface is and then technically extracts it in a correct manner. Better still if the machine extracting the sample could also run the sample."

"Maybe you should be an engineer, because that is exactly what I'm pursuing."

"Do you want some help with it?"

"How so?" asked Damian, now the puzzled one in this conversation.

"You know I do start-up companies - funding, advising, and finding staff to support someone who has a brilliant idea. You've been a one man show for a long time but if you had help you might finish this work faster."

"I've an interest in solving engineering issues and I haven't felt a sense of urgency to be first to market as I always seem to be first. But this latest idea is different. It's biomedical which is something I haven't dabbled in before, and I don't know if I'll be able to figure it out on my own. I've also met some people I'd like to work with - Natalie's son's fiancé and Angus Walsh, the ex-Aryan Brotherhood guy. In the case of a DNA test machine, I have an urgency to process test results, it's not about creating a new invention. Maybe it's time I built a research and design facility in Richmond or Oakland and hired a small group of people to help me pursue some ideas swirling in my head."

"I can help if you do decide to go down that path," Ariana said as she pulled up to the school where Hermione's swim meet was at.

Hermione was swimming in three different races this time. Her last meet qualified her for one of the regional meet races and today she wanted to nail the other two. She wasn't swimming for a place but to meet a time standard for qualification. Ariana and Damian had the numbers she needed to meet and were anxiously watching the clock with each lap. As she neared the last lap and appeared to be within reach of hitting the time, they stood on their feet cheering her on. In the end she nailed one of the races but not the other. Still as a fourteen year old, with a very disrupted life, they were thrilled that she'd even qualified for two races. The regional meet would occur over the coming weekend, so they discussed how they would get there. It was nearly 200 miles away so it made sense to get hotel rooms. Depending on how far Hermione advanced in the competition, they could be there all weekend. It would be a nice introduction to spending time with Ariana and Hermione for longer than a few hours at a time.

"I'll make reservations. Do you want to bring Miguel?" Damian asked.

Ariana looked around the area they were sitting to watch the meet, and decided it wasn't a great place for dogs. The dog would sit in the bleachers or the hotel room. If she took him to the river for a swim, she had no way to clean him up afterwards.

"No I don't think that's a great idea. I'll get my friend to dog sit him."

Damian nodded and they checked their watches expecting Hermione to come out of the locker room at any moment. She was nearly the last kid out carrying her gym bag, her short hair nearly dry.

"Did you see my time? I qualified for two events at regionals! My coach had all of us that qualified stay behind to arrange additional training this week. We weren't supposed to have practice after today."

"Congrats, Hermione! Damian and I just made reservations for a hotel in Fresno for this weekend so we can cheer you on."

"This is going to be so cool. My old school didn't have much in the way of coaching for swimmers and Mr. Bowman really helped me improve my start times and I bet I could shave some more time off of my start with some more practice. So there's a decent chance I'll swim even faster this week-end."

"That's really cool. Do you need our help? We could time you going off the platform at Ariana's house," Damian suggested.

She thought for a moment, than shook her head, "Mr. Bowman has a lot of suggestions to improve my ability so it's more than just reacting to the starter pistol."

"Do you want to go out to a restaurant now to celebrate your victory?" Damian asked.

She shook her head no and said, "I have a project due in two days and I had three weeks less than the other students so I'm cramming a lot in this week between my project and now extra swim practice and an away meet on Friday."

They went back to Ariana's home and she invited him to stay for dinner. Hermione would be studying upstairs, but the two of them could enjoy a class of wine.

Damian debated then shook his head and added, "I guess I'm like Hermione in that I was on a tear earlier thinking about my DNA test machine design and I'd like to get back to it. Besides I want to think about your earlier comment about setting up a company to manage my inventions."

Ariana nodded and they soon parted ways. She returned into the house to get some work done and eventually cook dinner. He was speeding across the bay in his zippy little two seater boat; his mind on adding some more items to his white board on the DNA machine. He was about two hours from sunset on a very windy day, so his boat was being tossed around on the white caps of water.

CHAPTER 40

With his life planned for the next three weeks between swim meets and the vacation to Cozumel, he decided to make a list of the pros and cons of setting up a company.

He suspected he would be helping Natalie on additional cold cases and he wanted to create a better technique for DNA analysis as that seemed to be the only way that cold cases were cracked. He had his wave technology targeted for helping third world countries and saving the earth by reducing greenhouse gasses. He was working on improving a drone to do bigger things like lift heavy packages over a longer distance, such as lifting a water hose to a roof top for firemen. He also had his pepper spray water gun that he'd like to promote to more people.

If he was to hire people to help him, what talents would he be looking for? Electrical engineers, physics majors, someone who could start manufacturing each of his gadgets? He'd need legal expertise both to set the company up and to deal with any laws governing the use of his gadgets, and then he needed a smart person who would just be a routine devil's advocate to push him and the team on by telling them it wouldn't work. Of course he would have to like all of these people and they had to get along. Heck maybe he should host an event at Pete's and invite all of his target future employees to see how they all got along with each other.

He also needed an HR expert and software to set salaries and benefits and pay people. He could privately fund the company for several years, as he didn't think he'd ever be ready to have outside investors telling him what to do. Maybe this weekend he would run his thoughts past Ariana and see what she said. She didn't know engineering, but she did know a lot about getting a company going.

He decided to head outside to fish for himself and the two cats. Nothing like a stiff bay breeze to blow the jumble of thoughts out of his head and since the fish were really biting today, he caught all the fish he and cats could eat for the next two days. He'd liked his idea of hosting an event at Pete's as a deciding point of whether to move forward. There was an upcoming Warriors playoff game and he could have Pete reserve a large booth that could sit as many as ten. He would invite Ariana, Trevor and Haley, Angus and a significant other if he had one and one other person he'd met while working on another invention. His question was what to do with Hermione. He'd like her to be there, but this was an adult gathering. She was old enough to stay home without a babysitter, but he wouldn't feel comfortable doing that and the day he had in mind was two days from now and she might still be working on her project.

He decided to check in with Ariana and her thoughts as she had a better handle on the girl. She texted back that the assignment was due Thursday, so Hermione would be free that night and would likely enjoy the event as she followed the Warriors. He reached out to the others and they wanted to join him both because of Pete's and the game at hand. He reserved the booth with Pete and sent a formal invite to all.

An email arrived from Natalie. It read,

An update on the Debbie Altman case - we got the DNA results back from the state lab and it's a family match to Debbie's brother. The DA was willing to issue an arrest warrant for John Avery. The SJPD have him under surveillance at the convenience store waiting for the arrival of Detective Shimoda and his partner. In fact they should be there as I write this email. I'm going to sit in on his interview. We may be close to cracking this case as well. SJPD is very happy with me and want me to continue working the cold cases.

Damian wondered if all of the car's trace had been processed. Sure they found a single hair, but it would be so much better if they found blood in the car. He asked Natalie that question and her email said,

They finished processing the car. They found blood in several spots in the car, but it's not that unusual to find blood in a car; because there were ten different areas of blood trace, it will take the lab longer to process those samples, the SJPD can hold him during that time.

Good enough thought Damian; they'll have this guy eventually for a murder he committed thirty years ago. What would be even better was if Mr. Avery confessed and told them where he'd dumped the body. Maybe he was hoping for too much. He also guessed that Natalie would be coming back to him for more help with her cold cases. After all, he'd first picked five cases for her to go after so at some point he'd need to circle back to those other three.

He enjoyed helping her on these cases both intellectually and personally. Perhaps as a side business of his future company, he'd invent stuff to make law-enforcement's job easier. Natalie was young - perhaps in her mid-fifties so she could work these cases for another decade. Certainly there were enough cold cases to keep her busy for quite some time.

He peered into the California prison network for the first time in about ten days. Looking at the prisoners expected to be released, he checked their original sentence and compared it to today's date. All seemed to be in order, then he checked into the

Brotherhood to make sure they weren't re-assembling a hit list that included he and Natalie. So far so good; the only names on the hit list were the prior leadership both inside and out of the prison walls.

He also took another look at identifying Hermione's parents. He'd spend the odd moment now and then looking for their identity, but hadn't come up with anything so far. The kid had not let anything slip so far as to their identity and his facial recognition and fingerprint searches likewise turned up zip. He thought that if they were in a witness protection program, that someone would have snatched Hermione by now. Were they part of an organized crime group that had them disappearing off the edge of the world? The kid was in a great place now but he couldn't imagine her parents not finding their way back to the kid.

Damian spent the remainder of the week devoting himself to all of his inventions. It was very freeing after the distractions of the last two or three weeks; really since the seventh anniversary of his family's murders. The worry about Hermione and the Aryan Brotherhood released his mind from dwelling about the loss of Jen and his two girls. He still grieved for them but like the wreaths floating on the water that grief was floating farther away as new people entered his life.

On Thursday, he had his informal gathering. It was really a very odd collection of people when he thought about it. A variety of ages, a newly minted college degree, an ex-Brotherhood member, an Assistant district attorney, a female venture capitalist, a teenager, and a Berkeley Professor in African-American Program, Nikki, who was Angus' date. What they all had in common was brain power and a love for Warriors' basketball. He quietly watched the conversation drift between referee calls during the game to the upcoming elections to gun control legislation. Yes, he thought to himself, he would enjoy working with Haley, Ariana, and Angus. Hermione, when she turned sixteen would make a great summer intern for the company he was thinking of starting. She hadn't been intimidated by the adults and discussed basketball stats with Haley and queried Nikki about life as a Berkeley professor. Over the coming weekend, he would use Ariana as a sounding board for his thoughts about setting up a company.

Friday evening found the three of them in Fresno for the swim meet. Throughout the weekend, Hermione advanced all the way to the finals in one of her races losing to an older girl. She was pleased with her performance and the thought she would do better next season; if she had a next season. She liked her school, but not knowing the status of her parents left her in emotional limbo; on one hand she was doing well academically and athletically and she would love to see how well she swam next year, but on the other hand that meant she would still be living with Ariana rather than her parents.

Damian spoke with Ariana over the weekend about his ideas for the company. Ariana showed her insight by asking if he was considering everyone that had been at the Warriors party and she laughed when he said he was even considering Hermione as a summer intern. She outlined for him the steps he would need to take and just like that he hired her and made her chief operating officer and gave her authority to march forward with everything she'd outlined.

"Thinking and acting so impulsively will get you into trouble in the start-up world. People want you to consider a wide range of options before making decisions; you're running with your gut which is a big no-no," Ariana said.

"Oh, come on, Ariana, you mean to tell me that all of those companies of yore that started out in someone's garage were successful because they considered a wide range of options before pursuing their passion? Bull shit."

"It's not bull excrement if you're spending other people's money. If you're planning to go at this entirely on your own, you are of course free to do what you please."

"I'll be a one man show with my money."

"Ok, in that case, I'll be happy to accept your title of chief operating officer. What's my salary?"

"I don't know. Figure that out and while you're at it, figure salary and benefit packages for everyone. Oh, and can you find me a 20,000 square foot warehouse for our headquarters?"

She laughed and shook her head at his cavalier attitude. They spoke at length about what he envisioned each person doing and what he wanted to do with the large warehouse. She had to admire how he jumped all in when he committed himself to something.

On the drive home, the three of them discussed Hermione's race results, her upcoming finals, her scuba lessons, and the announcement that they were taking a long weekend to visit Cozumel.

"Really? That's cool and now I'll have something to brag about to the other kids. They're really very spoiled and haven't hesitated to tell me that they're going to this place or that over the summer. Like I care, but that's teenagers for you."

Damian and Ariana had to laugh at her long suffering comment about her fellow teens. The they spoke about her aspirations for college and it was too early for her to know what she wanted outside of a swimming scholarship to UC Berkeley as that was the school of many Olympic swimmers. She didn't know what she wanted to study academically and she still had two years to decide. They spent the remainder of the drive thinking up names for Damian's new company.

Finals went off without a hitch for Hermione and she earned straight 'A's despite joining the school in the final third of the quarter. Damian took her to Monterey for her scuba lessons that Saturday. Since she was an excellent swimmer and she'd completed the online course, she was an adept student at scuba diving as well. A few days later they were boarding a plane for Mexico, excited to share with Hermione the wonders of the deep.

CHAPTER 41

Hermione was having a blast in Mexico. They were doing four to five dives each day and compared to Monterey, this water was clear and beautiful. The house Damian had rented had a pool in addition to the beach. The three of them swam laps in the ocean as well, with Hermione winning many races; the kid was fast in the water. They dined out at night and enjoyed breakfast and lunch prepared by the three of them.

Slipping into an exhausted slumber was easy each night with all of their exercise during the day. Still Damian had taken precautions when they arrived at the house; as much because Mexico had a reputation for kidnapping as for any worries about Hermione or the reach of the Aryan Brotherhood. He really hadn't thought the brotherhood would be a problem for a while as he periodically checked into their communications and they were fully focused on the new leadership. Natalie had sent him an email before they left on the vacation with the news that John Avery's vehicle that they had obtained from the salvage yard had trace blood in it belonging to Debbie Altman. Both the SJPD and the DA were thrilled with the case as it took a long time predator off the street, cleared a cold case, and disrupted a drug ring.

Natalie was embarrassed to take credit for Damian's sleuthing, but that was the way it had to be.

When they got back, Damian planned to meet with Angus and Haley individually to talk about his new company and see if they had interest in joining him. He was for the first time in seven years excited for his future rather than merely existing. On those pleasant thoughts he drifted asleep.

Rattling cans awoke him and he was instantly alert. By the time he reached Hermione and Ariana's bedrooms, he had his water gun in one hand and purple smoke bombs in the other. He opened Ariana's door and yelled, "Ariana! Wake up! Come into Hermione's room!"

In the dark, he saw motion and he heard curses near the front door. A house alarm was sounding as well. Ariana appeared out of the dark, with her own water gun in hand, and they backed into Hermione's room. Hermione was awake, alert and scared, with Miguel guarding her.

"Ariana! Quick, open the trap door in the ceiling closet!" Damian urged. He saw her do that as he listened for activity at the other end of the house. He heard at least three voices and one of them was in pain. Good, he thought! The man in pain got the bucket of pepper juice in his eyes.

When he looked for a house to rent, in addition to having at least three bedrooms, and beach access, he looked for a house with a safe room. This house had a ladder that folded down in the closet of one of the bedrooms. The room above had a steel floor, so even if someone shot bullets through the ceiling, they would be safe. There was a house alarm connected to a private security force that guaranteed a seven minute response and backup from the local police department.

The two women, he saw had the stair down and were lifting the dog up to the attic, which was not easy given the dog's size. Once he saw their feet disappear, he tossed a purple smoke bomb down the hallway and watched the corridor and living room quickly fill the space. Even in the dark, the hallway got darker. He ran to the stairs and was up in the attic in no time, pulling the stairway with him. When he viewed the mechanism upon arrival, he knew that below, a fake light slid into place covering where the access door was.

"Everyone okay?" he whispered.

Hermione had her arms around the dog and nodded 'yes' as did Ariana.

Poor kid, this must have been a replay of the night at her parent's house.

"The alarm company should be responding within three minutes by my calculation. Until then we have steel underneath us and these weapons. I think we can just wait them out."

"What happened to the men at the door? I thought I heard one of them moaning." Hermione asked in a whisper.

Damian smiled at her and replied, "Each night after you went to bed, I strung aluminum cans with pebbles in them across all doors. If someone broke in, we had an early warning in addition to the house alarm. I also placed a bucket of pepper juice with red dye over the doors, so that if someone broke in their eyesight would be harmed and they would be covered in red dye."

"Good thing I didn't go for a midnight swim," Hermione said with a surprising sense of humor given their current situation.

"I booby-trap every hotel or house we stay in, so you won't want to be sneaking out," Damian grinned.

Then they all quieted as they heard conversation below them. It was in Spanish which neither Damian nor Ariana spoke.

Hermione began translating in a whisper, "They said that Jose was unable to see as some substance fell in his eyes and he's worried about being blind. The other guy said so what that it was fewer people to share their fee with. They're looking for us wondering where we got to."

Then the color drained out of her face.

Ariana said, "What? What did they just say?" seeing the kid's distress.

"They said that Michael told them they were not supposed to harm me."

"What's wrong with that statement?" Damian asked puzzled with Ariana over the kid's distress and that indecision written on her face.

"That's my father's name," Hermione said. "Are my parents trying to kidnap me back to them?"

"I thought you told us your father's name was Jason?" Damian said.

"That was the name I was supposed to use when out in public. In private, his name was Michael and Mom was Laura," Hermione replied.

Damian and Ariana thought about the kid's statement and the name Michael for a moment and both shook their head.

"I think that it's just a coincidence. Your own father wouldn't terrify you like this. I know I wouldn't have done that to my daughters. I would fetch them myself; I wouldn't hire someone to scare them to death. I wouldn't trust anyone with their lives," Damian declared in a soft voice, adamant about the safety of his deceased children.

Hermione relaxed a little with his comment and concentrated on listening, but they moved on to other rooms in the house and she couldn't hear them.

They heard sirens in the distance as the police were approaching. They continued to listen, then Damian received a text from the security company.

'We are on site. We will clear the premises and let you know when it is safe to come out.'

The sirens sounded when they arrived at the house and then were shut off. No sense in waking up the occupants of houses near where the three of them were staying.

Damian relayed the information back to Ariana and Hermione

then said, "When we get the all clear, I'll leave this room, but I want the two of you to stay here until I contact you. Only listen for my voice or a text, ok? Is that clear?"

The two of them were clearly worried about Damian, which was sweet, but he had loads of tricks he could launch at any perpetrator. They nodded and he waited for the text telling him it was clear to descend. Less than a minute later, the text arrived. Damian quickly descended from the attic area and closed up the safe room. There were lights on everywhere and he could see both the private security force and the local police gathered around a suspect lying on the floor. He was covered in red dye and moaning in Spanish.

"Mr. Green, are you and your family okay? Do you need a doctor?" said a man wearing a security company logo.

"My family's fine. Did you catch any of the other men?" Damian asked.

"No there was a car that was fleeing the scene and Officer Gonzales and I decided to come to your aid first," said the security guy. Officer Gonzales appeared to wear the insignia of the Yucatan State police.

Officer Gonzales spoke up in heavily accented English, "What happened to this man? What is this red substance on him?"

Damian smiled and said, "Red food dye and chili pepper juice. I had it in a bucket in case someone broke through the front door. He must have been the first man inside. The dye will stay on him for about thirty days and he'll be able to see again in a few hours after his eyes get washed out."

The officer had raised his brows at Damian's explanation and he couldn't tell if it was due to admiration, puzzlement, or if he was thinking of some law that Damian had broken.

Damian added, "The security alarms sounded as they were supposed to, but the aluminum cans gave me a fifteen second jump on the alarm and then the bucket of dye and juice disabled one of the men and the other may still be suffering if they were splattered with the juice. Have you identified this man and his reason for breaking into my home?"

"No. He has no identification on him and he hasn't told us his name yet."

Damian had texted Ariana while they were talking and she and Hermione appeared in the doorway. It was probably bad for Hermione to see the one man in such distress, but he looked worse than he actually was. He met Ariana's eyes and she seemed to read his mind as she said to Hermione, "It's just dye and pepper juice, he'll be fine in a few hours."

She looked to Damian for confirmation and he said, "I brought a gallon of the pepper juice with me and I added beet and pomegranate juice with vinegar to set the colors."

She nodded and relaxed with that explanation.

"Why do you feel you need so much security Mr. Green?" asked Officer Gonzales.

This guy was smart, thought Damian, "Mexico has a recent reputation of kidnapping of tourists and I wanted to protect my family; seems that I was right to take the precautions."

"Perhaps you had trouble at home in the United States and brought it with you to Mexico," Gonzales observed.

That comment, while likely true, set off Damian's temper, "You think that if we were under threat that we would leave the United States and its police forces and safety and try our luck here? The answer is simply 'no.'"

Again, Gonzales had a way of expressing disbelief in his body language without saying the words out loud.

Instead he said, "May I see some identification for my report? Passports please."

Damian again in silent communication with Ariana left the room to retrieve their passports from the wall safe. He was going to leave Hermione's in the safe as he could think of no reason for the police to verify her identity.

He handed the two passports to Officer Gonzales, who opened

them up and wrote down their names, addresses, and birthdates. Then he handed them back and asked, "The child's passport, please?"

"I don't believe you need that," Damian said.

"How do I know she's your daughter if I don't see any identification? She might have been kidnapped from your country."

"Her passport doesn't state who her parents are, it merely gives her identity. Besides just ask her - she's bilingual, we're not."

Gonzales reeled off a few questions to Hermione in Spanish and she answered them in turn. Damian thought the cop asked her if she was with her parents and she said yes she was with her guardians and they had been scuba diving several times and she was happy and not threatened in any way.

The cop was still puzzled as to why he wouldn't show him Hermione's passport and Damian's only real reason was sheer stubbornness. He simply saw no reason that the cop needed to review her identity as she was a child of fourteen.

"Have you put out a police alert for the car that left this house?" Damian asked.

"Yes we have, but there are many places to hide especially in the dark of night. We may find the car in a few days or maybe not at all. It is the way with these kinds of searches."

Looking over at the security company guy Damian asked, "Do you have video footage of the two men?"

"We should, I'll get a copy," the representative said as he stepped away to make that phone call. Most of his company's security set-up had video cameras that were linked to a main switchboard, so he should be able to get a copy of the video quickly.

"When will you have this guy identified?" Damian asked.

"After we book him into jail," Gonzales replied.

"I'm going to throw some tap water on his face to wash out that pepper spray," Ariana said, unable to stand the guy's agony any longer.

"Officer Gonzales, can you take the man outside so we can wash his eyes out? I don't want any more mess on this floor," Damian said.

In short order, after multiple buckets of water the man's pain was reduced. He still couldn't see, but that would return in time.

Before he was hauled away to jail by another state police officer, he was asked his name again. He knew he was screwed both by his ex-partners and by the fact he had red dye on him which meant he would be bullied in jail. He had nothing to lose by snitching on his former partners. He supplied his name and theirs as well. He'd never met the men before so he didn't know if he had their real names.

"Mi nombre es Ricardo Garcia Corona," said the man in custody.

Damian wrote the name down to do research on later. He hoped it was the guy's real name. He said a little more to Gonzales, but Damian's Spanish was so limited he couldn't follow it. He looked over at Hermione to see if she was following the conversation. She nodded at him seeming to know his question.

"Ask the man who or what was the target in this house? Was it one of us or were they looking for stuff to steal?"

Damian listened to the questions and answers vowing when he returned to California to learn Spanish. It was a useful language and sheer laziness of brain had been the reason he hadn't learned it by now. Hermione moved closer to him and translated in a low voice.

"He says they were going to take all three of us and that there were four men assigned to the job," Hermione translated.

"Ask him how we were going to be transported out of here," Damian said.

"Why," Hermione asked clearly puzzled by Damian's question.

"I don't understand how seven of us would fit in a car. Were we going to be thrown in the trunk on top of each other or was another car going to arrive to assist in our transport? That tells us that more than the original four men are involved in this case."

"Okay," Hermione said then she asked Damian's question.

The conversation went on longer than Damian expected, but then Hermione seemed satisfied with Mr. Corona's response. Officer Gonzales was also taking notes on his responses.

"He said he was unaware of a second car, but he wouldn't be in the know if there was one. They were supposed to tie us and gag us but not hurt us."

"Does he know any of the names of the other people in on this job?"

Hermione asked the question, but her response made him think they were fake names as one of them was Jose Garcia, likely the most common name in Mexico.

The security dude re-entered the room with a tablet that he'd fetched from his car. "I have the footage of the attack on your house."

Damian and Officer Gonzales gathered around the tablet and they watched the four men arrive in a car. Three of them had hats on, and their faces were poorly captured by the video tape; the fourth man was the one under arrest. He must have been the sacrificial lamb as it was clear they sent him first into Damian's house. His face had been clear on the tape as he had no hat on to block the view. One of the other three men picked the lock or had a key.

"Can you send all the footage to my email address right now," Damian demanded. "After you do that, let's slow the video down at the front door and perhaps we can ask your suspect how they got into the house as it looks like they had a key."

The security company representative took a moment to forward the email he'd received from his command center to Damian and then they went back to watching the thug's entry into the house.

"It appears as though they had a key," Damian said. "Let's ask our suspect that question and what kind of weapons they were carrying. It's not like they could break into someone's house and they would willingly allow themselves to be kidnapped."

Gonzales asked the suspect those questions and then Hermione followed with one of her own, "Who's Michael?"

CHAPTER 42

Damian and Ariana froze when they heard the kid ask the question as it told them she hoped perhaps her father had engineered this kidnapping. They waited for the man to answer holding their breaths. Then they both let the breath out when they realized the conversation was in Spanish and they would unable to understand his answers.

"I don't know who hired us or who Michael is. I don't recall hearing the men mention that name."

"They mentioned it when they were searching the house," said Hermione firmly.

"Look lady my eyes hurt so bad I didn't hear anything and besides the alarm sounded. The only thing I heard was they were leaving without me."

"Who's Michael?" asked Gonzales.

"He's a friend of ours that gets carried away with pranks, but this seems too elaborate even for him to pull off," replied Damian. He could hardly admit that he was Hermione's father.

The Officer gave him an angry look and said, "I hope you do not plan to waste the resources of the Yucatan State Police on a prank."

"My family and I were terrified and hiding in our safe room. We certainly didn't think this was a prank."

Gonzales motioned to the other State officer that arrived to put Mr. Corona in the back of his vehicle and take him to jail. It appeared as though he was going to walk off without fingerprinting the scene or doing any other evidence collection. Wow, thought Damian. Okay then he'd make his own fingerprint kit and see if he could identify the suspects from his lab at home. Their vacation spoiled, he was going to cut it short by a day and head home now after he collected any evidence in the house. He'd study the video to locate the surfaces these guys might have touched.

Four hours later but still mid-morning, they boarded the jet to return to California. Damian doubted he would ever hear from Officer Gonzales and so before he left he collected all of the forensic evidence he could think of. He didn't own a DNA machine and he'd admit that he didn't know good evidence processing techniques so he would have to send it out to a private lab and wait a week or so for results at a fairly high cost as he had about ten specimens.

As for the fingerprints, he unfortunately didn't have all ten fingers printed for the suspects, but Mexico did collect fingerprints and he thought he could hack into their database to do a match. He had no idea how comprehensive it was or whether he might need Hermione's help translating Spanish. It would put him in a difficult position as he shouldn't be teaching the kid how to hack into computer systems. He'd see if he could figure it out on his own.

He debated telling Natalie about this incident. He didn't have a good explanation for Ariana and Hermione, but he sure could use her help as a former detective. He looked over at Hermione and she was looking out the window, with one hand on Miguel. Disappointment was written on her face. She had been having such a great time scuba diving; she was thrilled with what she saw underwater and it appealed to her swimmer's heart.

Damian said, "Next time we'll go scuba diving near the Great Barrier Reef. That should be far enough away to keep us safe from whoever wants to make our acquaintance."

Hermione looked over at him and asked, "Is that far enough away from the bad people?"

"Yes. Australia is a little harder to visit if you're a shady character. We could also fly into Papua New Guinea and rent a sailboat and sail to the reef. That would make us even harder to track."

Hermione brightened at that idea, "That sounds like a plan and Miguel would like sailing, although we would have to watch he didn't routinely jump overboard just to get a swim in."

Ariana smiled at that idea, "That does sound like fun. Maybe we could do that at Christmas since I assume that it's winter there since they're below the equator."

"It is winter, but this is a better time to go because it doesn't rain a lot and the water is still warm to dive. So maybe we can think of that trip in August before Hermione goes back to school. I'll look into sailboat rentals and a way to get there."

"That's awesome!" Hermione said. "It's good to have something to look forward to."

"Have you been sailing before?" Damian asked the ladies. Both shook their heads 'no'.

"I haven't either, but there's a first time for everything," Damian replied.

"Do you think the police will catch the men who broke into our house?" Hermione asked.

"I don't know," replied Damian.

When Hermione continued to look at him, he added, "I doubt it. Officer Gonzales was smart in one area, but I don't think he has the resources at his beck and call like an American police officer does."

"Are you going to solve the case?" she asked.

"I hope so. I'm going to consult the detective I mentioned before and explain that I was either here on business or to scuba dive and what happened. I don't plan to mention you or Ariana. Then I'll tell her what the Mexican State Police did and the evidence I have in my possession and see if she has any ideas that I didn't think of."

"Okay," Hermione said and then she returned to brooding while looking out the plane's windows.

The plane hit a few minutes of bad air pockets and the two women had a momentary look of panic, so Damian said, "Ladies, I had two different pilots check out this plane as well as a metal detector and I hired a bomb sniffing dog to search the plane before we boarded. This should be just routine air turbulence."

No sooner had Damian finished the sentence when the pilot announced that air traffic control advised them if they ascended another five thousand feet, they could avoid the turbulence.

Everyone relaxed with that announcement.

CHAPTER 43

With the return to the bay area, life returned to normal. Ariana was working with Damian to locate space and set up his company. He formally interviewed Angus and Haley informing them of his business plans and projected salary and job duties for each of them. Both accepted and were given start dates of two months hence as in the case of Angus he wanted to give his current employer plenty of notice and train his replacement and Haley along with Trevor had to find housing that would accommodate their commutes to two different bay area cities. The third person that Damian had in mind accepted as well.

Much to his surprise when he informed Hermione about the work he and Ariana were doing and her potential future as a summer intern, she wanted in on the research immediately. Damian spent a week discussing his theories for his wave technology and energy storage so that she would understand the physics principles at work. Then he cut her loose to work on the idea while he divided his attention between the new company and his ongoing investigation into the incident in Mexico.

He spoke with Officer Gonzales perhaps a week after he

returned to California and gained no new information. He didn't know if it was because the man had no information or if he was culturally not inclined to share. Meanwhile, the security company that protected the house sent him video footage of the driveway. They also maintained the security for two other houses in opposite directions from Damian's. From that footage, he gleaned that they came from the south and returned to the south. The license plates were stolen on the vehicle and there appeared to be no other van lurking nearby that would have transported the three of them. He was stuck with the theory that the three of them would have been deposited into the trunk of the single car involved in the raid... or perhaps, he and Ariana would have been killed and only Hermione would have been deposited in the trunk.

He was able to gain the vehicle identification number on the car and learned it was registered to someone known to associate with the Los Zetas gang. Cozumel was considered a crown jewel by the Mexican government given the amount of tourist dollars generated there by visitors. They had largely kept the gangs out of the city to keep tourists safe and in fact there were no U.S. State Department warnings about visiting that Mexican city.

In the end, Damian didn't know if theirs was a random kidnapping effort or if they were the target. He processed the fingerprints but they were random criminals according to the Mexican fingerprint database that he'd hacked into. Finally, in an effort of desperation to solve this mystery, he met with Natalie to go over the evidence.

"You mean to tell me you had a kidnapping attempt on your life a month ago in Mexico and you're just now asking for my help? Dammit! The evidence could have dried up by now," Natalie said. "Don't you trust my detective skills, Damian?"

"Of course I do and always will as you quickly solved my family's murder."

She let go of her anger with his response and said, "Show me what you have."

After much thought, she could think of no new avenues to explore and so the mystery remained. Was this in some way related to Hermione's parents or were the potential kidnappers after a well-heeled American family?

At the end of their discussion once they'd exhausted every last potential avenue of investigation, Natalie approached a new topic.

"Ah Damian remember when you analyzed the cold cases for me and picked five that I should focus on first?"

"Yeah," he said with a sigh, guessing what was coming in Natalie's tone of voice.

"Can you give me the other three to work on now with the reasons why they jumped to the top of your computer algorithm list?"

"Sure, Natalie, and I'll help where I can, but my plate is really full at the moment. You know I'm setting up a new company. I also made a promise to myself to invent a better DNA analyzer than the one you have now. I won't be able to help you as much as I did with the first two cases."

"That's fine, Damian; I appreciate any help you can give me. Good luck with your new company. Haley talked about it a little last weekend when they were over for dinner and she's real excited to work for you. Trevor is both proud and excited for her. He wishes you were operating the company closer to San Jose but he gets why you picked where you did."

He and Natalie parted ways, traveling in opposite directions to return home. He had a lot to think about on the return home. He was frustrated that with all his brilliance he could not solve the mystery of Hermione's parents nor the mystery of what went down in Mexico. He was excited to be reaching a turning point in his life. Impulsively he stopped at a florist on his way home to buy flowers. He needed to have a one-sided conversation with Jen and the girls about where his life was taking him and what the future might have in store for him. Instead of the usual red roses of a wreath, this time he was fortunate to find three leis. The scent of gardenias filled the cab of his truck.

That evening as the sun set over the Golden Gate bridge, the fog began to roll in. Usually the fog won the race and served to block the sunset, but not tonight. He sat on the edge of Red Rock Island, Bailey and Bella at his side, and tossed the three leis onto the bay. By the time he finished his conversation with his deceased wife and girls, the sun was long gone and the moon was now in a race to show itself before the fog blocked that too. He sipped some tea in a tumbler that kept it warm and petted his two companions.

What new adventures would appear in his life tomorrow?

~The End ~

ALSO BY ALEC PECHE

Discover my other books:

Jill Quint, MD Forensic Pathologist Series
Time's Up (prequel short story)
Vials
Chocolate Diamonds
A Breck Death
Death On A Green
A Taxing Death
Murder At The Podium
Castle Killing
Crescent City Murder
Sicilian Murder
Opus Murder
Forensic Murder
Return to the Scene of the Crime (short story)
Embers of Murder
Ashes to Murder
Mint Death

Damian Green Series
Red Rock Island
Willow Glen Heist
The Girl From Diana Park
Evergreen Valley Murder
Long Delayed Justice

Michelle Watson Series

Now You Don't See Me

Where Did She Go?

How Did She Get There?

Dog Humor

Eat, Play, Poop: Letters to my parents from camp

New Urban Fantasy Series - Stephanie Jones

The Awakening at Lake Tahoe (short story)

Witch's Medicine (2024)

ABOUT THE AUTHOR

I reside in Northern California with my rescue dog and cat. I love to travel, play sports, read, and drink wine and beer. I enjoy the diversity of the world and I'm always watching people and events for story ideas. All of my stories are generated by my imagination, I don't use AI to write books.

If you would like to sign up for my bi-weekly blog and announcement of new books, please follow this link: https://www.AlecPecheBooks.com

While you're waiting for the next story, if you would be so kind as to leave a review for this book, that would be great. I appreciate all the feedback and support. Reviews buoy my spirits and stoke the fires of creativity.

Readers that sign up for my blog receive a free prequel novelette for the Jill Quint Series.

Printed in Great Britain
by Amazon